THE RIFT

BOOK TWO OF ROOTLESS

CHRIS HOWARD

The Rift

For the forests

The Rift

PART ONE

CHAPTER ONE

They'd figured me to be some sort of savior. After I'd rescued them on Promise Island, put guns in their hands, and busted them free. But as the strugglers glared at me through the neon gloom of the cargo hold, anger bubbled beneath their faces like they were pots ready to boil, and I had no words to cool them.

They scowled at Alpha as she paced before them with her shotgun on her shoulder. They sneered at Zee, soon as she attempted to speak. And the whole Banyan being a savior thing seemed a long time gone, I reckon, after sixteen days pushing south on this lake, one sunrise after another, with still no sign of land.

The boat lurched through the water, turning things more sour with each side-to-side sway. Me and the girls had come in here to talk reason, but these strugglers didn't want to know how lost we were, or how close to starving we'd gotten. They just wanted out of the cargo hold. They wanted to piss in the wind instead of in a bucket in the corner, breathe the cold air as it wailed over the lake. And that would have been just dandy, except for who the hell were they? Sure, I'd saved them from GenTech, but they were still strangers. Nothing more. And that meant I'd be a fool to trust them.

"We fought our way off that island," said some dude with green eyes and a crop of red hair. "We fought our way free, same as you did. Left agents in pools of blood on the snow. And for what? For this?"

When he pointed at the walls of the cargo hold, I saw his left arm had its hand missing—was just a stump below the elbow. And I reckoned GenTech could have grown him a new hand to fix that for him, if they had been in the fixing people business. But GenTech was more in the use people to grow trees and control every last thing that grows business. And my own parents had been tangled up at the heart of it all.

"You think you can just lock us in here and we'll keep quiet? You think we'll cower in fear, on account of that shotgun you're wielding?" The redhead flicked his gaze at Alpha, his words shaking the crowd into a mutter and jeer.

"Damn right, Kade. You tell them, Kade." The strugglers jabbered on behind him, their voices pushing him forward, puffing him up.

And I could think of no right thing to say to them. Weren't my fault this lake stretched so damn far. And these folk didn't know the first thing about what I'd spared them, so they could stare daggers at me all day long—least they weren't being shipped back to the mainland as part of Project Zion. Least they weren't the start of GenTech's new crop of trees, covered in bark and shrubby with branches.

I pictured it for a second—all of them changing. Their human cells being used to grow a whole new species, forming the twisted beginnings of a forest, built for a world that hadn't seen trees in more than one hundred years. And you think they'd have believed me if I told them? No. Only way they'd believe me is if I showed them, and that secret had to stay in the hull.

"It's for your own safety," Zee called out, trying to make some sort of peace.

"A sweet sentiment," said this Kade guy. "If only it were true."

He couldn't have been much older than I was, but was the sort who acts like he's got a lifetime on everyone, taking deep breaths instead of just speaking, leaving big gaps for the words left behind. And considering he'd been dragged north by GenTech and drugged unconscious and almost never woke up, I reckon you'd have to admire the guy's spirit for still showing some fight. Gumption is what my old man would have called it. I called it a major pain in the ass.

"Quiet down," Alpha yelled as the rest of the survivors started to squabble and roar even louder. She pump-snapped her shotgun, and it shut up most of them.

Not all of them.

"What?" Kade took two quick steps forward, drumming a knuckle at his skull. "You want to put a hole in my head?"

Alpha leveled the shotgun at him. "Don't tempt me."

"It's a waste." This was aimed at me, and the dude was slowing himself down again, as if his head might explode if he got to talking too fast. "We're no use to you locked up in here. You should be putting us to work—we could help."

"Help with what?" muttered Alpha.

"Whatever it was that you stole."

"We didn't steal nothing." I tried to keep my voice as steady as his was. Reminded myself what I'd taken from GenTech was the remains of my father, and that man belonged to me, no matter what he'd become.

"I saw you rolling off of that island, bro," said Kade. "All three of you came up and over the hillside, riding on a big steel box with a nice set of wheels underneath. Impressive-looking machine, don't get me wrong, but any box is only worth as much as what's inside it. Am I right?"

He'd been inching closer and was now just a few feet from us. Alpha looked about ready to snap. I stepped in front of her, coming between her and the redhead so as to block him from the barrel of her gun.

"I know you're all angry," I said to the crowd behind him. Kade was too close now. I could smell the stale reek of his old sweat through the outfit he'd pieced together. We were all bundled inside clothes made for agents, the purple fuzz and bright white logos glittery beneath the pale neon lights. "And I know you're hungry. Hell, we're hungry, too. GenTech didn't exactly have the boat stocked for us to make our escape."

"And you'd like us to starve in silence, is that it?" Kade said it calm and with a grin on his face, like he was all handsome smiles and smooth talking, too wise to be bitter.

"That ain't what I meant. You just need to sit tight is all. Save your strength."

"My strength, huh?" He took another step closer and prodded me in the chest with the clubbed stump at the end of his arm. We were about the same height, but he was twice as broad. "And what am I saving it for?"

Hell, his guess was as good as mine. All I knew was we had GenTech behind us, and plenty more GenTech ahead.

The dude started laughing then. Head thrown back, teeth sharp and straight. "You've no idea, do you? You don't even know what's out there past the water."

"And you do?"

"Perhaps. Could be I know the northern wastelands like the back of my hand."

"And which hand is that?"

I shoved his stumped arm away, turned, and strode for the door, the girls falling in behind me, Alpha keeping her shotgun aimed into the crowd.

I was sick of them. Sick of their noise. And sick of the stench of the cargo hold, and the way the boat rumbled my guts as it rocked back and forth.

"Come on," Kade called after us. "I'm curious, bro. Where are you trying to lead us?"

"I'm just heading south." When we reached the door, I threw him a final look, then threw a look at the rest of them strugglers, trying to make myself real clear. "I ain't leading you people no place at all."

Outside, the wind still howled, and the world looked just as we'd left it.

"That went well," I grumbled, grabbing for the railing as my feet slid on the deck.

"Can't let them see you're afraid of them, bud." Alpha padlocked the door to the cargo hold and triple-checked it was sealed.

"I ain't afraid." I shook my head at Zee. "Going in there was a stupid idea, that's all."

"You're the one who said you wanted to quiet them down." Zee wound back her long hair to keep it from the wind. My sister was the only one on this boat whose head hadn't been shaved by GenTech agents, and it made her like the last pretty thing not messed with. "I still say we try leveling with them. Show them what we have in the hull."

"There's no leveling with that lot," said Alpha. "Red's got 'em too riled up."

Right on cue, the strugglers started hollering and pounding at the door to the hold again, stamping their damn feet on the floor. The sound could drive you insane, so I tried my best to ignore it. Started scouring the horizon instead, hoping for land but fearing I'd see GenTech boats rushing towards us. And yeah, the fear could also drive you straight crazy. Especially after sixteen days.

"But what if it's true?" Zee stared at the steel door between us and the strugglers. "You think that guy could know what's out here?"

"Only if he's an agent," I said. "GenTech kept us drugged the whole way north. And that dude ain't no agent. You saw the holes on his arms. He was plugged in ready for Project Zion, wired up to those purple cables just like the rest of them."

"We should give them a chance." Zee glanced at Alpha. "It doesn't sit right, and both of you know it."

I stared past the top of the cockpit to where the gun tower stuck up. And it almost looked like a skinny bit of scaffold poking at the rainclouds, like something me and Pop would have climbed to build trees as tall as our metal could fly. But I'd traded my scaffolds for lookouts, I reckon. Traded my tools in for guns.

It was up in that tower, wrapped in sheets of plastic, that we'd stashed every weapon but for the one Alpha had slung from her shoulder. Soon as those strugglers had first fallen asleep, we'd crept between them, gathering up their guns. Didn't see them wake up— we were out on the deck, the door to the cargo hold padlocked shut—but I won't ever forget the sound that they made.

"We can't trust 'em," Alpha said, following my gaze to the gun tower. "And we don't owe these people a thing."

"I know it," I said. Hell, they were lucky just to still be alive, and I told myself that over and over. Besides, there were only seven of those saplings growing out of Pop's dead body, stowed down below on this stolen boat. Seven last trees for a world made barren. And seven weren't enough to go sharing.

"We hit land, we'll make it so they can break through that door," I told Zee. "Then we leave them behind us, and they can fend for themselves."

Alpha leaned and spat off the deck as the wind rattled the water. "Can't come soon enough."

She was right. We'd all been stuck on this lake long enough to be praying for what lay beyond it, even though we'd no idea what that might be.

All we really knew was that at some point we'd have to cross the molten wastelands, the Rift. The lava fields where no one dared travel, the endless heat, the steam and ash and who knew what other flavors of hell. The Rift lay north of the dusty world we'd been plucked from, but it had to be somewhere south of the cold world we were in now.

I squinted at the low sun, then peered at the bow, and there was Crow, just like always. He'd been stood in the same damn spot, nearly all day long, for more than two damn weeks.

"Look at him," I muttered. "He's like a statue up there."

"Don't." Zee's eyes were watching mine, her brain guessing what mine was thinking. "You should leave him be."

"Ah, there's no stopping your brother." Alpha smirked as she tugged up Zee's purple hood, shielding her from the spray off the water. "He's what we call a glutton for punishment. Ain't you, bud?"

"Reckon I must be," I said, and I pushed off towards the bow.

CHAPTER TWO

I put my hands on the railing next to Crow's and stood with him at the bow, trying not to think about how deep the lake was, or how being no good at swimming makes you so good at drowning.

"How's the south looking?" I said, but got nothing from him.

Back when we were trying to find the trees and my father, there were plenty of times I'd have done anything to shut Crow's big mouth. In those days, most things he'd said had seemed like a lie. But that was before we'd become bound together, I reckon. Because now, his silence left me hollow.

"You're doing an awful lot of watching for someone who's all done being a watcher."

I'd made this joke before, and Crow closed his eyes for a moment, shook his head just the littlest bit. Reckoned that meant I was getting to him, though. Just had to keep on trying.

Even stooped, he towered above me. A bona fide giant, more than ten-foot tall now, on account of GenTech growing him his new pair of legs. His face had healed pretty good, too. The scars had faded on his dark skin. Still there, but not so bad, considering the burns and blisters he'd earned when Harvest's slave ship had exploded into flames.

"Didn't do a damn bit of good, waltzing into that cargo hold," I said. "I knew it was a waste of time. Some punk with one hand's the ringleader. Kade, they call him. Told him to watch out, or you'd head in there and kick his ass."

Finally, Crow turned to look down at me.

"Guess he weren't real scared of that prospect." There was no color in his voice, it was thin and bloodless, and when he cocked his head at the noise spilling out of the cargo hold, I tried to interrupt, but Crow weren't done yet. "And why should he worry? One hand's better than no legs."

"You got legs," I said, staring down at the lake. Anything but see the look in Crow's eyes.

"Sure I do. Big pair of wooden legs I can't use right."

"You're standing, ain't you?" I saw him grip tighter at the railing as I said it. "Hell, you used them before. Scampered all the way up the hill and off of that island."

"One time being better than never?"

"You'll get it back."

"Zee put you up to this?"

"What?"

"Always coming up here and pestering me?"

As the wind picked up, Crow wobbled against it, and he seemed to age a hundred years in one second. His fists clenched even tighter on the railing, and his voice became an angry whisper, like he was ashamed to even be speaking at all. "Even if I appreciated it, I don't need it, Banyan. I do not need it at all."

"So tell me what you do need."

"Nothing you can give."

I studied the horizon, searching for GenTech boats or a glimpse of land, so used to seeing nothing at all.

"You think you're the only one who lost something on that island?" I said. "I lost the father I'd come looking for, and a mother I never even knew I had."

"Well, I be the only one who ended up a cripple. I'm the only one who's a freak." Crow spat the words at me, then glared down at the thick tree-legs that had been forged to his hips. He'd covered them with strips of purple fuzz, hiding the knotted bark, the gray-brown grooves and ridges, and all across the fabric, the GenTech logo was stitched in tiny white letters, as if claiming ownership of their handiwork, and ownership of Crow.

"Freak of nature," I said. "So? You're one of a kind."

"Not nature, Banyan. Science." Looked like Crow had tears brewing on his eyeballs, but I told myself it was only the wind.

"They fixed you with that science. Best that they could."

"Aye. After they tore me in two."

"You'll be sprinting come springtime, you'll see."

"Spring, you say?" He shook his head. "Just get me to Niagara, little man. That all I be asking."

"Waterfall City, huh." Mightn't be a bad idea, I reckoned. The Rastas there had held onto some power, on account of all the fresh water they had to barter. Some said they even traded water to GenTech, forming an uneasy truce with the same folk they'd once battled real fierce. And agents kept out of Niagara, for the most part, anyways, so it mightn't be a bad place to plant us those saplings. We could keep them hidden there, amid the rivers and rocks. And even if the locusts found them, my mother had said these new trees weren't something the swarms could go eating, she'd said they were even stronger than the plants in GenTech's cornfields. So maybe someday, we'd watch our trees grow tall and see the branches bend down towards us, full of apples, limbs heavy with fruit.

Crow rubbed a hand at the scar on the back of his neck, where he'd once been burned with the red lion, the mark of the Soljah warriors who call Niagara home. "Sure, man. Waterfall City. Get me there, broken or not."

"Must be nice to have someplace to get back to," I said, staring at all the emptiness that lay south.

I sat in the cockpit and pieced together a small tree out of purple clips of wire, hung with pierced bits of white plastic I'd cut to the shapes of leaves. Thing was small, not a foot high, but it felt good to sit there and twist at it, even though I had to ignore the hollering in the cargo hold right beneath me the whole damn time.

That noise was a constant reminder of everything I wanted to forget—the locked-up survivors, the fear of never finding land, and the fear of running into GenTech. But I tried to put it all out of my mind and just focus on the wire and plastic I'd spread across the control panels, draping my little tree building project over all the gizmos and dials we didn't know what to do with. Boat had started steering itself once we'd hit open water, plowing south like it knew where it wanted to go. And even if we'd been able to change our direction, south seemed like the only place to head.

"Why'd you make it purple?" Alpha leaned over me, her chest pressed at my shoulder, her breath steaming.

"All the color I got." I tugged at the GenTech wires, resting my head against my girl as the cries leached up from the cargo hold. "I sure wish to hell they would shut the hell up."

"I know, bud. Me, too."

"You think Zee's right about telling them? Letting them out?"

"No. I think your sister's too soft for her own good."

"I don't know." I thought about what Zee did to that old bastard Frost, back on Promise Island. "You've not seen her with a nail gun."

"Crow say why he's giving us the moody?" asked Alpha, and we watched him on the bow through the glass eyes of the cockpit, as water sprayed off the lake and soaked him to the bone.

"Just said he's a cripple." A piece of wire broke off in my hand. "Thinks he's some kind of freak."

"He is pretty freaky-looking."

"Don't let him catch you saying it."

"But look at the size of him." Alpha slumped into a chair beside me, and that meant I was all done looking at Crow, because Alpha was by far the best thing to look at, just like she was by far the best way of forgetting all the pain that filled up this boat.

She stretched out her legs, propping her tall boots on the control panel, her thighs like pale gold beneath her purple rags and old bandages, and I felt sped up just at the sight of her. We'd fooled around up in the gun tower, when we could sneak up there and get away from Zee, but each time had just left me more frazzled and my lips more dry. I didn't know where to go next with it. And how the hell could I? My old man had barely mentioned women at all. He made sure I didn't stare too long at the ones we'd built trees for. Avert your eyes, he'd say. The good ones can burn you worse than the bad. But that was about all I got from him, all those years on the road. Still, seeing as what happened between him and my mother, I can't say as I'm surprised.

"So where do you think we'll put them?" Alpha said, swinging her boots off the control panel and resting them in my lap. Her skin had been tinged a whitish sort of green at first, after I'd unplugged her from GenTech's cables, but that was one thing that had gone back to normal.

"The trees?" I said. The caged voices in the cargo hold surged up even worse, but I could hardly think about nothing now my mind was on Alpha.

"Yeah. When we get back."

"If we get back. I don't know. Long as GenTech don't get them. Ain't right for there to be two things growing, the corn and these trees, and for GenTech to own both."

"Your sis says the trees'll start spreading."

"Supposed to. Once they get in the ground."

"And the apples?" Alpha crossed one leg over the other.

"They'll come. Once it gets warm."

"So we'll have to keep them hidden."

"Yeah." I pointed out the window at Crow. "Our buddy yonder's set on Waterfall City."

She frowned then. Tapped at my chest with the toe of her boot. "What do you think your old man would have wanted?"

"Pop?" I'd been trying not to think too much about him. "Man was a nomad. A drifter."

"So what about the statue? The woman he built in Old Orleans?"

"What about it?"

"We could keep the trees safe down there." She pulled her chair closer to mine. "And when we get the rains that far south, the mud runs dark and deep. Good for growing a forest, I reckon."

I wasn't sure what Crow would think about that—hiding the trees with Alpha's old band of pirates in their crumbling city on the southern plains. But what did I care? Long as the trees were kept safe, and kept out of GenTech's reach. I was just as much a nomad as my father had been, and a whole life spent on the road doesn't leave you with much allegiance to one place over the next.

"We get to Old Orleans, and then what?" I asked. "The rest of the pirate clans would all rally around? Said once, you'd be queen of every pirate army if you came home with fruit trees to grow."

"Sure." Alpha stretched her legs around me and worked her way onto my lap, wrapping me up in her. "And you'd be the king," she whispered, touching her forehead to mine.

"But I'm just a tree builder," I said, smiling as I held the fake tree between us.

And then we were kissing. Hungry mouths and chapped lips, and it felt like the morning sun was flowing through my veins. My plastic tree fell to the floor, forgotten, as Alpha put her hands on my hands, steering my fingers to here and there, soft and then hard.

We rolled from the chair to the control panel, and the gadgets and levers prodded us down to the floor. And it was there that Alpha began unwrapping the rags from around her, stripping down till her top half was naked but for my eyes on her skin.

I stopped kissing her then. Pulled back and just stared. Her body was like a whole world unexplored, so I just acted on instinct, tracing my fingers along the contours of her shoulders and her collarbone, working my way down, and down. And there on her belly, still a little green and pink but mostly the same golden-white color as her skin, was that patch of bark GenTech had used to fix her, the stiff patch of wood they'd sewn her up with after she'd been shot in the cornfields.

Alpha tensed as I touched the place where the flesh and bark met and one became the other. "Stop," she whispered, shrinking away from me and pulling bits of clothing back on.

"It's part of you," I told her. "There ain't nothing wrong with it."

"You don't need to touch it."

"So what do you want me to do?"

"Just pretend it ain't there."

The rest of the world seemed to flood back inside me—the moaning in the cargo hold, the secrets in the hull, memories across the water, and dreams at the bow.

"I love all of you," I said, my skin suddenly flushed hot and guilty. Sick that I'd upset her somehow.

"You don't know all of me."

I didn't reckon it was the knowing that mattered, but Alpha had finished tying her clothes back together, and as she pulled her knees to her chest, I realized that twice now, I'd told that girl I loved her, but neither time had she said the words back.

I heard someone on the ladder outside, clanging up the rungs in a hurry, and I tore my gaze from Alpha's brown eyes as the cockpit door flew open.

In burst my sister, looking all shaken up.

"What the hell's wrong with you?" I stood, glancing out the cockpit windows to make sure GenTech hadn't appeared on the horizon.

"It's not me." Zee's voice trembled. "It's the trees."

CHAPTER THREE

In the far corner of the hull, I could see Pop's tank looming in the shadows. Apart from a few crates and boxes, it was the only thing down there, and our footsteps echoed against the metal walls as Zee and I rushed down the ramp and ran to the trees.

Still cloaked in black steel and sat up on thick wheels, the tank was more than six-foot high and maybe five feet wide. And where the small viewing panel—a steel flap hanging down to reveal some glass and all that was inside—was popped open, red lights were pulsing and splashing out. So I reckoned that meant Zee was right to be freaked. Something was wrong, all right. The insides of the tank had always been lit up solid gold before now.

I peered in through the glass at the thin green saplings floating in the liquid. They were about two-foot tall and still tethered to the remains of Pop's body, which was crumpled at the bottom of the tank and bobbing up and down. Twiggy hair clung to his scalp, and his fibrous skin was knotted to his crooked bones, and somehow, it felt like looking in at the strange guts of this shiny machine. All of it strobing beneath the electric red lights.

"What's it doing?" I asked Zee, watching the lights flash gold but then red, the colors of a sky at sundown.

"I don't know. But there's something else." She pointed inside the steel panel, and shimmering at the base of the glass was a number—bright and white and blinking each second. A long number. Hard to work out.

"Can you read it?" I asked her.

"Almost three hundred thousand," she said, but before Zee finished, the number changed. "It drops by one each second that passes."

I watched the last digit change to a five. Then a four. And above us in the cargo hold, the strugglers stomped their feet and raised their voices.

"Those bastards need to give it a damn rest," I yelled up at the ceiling.

"Calm down."

"Calm? How can we be calm? What the hell's this thing counting down to?"

"Zero."

"I guessed that much. I mean, what happens then?"

"Your mother would have known."

But there was nothing left of my mother except this thing she had started. She'd sacrificed herself in the end, so I could keep living. And as I stared at the remains of my father, the echoes of something human bouncing around in the tank, I figured my mother only lived on in the same way that he did. She lived on in those bits and pieces of a dead man from which she'd grown the last trees on earth.

"They're bigger," Zee said, peering into the tank with me. And she was right—each sapling had grown a little longer since we'd left the island. Their thin, budding limbs stretched further out of Pop's flimsy body, which had in turn shrunk at their base, as if being used up as the saplings spiraled higher through the liquid, groping closer to the lights above. "Bigger has to be better, right?"

"Of course." Didn't take a tree builder to know that. I stared at the bark that had grown over Pop's skin, and it suddenly made me feel so lonely to see what my old man had become. Trees or no trees, bones or no bones, Pop was gone, and he couldn't get goner.

I tapped at the glass. "Could be this thing's low on juice. But I don't see no engine on it. It's like they had it charged up."

"Meaning the charge is wearing off?"

"Makes sense," I said. "Maybe the controller could help."

Alpha had taken the control pad off the tank and hooked it into the boat, back before she'd given up trying to hack into the boat's steering so we could change our course if we ran into trouble.

"It's up in the cockpit," I said. Seemed a long shot the controller would do any good. Thing was for steering the tank, not charging it. But I had to do something. And I hated the feeling of being trapped down there below deck, so close to the water, my guts churning as the boat churned through the lake.

"I'll go get it," I said. "We can connect it back in."

"And what should I do?"

"Make sure that number don't start ticking down any faster."

As I ran back through the hull, the whoosh of the water pressed tight at the walls, like the lake meant to crush me to death. I bolted up the ramp, back into daylight, feeling queasy and sucking in air, then stopping for a moment to clutch hold of the railing at the rear of the boat.

And I knew something was wrong soon as I started slipping through the puddles, heading for the ladder that led up to the cockpit.

The rain splashed out of the clouds, and the wind beat the sky, and the boat plunged on just like always. But it was as if the volume was messed, and the world had become louder in all the wrong places.

I heard voices at the bow—and that weren't right, it was only Crow up at the bow. And that weren't his voice. Or Alpha's.

Then I saw the cargo-hold doors hanging open, the padlock broken.

And I heard footsteps come rushing up behind me.

A fist crashed into my head and drove me straight down, and all I could see was black.

Someone was kneeling on me like they meant to split my spine open, and they were working me over, their fists like hammers, knuckles like nails. My bones screamed out, but my brain was all scrambled, and my mouth weren't working. And next thing I knew, I was being dragged across the deck, all out of focus and splayed out sideways, and when we got up to the bow,

I could make out enough to see that all hell had broke loose.

The guy holding me was a stranger—just a wiry knot of muscles, eyes like bruises—but I sure recognized the redhead who was pressing a knife at Crow's throat.

Crow looked helpless. Brought down by a blade tied off to a stump of bone. He was all contorted on the deck, legs useless beneath him. His head yanked back in Kade's one good hand.

But I spotted Alpha, too. Not ten feet from them. And my pirate girl had her shotgun pointed straight at Kade's head.

Standoff is what it was. Must have been about fifty strugglers stood around in scraps of purple turning slick in the freezing rain. They had a few clubs and one lousy knife between them. So that meant they'd not yet found the guns.

"Alpha," I called, and the dude holding me thumped me in the guts so hard, I nearly bit off my tongue.

"You look like me, bud?" she said, not turning her gaze even slightly. Never taking her eyes off the redhead with the knife. "Or you look like Crow?"

I tried to speak, but the bastard holding me clogged up my mouth with his filthy fingers. And for a moment, there was only the sound of the wind in the rain, and the rumble of the boat's engines as it burned up juice and stained the waters oily behind us.

And I wished that I did look like Alpha. I wished I had a gun in my hand and the world at my feet.

"Guess that means you look like Crow," she muttered, her gaze still fixed straight ahead.

I tried to make a moaning sound, loud enough she might hear it. And I knew she couldn't look at me, but

I wanted her to know what I was thinking from the look in my eyes.

We couldn't lose him. That's what my eyes would have told her. We couldn't risk losing Crow. I needed him. This man who'd been a warrior and then a watcher and who now was a cripple. This man who'd been turned into a freak and had somehow turned into my friend.

But it weren't Alpha's style to back down from a fight. And I imagined her weighing the odds, wondering if she could drop Kade to the ground before his knife even flickered, or wondering if Crow was a dead man, anyway, whether she laid her gun down or not.

"I'll kill every one of you," she called. "If you harm either one of them." But as she said it, Alpha hoisted up the shotgun and threw it out off the boat, into the water.

"I gave it up," she cried, as the ragged bodies swarmed towards her. "Now let them both go."

But Alpha could shout all she wanted and it wouldn't make any difference.

We weren't calling the shots anymore.

CHAPTER FOUR

Rain and blood filled my eyes as the bodies roared past me, feet trampling and voices arguing about what this posse ought to do with us now.

But what had we done to them? Hell, they'd have never woken up from Project Zion if it weren't for me. And I'd planned to let them go, hadn't I? Soon as we hit land.

Only now they'd find my trees. And my trees were in trouble.

I heard Alpha screaming. Then Crow was screaming, too.

Then silence.

I slipped my arm free as the rain made me slick. But Muscles wrapped a hand around my windpipe and squashed me flat on the deck.

"Keep him down," Kade said, and he appeared above me, his spine straight, head up, the rain bouncing on his shoulders as he gazed out at the lake.

"Did you kill them?" My voice was cracked and brittle as I stared up at him.

"You know what?" he said. "I hate this. Really, I do."

I struggled and strained, but Kade bent down and put his hand on my shoulder, his green eyes like deep pools of water. So calm, and somehow that made me even more scared.

Then he gestured behind him, and Alpha and Crow got sucked out of the crowd. Battered and bleeding. But still blinking, still breathing.

Kade leaned in closer, his stink all up in my face. "I don't do unto others what they don't do to me. Though I'm afraid I can't speak for the rest of my crew."

"Your crew?" I tried to pull my head away from him. "You folks had a vote or something?"

A fire came into his eyes. "Well, if we had, I guarantee not one of them would have voted for you."

My back was swollen tight from the beating. Had blood pouring out from a gash on my cheekbone, and bruises blooming all up my ribs. The pain made me stagger, but Kade grabbed my neck, shoving me down the ramp into the gloom of the hull.

In the far corner, I could see the outline of the steel box. Closed up now. Its secrets hidden for just a little while longer.

"Banyan?" Zee rushed towards me, but stopped cold when she saw who I was with.

"Long story, gorgeous," Kade said. "He'll tell you later."

His blade shone in the dim light as he gestured me forward. And by the time we reached the tank, more than a dozen folk had come down there to join us.

"Keep your distance, people," Kade told them. "Let me check this thing's safe."

They all held back, like his words cast a spell or something. I mean, some of them strugglers must have been twice his age. It was that voice of his. Like he was too confident to have to be cocky. The voice of someone who knew all the shit you did not.

"All right," he said, pushing me forward. "Go ahead and open her up."

"We were gonna let you go," I said. "Soon as we found land."

"Too late for that, bro. I want to see what you were so keen to keep hidden away."

"Clear your people out," I muttered, so only he'd hear me. "It's better to keep this thing secret till we get somewhere safe."

"Not the way I operate."

"You know these people? You think you can trust them?"

"Only person I don't trust is you." He stepped closer, raised the knife, and prodded it at my shoulder. "Now show me what's in there. Come on. Show us all."

I found the panel and set to prying it open, and as I did, the golden lights spilled out and turned red. The tank flashed and flared, and I stared at the numbers blinking on the glass. The first number was a two, followed by an eight, and all the way at the end, the last digit dropped lower with each beat of my heart.

I thought of that damn control pad, up in the cockpit. But could it do any good, anyway? All we'd used it for was steering the tank around. And if this tank that protected the trees was about to run out of power, then the only place I knew to charge it was back in the Orchard on Promise Island.

"You gotta get close to see it," I muttered, backing away so Kade could push up to the glass and peer inside.

If it hadn't been tied to his stump, I swear he would have dropped his damn knife. I could see his shoulders lose traction. His whole body went soft. And when he pulled his face away, the glass was steamed up from him breathing on it.

Then there was this moment where he tried to stop the bodies rushing past him for their own look at what was inside the tank, but Kade couldn't focus right or get his arms up, and when he spoke again, his voice didn't come out half as commanding.

"What is it?" he whispered, bringing his gaze to meet mine.

"You know what it is."

He rubbed his thumb in his eyes. "Tell me what you see in there."

"Same thing you see."

"It's real?"

"Kade," said one of his buddies. "You all right?"

"You saw it?" he asked them. He was scratching his left arm with his one hand, fingering the holes GenTech's cables had left behind. "You all see it?"

"It's trees," I said, just to shut him up. "Them are saplings, you damn fool."

I watched as the strugglers feasted their eyes on my father—the human skin turned green and craggy, the shoots coming out of Pop's hands and feet. They'd see the sapling curling from the remains of his stomach, and the one that had sprouted from out of his heart. And what did they think when they saw the little tree where his mouth had once been? Did it unravel their insides as it uncoiled towards them?

"How?" Kade's voice trembled. Not so damn sure of himself now.

A couple folk had dropped to the ground and bowed their heads to the floor, like they were praying to that tank and all that was in it.

"Science," I muttered. "GenTech."

"But the locusts ate everything." Kade shook his head like you do when you're trying to wake yourself up. "After the Darkness. Every animal and plant. The swarms ate it all when the sun came back. Everything except GenTech's corn."

He was almost right. Far as we knew, after the Darkness changed everything, the whole world over, more than a hundred years back, the locusts had consumed anything that tried to grow, anything that had somehow survived. Anything, that is, but for the engineered corn that grew with GenTech's logo stamped on the kernels.

Got so the locusts started feeding on human flesh, and GenTech grew powerful inside the walls of their city, Vega, stuffing themselves full of corn and brewing it into fuel, while most outside the Electric City struggled on in ragged bunches, trapped in the dust, with the surging oceans on both coasts, the massive South Wall sealing things off at the bottom, and the Rift pinning things in from up top.

"But GenTech found a forest on that island," I said. "And they fused a man with what was left of the trees."

"Why?" a woman asked, her eyes wild as she turned from the tank and looked to me for answers.

"So they could change the trees up, mess with them, make them too tough for the locusts. Then they could bring a forest back to the mainland and sell us apples like they sell us the corn."

"Apples?" Kade's gaze tightened, and I swear that dude's teeth chewed the air for a second, like his mouth was watering and his brain could hardly keep up. "Fruit trees?" He said it like he was ringing a bell to force himself back to business. "Apples? And you kept this good news to yourself?"

"Guess you'd have been throwing a party."

"You give me some apples, we'll have a party, all right. You ever heard of cider? Ah, yes. A drink from the age of plenty. The days of governments and law and order. The days of food growing everywhere." There he went again, like he knew everything you didn't. "Cider's sweeter than corn whiskey, I'll wager. Ladies and gents, do you realize what we've got here? Do you realize what our young friend stole?"

"I didn't steal it."

"Then GenTech Corporation must think mighty highly of you."

I pointed at the holes they'd drilled into his skin. "They were gonna do this to you. All of you. You were gonna be used up for their forest. Until I yanked their damn cables out of your arms."

"Needed our help, I suppose." His eyes flickered to the tank. "So you could get this thing out of there."

"It ain't a thing. It's trees. All of the trees we're gonna get. And that man who died in there was my father, so maybe you ought to show some respect."

"Your father?" Kade's eyes were like a battle between crazy and calm. "Well, who the man was does not concern me. Apples, on the other hand, certainly grab my attention. How long till we see one?"

"Never." Zee stepped up beside me and sounded about as spiky as she looked smooth. "Unless we stop arguing and start to work things out."

Before Kade could respond, someone was hollering his name from up on deck. I turned and saw Muscles running down the ramp towards us. "You gotta come," he was shouting. "Kade. Come quick."

"Boats?" Kade asked. "Or land?"

"Neither. There's a message coming in."

CHAPTER FIVE

Kade made me scamper up the ladder to the cockpit, and once he pushed me inside it, I found Crow and Alpha on the floor with their backs pressed together, bound with the same purple wire I'd built my little tree from.

"You should go easy," I said to the strugglers messing with dials and switches on the far wall. "Before you break something."

"Never mind him," Kade said, bumping fists with his cohorts. "He's had a rough day. Now, what do you have for me?"

"Can't get it back." This was some bucktoothed geezer. "But there was a voice coming in. That screen over there."

A transmission? Out here? It could only be GenTech. And there could be no worse news.

"Untie my friends," I said to Kade as he tapped his knife on the monitors. "You're gonna need our help."

"Doesn't work that way, bro. The girl's a little too feisty. Even for me."

"Just eating this up," I said. "Ain't you?"

"No, sir." He jabbed his stumped arm at his belly. "I'm saving myself for those apples."

"Half the hands," Alpha muttered from the floor. "And twice the mouth."

"Funny. I don't remember you and my mouth getting acquainted. But maybe we can find time for that later on." Kade turned from the monitors so he could flash her his handsome grin, but then the screen behind him was sparking to life.

A noise had rustled up out of nowhere. Weren't just sound, neither. A scrappy picture was beaming in through the static, crackling like flames in a snowstorm. And as the blur turned into an image, the noise became words, and the voice weren't just talking, it was talking right at me.

"I see you, tree builder," the man said. "I see you."

The whole place ground to a stop. And I just stood there. Staring at the face that hovered and flashed on the monitor. A face I recognized, even though it had changed.

A dead man's face that was all too alive.

King Harvest's scalp was as pale and hairless as it had been, but below it, his cheeks and nose were now twisted and curled, as if the flesh was trying to drip off his skull. He'd been burned. Scarred. But he was still alive, all right. Hell, he was right there on that monitor and staring straight at me.

"Yes." Harvest's voice cracked through the static. "I remember you, boy." He reached a hand to his melted cheeks, pinching at the bloodless skin. "You left me with this souvenir, after all."

Had thought I'd seen him shot down. Knew now it had only been one of his damn replicants, those pale King Harvest copies he surrounded himself with. Meanwhile, the king himself must have escaped his slave ship and scuttled away—though not before the explosions tore up his face.

"Should've stayed out of Old Orleans," I said, glancing around, trying to figure out how he was able to see me. Had to be some sort of camera somewhere, hooking into the transmission.

"And you should have stuck to making trees out of metal," he said, before a bout of interference severed our link.

I turned to the others. Crow was staring at the monitor, just jumbled there in a pile on the floor. And Alpha was trying to arc her head around so she could see the screen—but I figured if she could see him, then maybe Harvest would see her, and I felt an urge to shield her from his gaze, as if that might keep her safe.

"Keep him talking," Kade whispered, and I turned back to the monitor as the fuzz broke clear. I looked into the pits of Harvest's eyes. The black-and-white image became color, but it didn't make much difference, since everything about that man was some shade of smoke.

"So what's up, Candlewax?" I said.

His melted face attempted a smile, but the scars wouldn't let it happen. "I'll let you keep the boat, tree builder. And everyone on it."

"Bastard wants a trade," Alpha said, and suddenly Harvest's eyes started to dance around, like he was trying to peer out of the screen.

"All we got is the boat," I said, grabbing back his attention. "Don't know what else you'd be after."

"Oh, I'm quite sure you do know. Glass tank. Roughly six feet high and five feet across. Illuminated by golden lights, and full of clear liquid. Something very special floating inside."

"You still working for GenTech, old man? What they giving you to come out here?"

"Don't presume to know anything about why I'm here, boy. I'm offering you a chance. And I suggest that you take it."

"Does sound like quite the opportunity."

He nodded. "I'm glad you see reason."

"Except I'd rather see you in hell."

Harvest's face disappeared for a bit, washed out in a sea of gray splinters. And when he came back, he looked neither angry nor surprised. "Very well," he said, like he was distracted by something. Like he was too busy all of a sudden to play any more games. "I'll take what I came for, then blow your boat from the water."

"You'll have to find us first."

"My dear tree builder," Harvest said, "I already have."

The image shrank off the screen like it had been sucked down a drain. But before Harvest's face spiraled all the way gone, me and Kade were peering out through the windows, our faces pressed up against the glass. I strained my eyeballs, but there was no sign of nothing. Not to the south, anyway. I peered west—nothing but the endless water and sky. I stared east—empty. Then I ran back through the cockpit, swung outside over the ladder, and gazed behind us, my eyes turning watery in the wind.

"We can expect company," Kade called after me. "Just a question of when."

I leaned back inside and watched as he untied the knife from the end of his arm.

"Cut your friends loose." He threw the blade in my direction, and it jangled onto the floor. "Then fetch us our guns."

"You're letting us go?"

"I'm doing what you should have done to begin with," he said, pushing past me as I picked up the blade. "There are enough enemies out there. We can't afford to make more of them."

I weren't ready to trust this smooth-talking redhead who'd put a knife at Crow's throat. But I reckoned he did have a point.

"If we're working together, you should know that tank seems to be running out of power," I said. "And it's all that's protecting the trees."

"All right. I'll see if there's someone who knows how to rig a charge to it."

I grabbed the tank's control pad from where Alpha had left it, handed it to Kade. "This might help."

He coiled the control pad's wires around his shoulder. "Anything else I should know?"

"The boat's steering is locked. Keeps heading south, no matter what."

"Some escape plan this was. Man, you really thought things through, didn't you?"

I pointed at the steps that ran up through the ceiling of the cockpit and into the gun tower. "There's a scope up there. Big old sub gun. Your weapons. I don't know what else to tell you."

"Then let me know what you see through that scope. I'm heading below."

"That's it?" Alpha called after him. "Face on a screen, and you run off and hide?"

"Oh, I'm not hiding." Kade swung outside, gripping the ladder with his one hand and waving his damn stump in the air. "I just think we'll need all hands on deck."

"Thought I saw Harvest die," I told Alpha as we climbed to the top of the gun tower, moving as fast as we could. "I thought Jawbone shot that freak full of lead."

"Bastard's been slippery a long time, bud."

"You see that scar on him?"

"Could only hear him. Heard that voice every year of my life, remember?"

And I did remember. He'd come trading with the pirates at Old Orleans for slaves he could sell to GenTech. He'd snatched Crow and Zee off the road, and Hina—Zee's mother, who'd been such a perfect copy of my own mother that I reckon Pop had fallen in love with the same woman twice.

I remembered dragging Hina out of the wreckage of Harvest's slave ship. I'd saved her then. But I hadn't been able to save her in the cornfields, when the locusts had come.

"Zee's gonna take it hard," I said as we reached the bundle of guns we'd tied in plastic and stashed out of sight. "I saw how Harvest had them locked up in cages."

"You want me to tell her?"

"No," I said, figuring I should be the one to do it. "You better get folk ready for battle. Don't want them shooting themselves in the foot."

"They did all right getting out of that bunker."

"But it'll all be for nothing if we all die out here."

"You meant that about the tank running low?"

"That's what it looks like," I said, picturing those red lights flashing like some sort of alarm. "I'm hoping maybe the controller can fix it. Or that we can charge it back up."

"We can do that?"

"I don't know."

She began to lower the bundle of weapons down towards the cockpit. "I'll teach people how best to use these things. You keep a lookout for Harvest. And keep your eyes on Red, too."

At the top of the tower was the meanest sub gun you ever seen. Whole buckets of ammo fed into the gun's belly, and its mouth was fixed to point out off the boat. You could swivel the gun all the way around, and I sat in the control seat and pushed my eye to the scope. Started north, then turned my way to the east.

The skies had cleared some, but the low western sun was about to sink into clouds. Everything on the horizon was blank—empty and shadowed. But I kept turning the scope. I angled due east. Southeast. And then, on the far edge of the world, I saw a smattering of small black points, static and sticking out of the water.

And what was that looming behind them?

I pulled my face off the scope. Jammed it back on again. I twisted at the focus wheel until I could see. The black points were dotted in a clump across the horizon—rocks, maybe—but behind them was a smear of brown and gray and little pieces of white, and hell, yes, that was dirt and snow I was seeing. I almost yelled down into the cockpit that we'd found land, at last. But I figured I should keep on with my scanning.

And as I steered my sights south, I spotted the fleet of boats that was coming our way.

CHAPTER SIX

Even in the dim light, the boats sparkled against the sky and chopped up the water, as if they were shattering some vast sheet of glass. They were far off—took my eye from the scope, and I could see nothing but the pale bend of the earth. But the boats were heading right for us, there was no doubt about that.

I pressed up at the scope again. In the middle of the fleet, the biggest boat was darker in color, and seemed to be out ahead of the rest. I pictured Harvest on that boat, leading the charge, and I imagined him on its bow, his scarred face pressed at a scope like my scope. His eyes cheating the distance. Hell, perhaps we were staring straight at one another, as if to see who might flinch first.

I climbed down into the cockpit and glanced out the window. Down on the deck, the survivors stood stone-faced and silent, guns squeezed in their fists as Alpha marched between them, going over how to load up and aim the weapons, and making a big deal out of how few bullets we had left.

"So you wait till the shot's for the taking," I heard her say as I slid down the ladder. "But don't wait a moment too long."

The sun had turned the sky to ash and embers, and it was getting colder by the second as I pushed through the crowd and found Crow at the bow.

Kade was there with him. Not long ago, the punk had a knife at Crow's throat, but here we were all partnered up. Too many enemies already, I reminded myself. No room on the list for new ones.

Not yet, anyway.

"Five boats," I said, coming up to the railing and pointing south. "Each one probably bigger than this one. And we're heading straight for them."

"Then it's a good thing the girl makes a good general." Kade nodded over at Alpha. "A fine-looking one, too."

"Shouldn't you be doing something useful?" I said, burning up when I saw the way he was staring at her.

"I've been searching for someone to work on the boat, if you must know. Trying to find someone who might know how to power that tank up, too."

"Out of this bunch?" Crow muttered.

"Hard to tell where people have been. Or what they can do. I counted one Soljah, for starters." Kade glanced up at the scar burned on the back of Crow's neck. Then he turned to me. "Oh, yeah, I hear we have a tree builder, too. That should come in handy."

"And what did you used to do?"

"I was a scholar. A poet. A thief and a fighter."

"Ever work with mechanics?"

"And get my hand dirty? No, thanks. But I found a woman who used to work with the Salvage Guild. She's down there now, cracking open the steering shaft. Trying to snap off the automatics, move out the rudders. Said she used to work the Heaps, before she got taken."

I might have been impressed, if I'd believed the Heaps existed. Never seemed to me like the Salvage Guild would keep all their best stuff off-limits, though. Their whole business was based on scavenging up old machines and gadgets, fixing them, then trading them for water, corn, old world Benjamins, even slave labor. So why would they keep their finest prizes all hidden away?

"If she gets the steering working, point us southeast," I said. "I saw land through the scope."

"And there was me thinking you'd just get in the way."

"You know this man? Harvest?" I asked, trying to ignore Kade's needling.

"I know of him." His green eyes turned squinty as the wind cut cruel. "Man who calls himself king."

"We should get folk inside," Alpha said, joining us. "Before they all freeze to death. They're as ready for battle as they're gonna get."

She shoved a pistol into my hand, then held one up to Crow.

"No," he said. "Give mine to the redhead."

"I know what you're thinking." Kade flashed his big smile at Alpha, seeing her hesitate to hand him the gun. "But I suggest you let me earn your trust."

He grinned even bigger once she'd handed the gun over, then he spun it around on his finger in a way that said he knew how to shoot pretty good.

"Nice work, getting them ready," he said, nodding at the rabble Alpha had lined up on the deck. "I'm taking it you've seen some action."

"I've seen plenty." Alpha put her hand on Crow's back, trying to make him quit wobbling. "We all have."

"There comes a time when plenty's too much." Kade was staring at Crow when he said it, but Crow's gaze was stuck on the horizon, watching the end of day and the beginnings of night.

"Where's Miss Zee?" Crow asked.

"Ah, yes. Her." Kade frowned. "Been meaning to tell you. We have another problem below deck."

I hadn't realized how many folk were still down in the hull. They were hunkered together at the far end, forming a scruffy circle around the tank, and one woman was singing a song about redemption and the blood of Zion, so I could tell she was Rasta. I mean, you couldn't tell by looking at her, since GenTech had shaved off her dreadlocks, and she was dressed all in purple, not in red, gold and green. Most of the others were kneeling and praying, their hands drumming slow on the floor, and it didn't seem like these folk were getting ready for battle. Sounded more like they were getting ready to sleep.

"We should find guns for these people," I said to Kade.

"Guns aren't the problem." He pointed through the crowd. "She is."

Zee was stood next to the tank, in the center of everything. The panel on the steel box was still hanging open, and the lights still flashed inside the glass, and I'd no doubt those numbers were still blinking down, too.

"They want to surrender," said Kade. "Her most of all."

"I'll talk some sense into her. You wait here."

I worked my way into the middle of the strugglers, joining Zee in the space these folk had left around their steel-box shrine.

"You got it hooked up," I said quietly, when I saw she'd wired the tank's control pad back in.

"Didn't do any good." Zee pulled her long hair back with her hand.

"Had a feeling. But I heard someone might be able to charge it back up."

"No luck so far," she said. "I feel like we're losing him."

"Him?"

"You know what I mean."

A woman shoved past us, huddling up at the tank to press her dirty palms on the glass, then smacking her wet lips at the steel.

"Give us a second," Zee said to some of the others hovering around, and they pushed away, giving me and her a little breathing room.

"It's Harvest," I whispered. "He's coming for the trees."

"Harvest?" She kept her voice low, as if she didn't want to disturb the singing none, but her eyes were wide, and she was biting her lip.

"Don't you worry. I ain't gonna let him hurt you."

"People said it was GenTech," she said, and she almost looked disappointed.

"Could be they're the same thing."

I peered into the tank. There was a little space above the liquid, an air pocket nearly a foot high, and I watched one of the saplings reaching for it, as if trying to break free. Then I glanced down at the bottom, where the remains of my father were all freaky and faded, and all of me ached for my old man to still be alive and be stood there beside me. He was the one who'd come north to try to put things right. All I'd come for was him, and the promise of someplace that was different.

"Either way," Zee said, leaning against the tank. "I suppose Harvest could know."

"Know what?"

Her eyes were gray and shiny, like bits of scuffed chrome. "How to keep this tank working."

My heart sank down to my toes when she said it.

"We can't fight him, Banyan."

"We fought him before, and we won. What? You don't remember what it looked like in the pit of his slave ship?"

"I remember," she said, her voice turning sharp as her face turned away from me. "It was the last time I saw my mother alive."

"That's why we have to keep fighting."

"No." The red lights from the tank played on her brown skin. "We have to keep these things safe."

"You just want to surrender?" I stared past her at all the people singing and praying. "After everything we've done?"

"If that's what it takes. Give him the trees, and the trees get to carry on. It's the best hope we have."

I turned back to the tank, watched that tallest sapling trying to float its tip into the air at the top. "You want to just give these away? To that slaving son of a bitch?"

"They're all that's left, Banyan."

"You mean, because I fired up and burned down the rest of them? And you don't think that keeps me up at night?" I remembered the shells of those white trees burning on that island, creating a distraction so we could get the people free and steal ourselves a future from GenTech. I could still smell the smoke from the fire, and still feel the weight of my mother, dying in my arms.

"We sacrificed too much to give up now," I said.

"But the trees are more important than who gets to control them."

"I don't want to control them. I just don't want GenTech to hoard them away."

"You don't know he's with GenTech."

"Might be he's even worse. Who knows how many people he sent off to that island? And what about the ones who didn't make it that far? The ones who burned in Vega. Like Sal."

"Don't."

"They threw him in a pit full of flames, and I watched them do it. And how many others died just like him because of men like Harvest and GenTech's greed?"

"So we stop fighting—then no one has to die."

"I thought you changed your mind when we busted off of that island. After all we did, and now you just want to quit."

"I want to live," Zee said. "And I want you to live, too. And Crow and Alpha and everyone on this boat. And the trees, Banyan. You said you'd keep them safe." She pointed at the saplings through the open panel. "You told your mother you would. I was there when you promised."

"Giving them to that bastard ain't keeping them safe."

"Nor is letting them sink. The world needs them, Banyan. Not just you."

"He was my father," I said.

"And what? He was just some man that left me?"

The singing had stopped and the drumming broke down, and I could feel everyone's eyes upon us.

"He didn't know about you," I said, trying to lower my voice. "Or he would have come found you."

"It doesn't matter."

"Yes, it does. And I would have come for you, too."

"You did." She smiled at me, but then she quickly looked away, and I was losing her all over again. "All these people around us, they're pieces, like the scraps you built trees out of. It's when you put them together that they become something special. That's what a family is, Banyan. Not some man who ran away."

"He ran away so he could fix things."

"And you're still running after him." Zee put her hand out. I thought she was reaching for me, but instead she touched the black steel that cloaked the tank. "But he's gone. And we can't afford to lose what he left us."

I started to back away from her.

"Please," she said, her pretty face made ugly by the things she was saying. "He'll destroy us. It'll be even worse than before."

"Not if I can help it."

I stumbled through the crowd, heading for the ramp, and I knew Zee wouldn't follow. I could sense it, I guess. That lass was the last bit of blood that I had.

CHAPTER SEVEN

The big moon was blocked by clouds and drizzle, but despite the darkness, I spotted Alpha at the bow right away. She was leaning against the railing and peering into the night, and as I stood back, watching her stretch her shoulders and flex her legs, I wondered if there'd come a time when there was no battle to limber up for. A time I could hold onto that girl and never let go.

"What is it, bud?" she said.

"How come you know it's me?" I stepped up to the railing to join her.

"Maybe I just hoped it was."

"You see the boats yet?"

"You'll be the first to know."

I put my hand on her back, trying to make like it felt natural, but there was something awkward in the gesture. Maybe because of the way Alpha just stood there, like she was frozen solid beneath her damp rags.

Or maybe because what I really wanted was to feel her whole body against me and seize some last sweetness.

"There's a girl inside," she said. "In the hold. And she's too young to have a gun in her hand."

"We'll get her down in the hull." I figured the girl had to be tiny, seeing as how small some of Alpha's own clan had been. "There's a bunch of them down there who ain't planning on fighting. And guess who's heading them up?"

"I know this kid," said Alpha, clearly not in the guessing mood. "I mean, I seen her before. We traded her down in Old Orleans. Year before you came."

I figured there weren't no wonder the little lass had a gun in her hand then. Snatched up by pirates, traded to Harvest, then hauled north by GenTech. And now here she was, about to face Harvest again.

"Ain't your fault she's out here," I said.

"I don't know. I'll take my fair share of the blame." Alpha's voice was barely louder than the wind. "Where's Red at, anyway?"

"Overseeing work on the boat, trying to free up the steering."

She glanced about, making sure it was just us out there.

"I'm worried about Crow," she said. "It's like he's given up or something."

"We get him back to Niagara, he'll be all right."

"That's a long ways from here, bud. And I don't get how he wants to head back there, anyway. Didn't he say he got banished?"

"Yeah," I said. "Thrown out."

"So that makes sense to you?"

"What you trying to say?"

"I'm saying Crow ain't what he was. And he might not hold much sway with the Soljahs."

My hand was still on her back, and my arm was shaking, and her back was trembling, and everything was shivered to the bone. I leaned into her, put my arms around her.

"You're with me, though," she said. "All the way, right?"

"All the way."

"And if something happened to me, you know I'd want you to head back there. To my people. To Old Orleans. You and the trees would have the protection of all the pirates on the plains."

"Don't talk like that."

"They deserve them saplings."

"You're getting way ahead of the game."

"Promise me, Banyan."

"Promise what?"

She kissed me then. She was as warm as the air was freezing, and it bloomed me up on the inside, filling me with feelings that weren't born out of fear.

"You and me," I whispered to her. "We'll grow that forest together. And I'll build us a home in the treetops, you'll see."

But the moment was over. Alpha weren't even listening. She just pointed across the water, and I could see the five boats, creeping out of the void like bad-luck stars.

We found the girl in the cargo hold and took the gun off her. And she was tiny, all right. All elbows and ears. Alpha took the extra pistol. Rounded up a couple other kids we thought were too young to be fighting. Then we herded them to the back of the boat so we could send them down the ramp that led into the hull.

Top of the ramp, we ran into Kade and the Salvage Guild woman he'd found. Her purple rags were covered in oil, her knuckles all torn.

"Any luck with the rudders?" I asked them.

"Luck's got nothing to do with it." The woman looked like a piece of salvage herself, useful but rough at the edges. She rubbed her big hands together and grinned. "But if we get up in that cockpit and start steering, this old beauty will point wherever you want it to go."

It did, too. And by the time the sun rose, we were heading southeast and really hauling ass about it, the boat's engines hollering and grinding, the air stinking of burning juice.

But no matter how fast we moved, Harvest's boats moved faster. They were still a mile or so behind us, but closing the gap much too quick.

The Salvage Guild woman had fallen asleep in the corner of the cockpit, and Crow had joined me and Alpha, peering out through the glass. Kade was there, too, of course. Hanging around like a bad smell. We all squinted through the cockpit windows, watching land appear on the horizon, silhouetted against the searing dawn sky.

As we got closer, we could make out those floating points I'd spotted through the scope. Looked like pillars now. Taller than our boat. Stony islands, maybe, scattered between us and the shore.

"What are those things?" Kade said, shielding his eyes from the glare of the sun. "Rocks?"

"I don't know. But I reckon I should see if the trees are set for moving," I said. "We hit land, that tank needs to be ready to roll."

"You want me to come down there?" Alpha put her hand on my arm. "Talk to Zee?"

"It's all right. I'm done talking to her, anyway."

"Don't see no lava." Crow was still focused on the horizon, his eyes squinting a little less as the sun inched up. "Them hills be brown. Snow in the distance. No steam. No ash."

"So we're a ways above it," I said. "The Rift's further south."

"Ain't just that," he said. "Look at them rocks now."

We leaned over the controls and out through the window, peering into the brand new day.

"What about them?" Kade said.

"They ain't rocks."

And Crow was right. They weren't.

They were buildings.

CHAPTER EIGHT

It was a city. What was left of one, anyway. Sticking up out of the water were buildings as tall as the ones they still have in Vega and the northern Steel Cities. And those old scrapers were blocking us from the shoreline. The jagged remains were too thick to travel through, and they stretched too far for us to try to cut around.

"It's a mess," said Alpha, peering over my shoulder.

"Aye," Crow said. "And there'll be more of it below water."

Sure enough, there'd be other, shorter buildings just below the surface. A hidden sprawl, waiting to puncture us if we tried to weave through the maze.

Crow was bending back on the throttle, easing our speed.

"You insane?" I turned to him. "Harvest's fleet's right behind us."

"No way we can make it through that city," he said, and I figured it was like Alpha had said, Crow was

60

just giving up. Hell, I should have had him run down there and hide in the hull with Zee and the rest of the cowards. Maybe he could watch over her like old times, when Frost was beating her ass and Crow never did a thing to stop him.

I stared back out at the city. Looked like concrete fingers reaching into the sky. And as I peered at those old world towers, I could see the tops were connected— thin bridges dangled between the scrapers, stretching from rooftop to rooftop, suspended in the air and stitching the skyline together.

"If we can get in there," Kade pointed at the buildings and then up at the bridges, "those could be our escape route. Get inside a building and get to the rooftop, then we follow the bridges toward land. Unless one of you has a better idea?"

"You be as crazy as Banyan," Crow muttered, but he limped aside so that Kade could ramp back the engines.

There were a couple dozen folk lined up along the back of the boat, and there weren't much to their formation. They just stood there and fiddled with their weapons, ammunition counted out in buckets beside them, near-empty packets of corn in their fists.

At first, those stragglers had all looked the same to me, their shaved heads stuffed inside purple hoods, their thin bodies wrapped in fuzz and GenTech logos. But I realized now that each one of them was as different as they were desperate. Different shades to their skin and their stubble, whole different worlds in their eyes.

Kade told them we'd soon come crashing into a sunken city, and he outlined his vague plan for what we'd have to do next. And once he got done, I didn't head to the hull like I'd planned, to make sure that tank of trees was ready for moving. Instead, I stood with the rest of the crew and stared at the four silver boats and the black one in the middle, glinting in the harsh morning light.

The fleet was so close now, I could see the glass of their cockpits and their towers of guns. None of those boats were GenTech purple. But nor was the boat I was standing on. These were old world machines, the same color as when they'd been salvaged. And whatever color his boat, I reckoned Harvest had to be working for GenTech. How else would he know to be out here, in this forgotten, frozen part of the world?

I saw the shiny bald heads of the king's replicants, lining up on their boat decks, all dressed in gray and brandishing guns. And there were so damn many of them. Got close enough and I could see they didn't have Harvest's burned face—they looked just how he used to. Each one of them, a perfect dead-eyed copy.

And then those replicants weren't just lining up across from us, they were down in the water and hurtling towards us—riding on the back of one-man pods shaped like missiles, sleek and slippery machines that soared through the waves.

"Hold your fire." Kade's voice rang out and took charge. "Wait till they're in range."

I was supposed to be seeing if the trees were ready for moving.

But I pulled out my pistol instead.

The Harvesters' gleaming skulls zipped across the lake, the pods trailing dirty foam in the white wake behind them, the wail of their engines growing loud in our ears.

"Now," Kade yelled from the far side of the boat, and as the rifles boomed and busted, I took aim myself.

The first Harvester was maybe forty yards from us, but as we fired at him, he drove his pod under the water and stayed down. Submerged. For maybe three seconds. Then he broke free, arcing out of the lake and skimming across the surface, speeding towards us.

And he kept spinning under the water and whirling back out as we unloaded into the last place we'd seen him. Not a damn one of us conserving our bullets. And not one of us even slowing him down.

"This way," a woman screamed from the far side of the boat. "They're this way."

But they were every way, and everywhere. Their jet pods drilling through the water and diving beneath it as our bullets rained down.

Chaos clawed through our voices. Everyone shrieking and spooked. But then our hollering got drowned out by the sub gun opening fire above us, and when I glanced up at the gun tower, I saw Alpha working in a new line of ammo and crackling a fresh round loose.

She made a hit. Showering up a bloom of red in the water. Sending up a plume of smoke. The pod she'd hit reared up with no rider and bounced itself to a halt.

"They're frontside," Crow was yelling, sliding down the ladder to join us. "The bow. Get to the bow."

He hit the deck and crumbled, his legs collapsing. And I ran to him, the sound of the jet pods screaming in my ears.

"Get off me." Crow shoved me away. "They're almost onboard. And we're almost into that city."

"Then do something," I shouted, sprinting for the front of the boat. "Get the tank ready. Get Zee."

Before I reached the bow, I spotted the grappling hooks spinning onto the railing. Two of them. Three of them. Then there was hands. Heads. Whole bodies climbing up. And I was running towards them so fast, I couldn't aim my pistol straight.

I hit one of them, though. Got lucky, I guess. But the other two Harvesters kept coming. Raising up guns of their own and opening fire.

I hung back by the door to the cargo hold, ducking against the wall. Alpha was trying to swivel the sub gun down on the two replicants, but she couldn't point it low enough. Thing weren't built to shoot up its own boat.

So I charged back out with my gun blazing. Kept low and kept firing.

Until I got thrown in the air.

The boat had hit something. No time to hold on as the front end plowed downwards, the howl of steel tearing apart somewhere below me as I slammed back onto the deck.

And then I was rolling and sliding, and I never stopped moving. Just kept bouncing all the way to the edge.

CHAPTER NINE

There was whole seconds when the wind rushed and gusted and I spun in the air with my eyes sealed shut. Then I hit the lake like an explosion. The sound of water smashing into my brain as my legs snapped at the surface and dragged me below.

First time I'd nearly drowned, in a river too deep, my old man had been there to save me. Second time, in a muddy pool, it had been Sal who'd hauled me back out. But I knew the third time, I'd not be so lucky.

Unless I could save myself.

I thrashed my arms around, kicked my legs. Clothes dragging at me, heavy boots pulling me down. Everything was muted. Distant. Couldn't hardly see nothing. Just bubbles. Brown and green and blue. But a clear light wobbled above me. And below was a blackness that kept tugging me closer.

I was moving my arms in frantic circles. Swinging about, getting nowhere. Losing the frothy last gasp in my lungs. But when I felt something at my shoulder, I spun around till I had my hands on it. Heavy steel, spiky in my fingers. I peered through the swirling murk and realized I'd found a damn hook, one of the grapplers the Harvesters had slung up to the railing. I caught the hook between my knees and grabbed at the steel wire floating behind it, pulling the wire down, making it taut. And that meant it was attached to something above me.

So I used it to pull myself up.

One breath, not even a full one, was all I had to go on. And it was like it had seeped out already, I was so empty and aching. My brain throbbed and my chest got stiff. But I didn't stop putting one hand over the other, following the wire back to the surface. The water so cold, like it might freeze me inside it, as I kicked at it and kept reaching higher, crawling my way to the light.

My senses all shattered as I broke through the surface. I burst into the air and coughed and spluttered and damn near swallowed the lake. But I held onto that steel wire as I held my head out of the water. And I found what the wire was fastened against.

A jet pod. Black and steel and slippery. Its engine was still warm, and there weren't no one on it.

Not until I hauled myself up.

You had to lay flat on your stomach on that Harvester machine. I hooked my feet at the rear, stretched my hands to the front, then tried to get my bearings.

The flooded city lay straight ahead and not fifty yards off, all decayed walls, broke-glass windows, and rusted steel-bone frames. And our boat was spinning into that city, about to disappear in the shadows. Smoke and screams poured out of the hull, and I could see as many Harvesters as survivors on the deck, their bodies all wrangled together.

Then the boat was gone from view. Lost between the towers.

I jabbed a thumb at the pod's ignition. Flipped a red switch and grabbed on tight, revving the engine beneath me with the grips in my hands. The pod shuddered as it bounced forward, and I thought it might stall, but pretty soon I was getting the hang of it, racing across the water and skipping through the boat's wake, engine shrieking like a chainsaw and spewing smoke.

I clamped the pod with my thighs, throwing a glance over my shoulder as I bucked and thrashed towards the city.

Behind me, Harvest's fleet had stopped a safe distance from the buildings, the troops on deck peering at the old world remains. I glimpsed a figure among them dressed in long gray robes, and I reckoned it was their leader, their king.

No sign of agents, though. No purple. No GenTech logos. So was Harvest working for GenTech or working for himself?

Didn't matter, I told myself. Either way, he was after our trees.

When I spun back around, I had to bank left. Hard. Just missing a clawed rod of steel. I needed to pay better attention, damn it, now I was inside the maze.

I shook the spray from my face and spotted the boat up ahead, its entire bow under the water. So I cranked the throttle as throaty as the jet pod could muster, catching up to the boat and pulling alongside it, throwing glances up at the deck and hollering out.

Looked like the Harvesters onboard were losing the battle. But it wouldn't matter who won if the whole boat sank. We needed to get that tank into the buildings and up to a rooftop. We needed to get the trees to those bridges and find some way to reach land.

I swerved to the right of a rusted steeple. Plowed through a floated-up pile of junk. Still, the boat spun. Still, it bounced at the buildings, slowing down a little more with each shudder and crunch.

Biggest damn tower was straight ahead, though. And I reckoned I had to get to that scraper before our boat hit it. It was the only way I might get back onboard in time and get to the trees.

I wouldn't have long inside the building—once the boat rammed into it, I'd have minutes at best before the boat finished sinking. So I pulled away from the boat and sped faster. Took aim at a shiny column of windows in the tower ahead, hammering at the front end of my pod to get the thing slapping at the water. Faster. Harder. Then I was kicking down, launching up—and not ten feet from the building, I was airborne, arcing upwards and driving the pod through a great wall of glass.

The windows sliced and slivered, and I covered my face with my hands, bailing before the pod slammed into the far wall of the room I'd entered, the impact shaking the ceiling and filling the air with debris.

I landed hard. My bones battered, but nothing broken. And soon as the air cleared, I began busting past tables and chairs and old gadget salvage, working my way out of the room and hunting some stairs.

I had to climb up—higher than the boat's deck—if I was going to get back onboard when the boat hit.

The stairwell switchbacked up the inner core of the scraper, and it was crowded with bones, old bodies cluttering the steps, arrows all down the walls. The remains of some battle, I reckoned. But I had no time to ponder it as I raced up, clearing four steps with each stride. Just had to get high enough before the boat hit. Then I had to get the tank off the boat and into this stairwell.

These steps were our only way up to those bridges.

And the bridges would be our only way out.

When the boat smashed into the scraper, the whole building groaned and bent, as if it might topple from the impact. But I pushed on through the carnage, staggering into a room full of plastic booths, then kicking my way through them, crashing towards the boat as the boat crashed through the room towards me, like it was eating its way through the walls.

The back end of the boat was the only part still above water now, and strugglers were pouring off what was left of the deck, vaulting over the railing, then rushing into the building, their purple coats stained with blood, dead Harvesters mangled between them.

I saw Kade leap from the deck onto the railing, the sub gun strapped to his shoulder, his hand reaching out to keep his balance as he readied to jump into the room.

I rushed towards him, fighting through the strugglers swarming past me in the opposite direction.

"Where's the tank?" I yelled, because it was always those trees that seemed to matter most to me. Even more than my friends, or the little kids I'd smuggled into the belly of the boat.

As Kade landed in the room beside me, he pointed back through the confusion, back onboard.

And there, rolling up the ramp out of the hull, came our big black box—the tank of trees, cloaked in steel and in motion. Zee was riding on top, the controller clamped tight in her fists. She was wheeling the tank back and forth across the sloping deck, trying to keep it steady as the boat slumped and sank beneath her.

She had Crow bundled beside her and was ramping up now, trying to steer through a hole in the deck's railing and get off the boat before it sank too low.

But as soon as she touched down, just inside the torn-up room, the tank's wheels skidded and snagged, and I knew they weren't going to make it. They'd landed much too close to the edge.

I raced towards them, wires and sparks thrashing out of the walls and ceiling. And when I reached the tank, I grabbed Zee's leg and pulled her off, dragging her towards me, Crow coming, too, the big guy landing in an unconscious pile at my feet.

But the tank was creaking and swaying and leaning back the wrong way, ready to topple and follow the boat into the freezing depths.

I grabbed the controller from Zee and spun the tank's wheels in the right direction, keeping it upright, working it further into the room. Moving it away from the edge, steering it to safety as the last bits of the boat disappeared into the lake.

"Where's Alpha?" I screamed, throwing down the controller and staring at Kade. The last of the survivors scurried past us and raced up the stairwell. Anyone still on the boat was trapped below the surface. Lost in the water.

Kade had reels of bullets hooked onto his arm and strapped on his back, and he had the sub gun resting on his shoulder. The sub gun I'd last seen Alpha using.

"Where is she?" I yelled at him.

He just shook his head.

I stared out of the shattered windows at where the boat was now just bubbles. I waited till it was nothing but gone.

Dread shivered my spine.

"She couldn't have been onboard," I whispered.

Everything seemed so quiet without the whine of engines. Everything was still for a moment, and everything was wrong.

"You think they have more of those speeders?" Zee sounded frantic, barely holding it together.

"Harvest'll find a way in here." Kade started shoving debris out of the way, trying to clear a path for the tank through the remains of the room. "We don't have much time. We have to get up to those bridges."

"But we have to find her," I said.

"There's nowhere to look, Banyan." Zee had blood on her hip. Her whole body soaking wet and shaking as she grabbed at my arm. "You think Alpha would have wanted us to stay here?"

She started pulling at me. Every inch of her stained thick with fear.

"You can't say it like she's already dead."

"There's only one way to go." Zee pointed at the stairs. And the steep way would always be my way, I realized.

I felt pressed into nothing, as if the sky was crashing upon me and the ground refused to yield.

I watched Zee shake Crow, checking to see if he was still breathing. But hell, she should have been checking me, too. If Alpha was in that lake, then she was nowhere, and I was nowhere without her.

My sister snatched up the control pad and punched it to life, the wheels beneath the tank clicking into action.

I'd never even known what to do, I realized. I'd never been able to show her or tell her in the ways I had wanted. There'd been no words to describe right the way that girl made me feel.

"Alpha," I yelled out, turning back to the lake and the remains of the city. I screamed her name at the drowned buildings and the damned lake and the big empty sky.

"Get him up," Zee called, and when I finally turned from the water, I saw Kade helping her shove Crow on top of our steel-cloaked tank of trees, while I just stood there, useless.

Then my sister grabbed hold of me again, pushing me through the furniture and junk, following behind Kade as he steered the tank through the rubble.

And I just let Zee keep me moving. As if there was nothing else I could do.

CHAPTER TEN

We had to pile up the bones in the stairwell, creating a crumbling ramp for the tank's heavy wheels. Then our big black box cracked and crawled its way upward, Crow slumped unconscious on top of the thing, and the wheels spinning out underneath if we didn't angle things right.

The remains of the dead were crisp and brittle beneath the weight of the tank, popping and snapping as we pushed higher. I peered back past the switchbacks, searching for signs of life behind us, but all I could see was the old bones, arrows pried into the eye sockets of skulls and skeleton ribs. This city was a graveyard, a place to rot and be forgotten. We were just rattling around in a tomb.

The scraper might have once been real pretty from the outside, all that glass and steel towering up to the clouds, but the roof was just flat, ugly concrete, vented with old shafts and exhausts. And it was littered like the stairwell had been—more bones and more arrows, even some broken old spears.

I hunched down on a pile of cinder blocks, gripping my knees with my hands so I might quit shaking. But the fear was spreading through me. The pain and the loss and the knives of the feeling. I stared up at the sky, and it was some of the prettiest blue I ever had seen, but I knew that everything pretty ended up like this building, ugly and wasted and ready to fall. I leaned over and puked, retching and wretched, covered in sweat but so damn cold.

I forced myself to stand, though. Shivering in the wind as I scraped what was left of me back together to keep pushing on.

There were three bridges leading off the rooftop, each one woven out of thick steel cables and anchored to the concrete with rusted bolts. Each bridge stretched to a different building, creaking and sagging in the middle and not looking too stable. They were narrow, too. Just about wide enough for the wheels of our tank.

I was so damn lightheaded, I thought I might float away, but when I bent down and checked the steelwork, the feel of the metal seemed to ground me a little. Reminded me of all the years I'd spent building trees with Pop.

I stared out across the rooftops, watching the bridges drooping and swaying. They formed a web, patched across this old city that drowned. And it made me think of another old city—the city on the plains where Alpha had made me promise to return. She'd wanted me to get the trees to her band of pirates in Old Orleans.

But could I do that for her? Could I do it without her?

In the distance, I saw the strugglers who'd escaped off the boat, already disappearing into the skyline maze. Same people I'd locked up. The people who couldn't be trusted. Until something worse came along.

And where would they go now? What would they do? Out there, past the eastern edge of the buildings, I saw hills as old as time. Land. Just like we'd wanted. Brown dirt. Snow on the high ground. But how did we get there from here? And then what? Then where?

"Which one do we take?" Zee said, the wind whipping her wet hair all around her. She pointed at the bridges, but I just stared down below.

We were a good hundred feet above the water, and part of me wanted to topple down there and smack at the surface, then become withered and shriveled in all that blackness.

"Thought you wanted to hand the trees over," I said, my voice shaking, as I turned to face Zee. "Thought we were supposed to give them to Harvest."

"He's going to kill us," she screamed.

"So he kills us, takes the trees, and the trees keep living. Ain't that all that matters to you?"

"I never wanted to die."

"Nor did Alpha."

"Stop."

"We could have used your help fighting."

"Fighting was your idea." Her voice fought the wind to see which one was louder. "Yours."

"Just pick a bridge," said Kade. "Whichever looks strongest."

He combed the city with the scope of the sub gun, still trying to keep things together. Still playing the fearless leader, even though he had no one to lead. And how had he ended up in that gun tower, anyway?

How was he the one ended up with that gun?

"This one," Zee said, turning from me and stomping her foot at a bridge.

"No," Kade said. "We go west."

"Away from land?" cried Zee.

"Away from them."

Kade pointed at a rooftop just east of us, where pouring out of a doorway stormed a whole crew of Harvesters.

The bridge swayed as the tank rolled onto the woven cables and balanced above all the nothing below us. And as Zee stepped onto the bridge, it lurched even worse, swinging from side to side.

"Climb on top," Kade told her, adding his own weight to the cables. "But go slow."

Zee clambered for the top of the steel box, then Kade crawled up onto it after her, everything bobbing and weaving each time they moved.

But how much weight could these bridges handle?

I heard the Harvesters racing behind us, boot heels slapping at concrete.

They wouldn't shoot at us, though. They couldn't risk losing the trees, and they'd lose everything if this tank fell into the waters. But I reckoned they could catch up to us, wrestle the tank from us. And it sounded like they were getting real close.

So I shuffled out onto the bridge. Got my hands on the steel walls of the tank, steadied myself, and dragged myself up. Then we were all huddled together, our knees pinning Crow in place as Zee gently rolled the tank forward.

The bridge was barely wide enough. Cables corralled us in place, but we were tripping and tipping, the tank teetering this way and that.

The wind sucked us inside its noise, and Kade's sub gun cracked like thunder when he fired at the Harvesters on the rooftop behind us. But it should have been Alpha with her finger on that trigger. Not this son of a bitch.

The bridge sank real bad in the middle, like the cables had all gone slack. But we made it across, rolled up onto the next roof with a bump, went wheeling across it, then began rattling down a bridge even longer and more scraggly than the last. It kept us away from the Harvesters, but it didn't lead much closer to shore.

Replicants were popping out onto rooftops all over the city, crawling over the buildings like a disease, multiplying and festering and closing in quick.

Kade took aim at a bridge across from us that was chock-full of troops, and as he opened fire, the steel cables beneath us began to pivot and swing so bad, I lost my grip on Crow.

I grabbed at him, hauling him against me with one hand while I held onto the tank with the other. And when we rolled up onto the next roof, Zee started to cut to the east, but I grabbed the controls from her and ground the tank to a halt.

"Land's this way," she yelled, trying to snatch back the controller, scratching her nails at my fists.

"I know," I said, because the bridge before us stretched away from the city and down to the shoreline. "But what about them?"

I was staring back across the web of steel to where a group of survivors were running towards us, racing across a bridge, steel cables shaking beneath their pounding feet. I was checking their faces. Searching for Alpha. Knowing they were all that was left.

Out in front, I could see a woman sprinting along with a kid in her arms, and it was that mechanic from the Salvage Guild. The one who'd fixed the boat so we could steer straight into this mess.

I saw Muscles limping along, a girl hooked on his shoulders.

There were others I recognized. But no one I knew.

"Come on, bro." Kade thumped me on the back.

"Ain't they your people?" I said, watching the poor souls from the boat. Folk who'd fought their way off Promise Island, then fought their way up here. And I reckon I should have trusted them all to begin with, because now I saw the fear in their eyes, they didn't look like strangers, they looked just like me.

"They don't belong to me," said Kade, and I let Zee steal back the controller.

I reckoned those strugglers belonged to no one at all.

We were midway down that last bridge when I felt it go sloppy. Punched too wide and pinched too thin. There was too much damn weight on the cables, but here came everyone behind us, anyway—the last of the survivors, the Harvesters—all squeezing onto the bridge.

"Hold on," Kade shouted as Zee forced the tank to go faster. The cables were moaning, shredded and rusty. And land looked so close now. Mucky and solid. I could almost taste the dirt and the rocks. But the cables started snapping and screeching, and then there was no more damn bridge at all.

We were hurtling through the air. And when I crashed down, I landed in the water, just shy of the shoreline.

I stood, up to my hips in the water, and stared back at those who'd been on the wrong side of the bridge. Those who'd managed to hold on had been whipped back to the buildings. They were sliding down the concrete walls and smashing into the lake.

So we'd got separation from that Harvester posse, but we'd lost our survivors. The ones who'd made a stand and the ones who'd sat singing. They were gone. Just like Alpha.

I pictured the little thing with the sticky-out ears, remembered prying the gun from her too-small fingers. And what good had it done? I'd failed them all in the end. Left them all behind.

I staggered and fell through thin bits of ice, slipping on the cold rocks beneath.

"Alpha," I whispered, like her name was tears I was crying. I sank to my knees, but there were hands on me, lifting me.

"Help," Zee said. "I can't find Crow."

CHAPTER ELEVEN

We found Crow facedown in the water, and we spun him upright and hauled him to shore. Gray clouds crept across the sky, and the cold wind moaned. The three of us were shivering, but Crow weren't shaking at all. Hell, he was hardly even breathing.

Zee shoved at his guts till water came heaving up out of him, then we pushed him onto his side, his eyes still shut down and fluttery, his chest moving slow, and his lips gone blue.

"His legs," said Kade. "Look at his legs."

The rags Crow had wound around his tree-legs had come all undone in the water, and Kade was picking at the knots and grooves of the bark. He pinched water out of the wood with his fingers. "GenTech?" he whispered, his green eyes wide and his mouth wide open. "They did this?"

"Get your lousy hand off him," I said.

"It's wood, though. Real wood?"

"I said leave it." I went to shove at him, but he gripped my wrist with his fingers. It was like his one hand held the strength of two.

"Careful." Kade stank worse than ever of old sweat and hunger, and he tugged me closer, clamping down on my wrist as if to snap off my hand. "I'm all the help you've got left."

It was like a switch got flipped inside me.

"What did you do to her?" I whispered.

"What?"

"She had that gun before you did. I know that she did."

"Banyan." Zee tried to stop me. But it was too late. I swung my fist at Kade's head, breaking his grip. Then I dragged him by his ears and smashed his skull on the rocks.

I pinned my knees on his chest and beat his face bloody. Zee quit holding Crow and started dragging at me, shouting, but I just shoved her aside.

"What did you do to her?" I screamed at Kade, spit flying out of my mouth.

His eyes bulged as I throttled him. He was fighting back with his one hand, wrestling me off him, trying to get up.

"I'll kill you." I roared the words in his face. But then there was Zee's voice behind me.

"I saw her, Banyan. She came for the children. In the hull."

I let Kade pull away from me.

"It all happened so fast," Zee said. "We were sinking."

"The water," I whispered, staggering backwards and spinning back to the lake. She'd been below me, in the water. I could have looked for her. I could have jumped aboard that boat even though it was sinking. But I didn't. Not once I had my hands on those trees.

"Please," Zee said. Maybe she was sobbing. Hell, I don't even know. I had no juice left. I was shaking and crying and couldn't think straight. And I couldn't look no more at that city. Not if my girl was cold and heavy beneath it. Lost in the depths I could not fathom.

I glanced at Zee, and she seemed to cower below me. As if I were a stranger. Like I was no longer Banyan and would have to be somebody else.

The trees. That's what I'd gone after. That was the path I had picked.

I splashed back into the water, and the cold slapped at me as I reached the tank. The control pad's wires were tangled and frozen, and I worked them loose with numb fingers, slowly untying the knots. Then the tank moved forward, when I punched the right buttons. It ground up onto the shore, and there were bones as well as rocks on this beach. Skulls burst under the tank's heavy wheels, and the sound mingled with the sound of dirty water lapping at the shore, the muted sounds of the dead.

I pulled Kade off the crusty ground and handed him the sub gun. His face was frosted and bleeding. A handsome face I'd made ugly and weak.

Zee scrambled between us as Kade checked the gun. "We have to work together," she said. "We have to stick close."

Kade spat a wad of dark blood on the rocks.

"You owe me a beating," I told him as he propped the gun on his hip. "Put a hole in my head if you want to."

"What?" His voice cracked. "And let you off easy?" He was holding onto the gun with one hand and trying to wipe the blood off his face with his stump.

"We'll put Crow on the tank," Zee said, tugging at me. She stared into my eyes like she was wanting to find me in them. "I'm sorry, Banyan. I'm so sorry. I know you loved her so much."

"You don't know shit."

"I know she was special. Strong." Zee blinked up at me. "And I know what it feels like."

"Please shut the hell up."

"I lost my mother." Her voice snapped in the middle. "I lost Sal."

"This ain't like losing some fake little brother."

"He was more of a brother to me than you."

"You can't say that. I weren't even there. I didn't even know you."

"But you're here now, and I need you. And when you lose someone, you have to bring the rest close."

"The rest?" I would have laughed at her if I hadn't been crying.

"You can lean on me."

"I don't want no one to lean on. All that happens is they leave in the end."

I was blank as I'd ever been. Like a blind man blessed with sight for one day only, and now night had fallen too soon.

"Think about Crow," Zee said quietly. "Think about me."

"You're wasting your time with him." Kade was studying the angle of the sun and the shadows. Same way that Alpha would have done it. And he kept sniffling and snuffling, like he was dead set not to cry. That was

Kade. Our damned fearless leader. He pointed the sub gun at the slope of frozen mud. "South is over these hills, and we have to start moving. If we're to honor those that fell behind."

I broke free of Zee's grip and stumbled over to the tank, my fingers shoved under my armpits, trying to thaw out my hands before I set them to work. Then I scraped at the panel till I pried the steel open.

There was a crack down the far side of the glass, near the top, and the tank had lost about a third of its liquid, and the damn red lights still flashed at the gold and the green. And there at the bottom, the dwindled remains of Pop's torso had gotten tumbled and mashed, the saplings unruly and too bunched together.

"What about the counter?" Zee said, and I stepped back from the glass so she could see it. "Nearly two hundred thousand," she said, which meant nearly two hundred thousand and not nearly enough.

"And what happens at zero?" Kade was still smearing the blood off his face with his fingerless stump. "If the charge runs out?"

"We don't know." Zee glanced at me as she said it.

"Sure we do," I muttered. "Everything we fought for gets taken away."

CHAPTER TWELVE

The only thing was to head south, and so that's what we did. Never stopping. Never resting. We just made soggy strides through the crusted mud, working our way up from the shoreline, heading for the frosted hills. Zee steered the tank as we trudged along beside it, and me and Kade had to keep making sure Crow didn't fall off.

Got high enough we could see back over the scrapers and all the way to where the boats still bobbed on the water. I gazed at Harvest's fleet, wondering if he could see us now, wondering if he was watching us through some magnified lens. And just in case, I quit breathing so hard and looking so bent full of sorrow, though the truth was, sorrow had just about snapped me in two.

"Pass me the gun," I said to Kade, but he wouldn't hand it over. Not all the way. He just held it for me so I could peer through the gun's scope, tracking over the buildings to the place where our boat had disappeared.

I felt like sobbing again. The feeling kept catching me unawares.

"Let's go." Kade tried to pull the gun away from me. "There's nothing to see."

He was right. There weren't nothing to look at. But I grabbed hold of the gun's scope and kept staring at the lake as if Alpha might emerge from it, shaking the water off her golden-white skin.

Kade thumped me in the gut. Snatched the gun away. "I said, let's go."

"And you're in charge now?"

"Even if you were the one with this gun, you're in no shape to be calling the shots."

What did it matter? I stared at the landscape ahead. Rocks here, a muddy patch there. Mostly, though, as the hills drifted higher, the ice shone thicker and the snow grew more deep.

And behind us, we were tracking a mess much too easy to follow, leaving footprints and wheel ruts in the mud, and there weren't any way to clean that mess up. Not unless it rained, maybe. I peered at the cold ceiling of sky. We only had a couple more hours of daylight. And rain would be bad, even if it covered our footprints. But snow would be a whole lot worse.

We stumbled on without speaking. Breath steaming, bellies tight. By evening, a mist rolled inland off the lake, soaking up what was left of the sun and making my GenTech clothes even damper, the wet fuzz binding my limbs together and chafing my skin. The sleeves of my jacket unrolled into gloves, and I shoved my hands inside them, but it didn't stop my fingers going numb.

End of one hill meant the start of another. The bottom of each slope turned into straight back up. So we made hard work of cresting each ridge, and by the time it got all the way dark, you could even smell the cold getting worse.

The icy air pried at my lungs and pressed at my bones, making everything ache and sting. My face was all snotty and raw, and I started picturing big bags of popcorn bursting with steamy flavor, me shoving my face down into the hot food. But then I forced the image from my mind. Tried to imagine apples instead.

We stopped now and then to peer through holes in the mist, trying to get our bearings, and if he was feeling generous, Kade would hold the gun's scope so I could stare back the way we had come.

"Give it up," Kade said, when I asked to stop one time too many. "Please. There's nothing back there."

"What? You don't reckon Harvest's behind us?" I watched the wind blow across the hills, moving the mist in sheets around us.

"Oh, I'm sure he'll keep hunting," Kade said, because he always had to let you know he was so sure about everything.

"You think he's working for GenTech?" Zee asked him.

"I doubt his allegiance is to the Executive Chief. I'd say he's more likely biting the hands that feed him. Trying to exploit some weakness in the GenTech Empire he's been trading with for years."

"So how did he even know to come up here?" I said.

Kade shrugged. "How did you know?"

"I didn't. Just got dragged up on that boat. But you know all about what's out here. Right? You know these wastelands like the back of your hand."

He pulled up the sleeve of his coat to show me the stump at the end of his arm. "Wrong hand, I suppose."

"Meaning you're as clueless as we are."

"At least I still know which way is south."

"And how do we even know that's true?"

"I'm not pretending at anything, bro." His smile weren't so fine-looking since I'd smashed up his face. "Look at me. I'm an open book, same as you."

I just stared at him. Never knew the expression.

"Means he's honest," Zee said.

"Great." I started pushing on again. "Open book. Gets cold enough, we got something to burn."

Zee started to stagger and shrivel, and Kade had her sit up on the tank, telling her to make sure Crow was still breathing, as if Kade gave a damn about Crow.

And it slowed us down even more, the tank slipping worse in the mud and old snowy patches. I found myself cursing Zee and her skinny ass. Alpha would have still been walking. Hell, she'd have been out there ahead of us, coming up with a plan by nightfall.

But night fell with no plan. Just a black, damp sky clamping around us. And still I stomped and strode and shook.

"She's going to die," Kade said quietly, pointing at Zee as she coughed on her fragile lungs, slumped up on the tank, ahead of us. We'd reached a plateau, the hills leveling out into something flatter. For now. "Your friend will, too. If he's not dead already."

"So what else can we do?" My voice was as weak as the rest of me. "Stop, and it'll get colder."

"There's colder?" He made a wheezing sound that was meant to be laughter. "You might make it through the night, but she won't. Can't you hear her breathing? Crusted lungs, bro. She's as rough inside as she is good looking."

"Take it easy," I said. "That's my sister you're talking about."

"You don't act much like her brother."

"And you're some sort of expert?"

"Could be a little nicer to her, that's all," he said. "Soon as you get done feeling sorry for yourself."

"Guess there's not a whole lot of nice going around."

He pointed at his busted face. "You should learn to use your anger in the right direction. I told you before—too many enemies to keep making new ones."

"Man, you're just full of advice."

"I mean it. Your own sister's scared of you. Good thing I was there to take the brunt, I suppose."

"Shut your damn mouth." I quit walking and stared at him, my breath puffing out like white smoke. "I wouldn't ever hurt Zee."

"I thought stopping was a bad idea."

"So is you talking."

Kade shifted his sub gun from one shoulder to the other. "Meaning you don't want to hear my plan?"

"Here we go."

He whistled, and Zee brought the tank to a stop. Then Kade strode up to it and tapped its steel walls. "This thing come off? The metal?"

"Sure. You want to carry it? This walk ain't been hard enough for you?"

"I'd like to use it as a shelter."

"You're crazy. That steel's keeping the trees safe. There's just glass underneath."

"No. Wait," Zee called out, sliding off the top of the tank. She tried to clear her lungs and breathe easy, but she was all gurgled and filled up with spit.

The air was clean out here, but it was so damn cold, it was hard enough for me to breathe proper. And that meant it was way too hard for Zee, whose lungs had been wrecked by the dust storms and hazard winds that blew across the barren lands we were trying to get back to. And so that was one more reason to feel like a bastard. I'd led Alpha nowhere but down to the bottom of that lake. I'd managed to lose the rest of the strugglers. And now my sister might not make it till morning.

"Take your time," Kade said to her, shielding Zee from the wind.

"It's the liquid that protects the trees," she said after she got done coughing. "Not the metal. The liquid preserves the microclimate."

"The metal got put on this thing for a reason," I said, shuffling over to them.

"We won't move it," said Kade. "Not during the night."

"We could get warm, Banyan. Out of the wind." Zee's face trembled inside her big purple hood. Her eyes big as fists. Kade reached an arm around her, trying to rub some heat into her, and even miserable as I was, seeing him touch my sister like that sparked something inside me. I mean, it looked a little too damn friendly, if you asked me.

"It's too risky," I said. "For all we know, Harvest's troops are right behind us. We gotta keep moving."

"She can't keep moving." I could hear the scowl on Kade's face, like he was all out of patience. Like I should be cheering him on for bossing at me.

"He's right, little man," said a voice above us, and Crow was leaning down off the side of the tank towards me.

"Decided to wake up, did you?" I might have smiled at the sight of him, but my jaw was frozen stiff.

He peered about at the black sky and the dirty slush. "Where are the others?"

"Gone," Zee whispered.

"All of them?" Crow said, and I saw he was shivering like we were. Made him look smaller, somehow, like he was being eaten away by the cold.

"Everyone," I told him, and the word was like a splinter. Got worse the longer it sat.

Crow shut his eyes. Couldn't look at me. "Some folks be precious, Banyan. But no folks be for keeping."

I felt frosty tears on my cheeks, a sick, sad knot in my gut.

"The redhead's right," he went on. "The night's too cold. I'm gonna die and so are you, and the trees won't get nowhere if we all be dead."

"You want to stop?" I asked him. "Make a shelter?"

"Not a want, it's a need."

"Fine," I said, because I couldn't risk losing him, too. "But you better drag your ass down here. We can't lift off this steel shell with you sitting on top."

CHAPTER THIRTEEN

The snow began to fall. Hard and mazy. White flakes clouding the darkness, trickling inside our hoods and sneaking up the sleeves of our coats. We had to unclamp where the metal was paneled and latched beneath the tank, frozen hooks and fasteners connecting the protective steel cloak to the glass and sealing things tight. Took ages, working the right pieces loose, especially around the tank's wheels. And when I stood back up, the snow was already half as high as the top of my boots, and coming down in a bright white spiral.

Zee kept clutching her chest and coughing, while me and Kade grappled with the metal box, working the shell upwards, the steel squeaking on the glass. As we unpeeled the tank, its lights spilled out, red and gold, glowing like a fire in the dark.

"Quickly now," Kade said, because I was just standing there, staring through the glass at the sapling that grew from Pop's mouth. What was left of my old man's face was bent up as if he was looking straight at me. As if he still had eyes that could see.

"Banyan," Zee said. "We have to get out of this cold."

"Hold on," I told her.

I inspected the glass, making sure it had not got too damaged in all the ruckus and sprung itself a major leak. That steel cloak had done its job, though. And this GenTech-grade glass had been built too hard to shatter. There was just the one crack in it, and the tank was still two-thirds full of liquid. The glass was real warm to the touch, too, like the tank was being heated. It was certainly a sophisticated machine. And I knew one day, if we were lucky, we'd get to lift those saplings out of this tank and watch them blowing in the wind, instead of floating in liquid. There were hinges on top where you could peel the glass open, and I tried to picture myself tugging the trees free.

"Anytime you feel like helping." Kade was still wrestling with the steel box. So I went over and gave him a hand.

We got the thing upright, its opening facedown on the stamped-down snow, and the shell formed a decent shelter. All sealed up but hollow inside. It was just about big enough, too.

We had to lift up one corner so Zee could get Crow in there, dragging him through the snow. Then Kade slid in after them, and I took one last glance at the tank, the trees, then scooted in, too, the walls sealing tight around us.

We bunched up cowering against one another, huddling against the cold steel walls. And as the air got stale, we began to get warmer. Little by little, I felt my joints thaw, and my heart slowed down as my bones quit shaking.

"You think we might run out of air?" I asked.

Crow was out again, shut down already, curled up in a bulky ball. And I could hear Zee wheezing, bent crooked as she slept beside me.

Only Kade was still awake, his face just inches from mine.

"We could open that panel," I said. "The one we used for looking in here."

He was worried we'd lose too much heat, but once we popped the panel loose, it weren't so bad. You could hear the gusts outside but not feel them. Snow puffed in on occasion, but not enough to freeze us out. And this way, if we were discovered out here, I figured at least we might hear Harvest's troops coming. Though there'd not be much we could do about it.

I twisted my head back to watch the snow flurries through the opening. I could see the snow change from white to gold to red, and I sat that way for a long time, watching the glow from the tank, going over things in my mind, like I was hammering a nail into place.

"You awake?" I whispered, to see if anyone might answer.

"Try to sleep," Zee said softly, her head at my shoulder.

I thought about what Kade had said about me being nicer to her, and if Harvest did find us in the night, I'd not likely get the chance again.

"You all right, sister?"

"The cold sits tight." I heard her thump at her chest.

"Least it's not dusty," I said. As if there was some positive spin to be found.

Back on Promise Island, I'd told Zee I'd keep her safe, but now look at us. Freezing and lost, hunted and starving in this winter wasteland.

"You still think we should have given them up?" I asked her. "Handed the trees over?"

"It's too late, Banyan."

"I mean, if we had to do it over."

"I know what you meant."

"I miss her so bad." I cupped my head with my gloved hands. "I miss her so bad, and I don't know what to do."

"I miss her, too." Her voice was almost not there at all, and it surprised me to hear her say it. Made me think I didn't know Zee even nearly enough. I mean, she was my sister, and I knew I should love her and take care of her, but we were so different. Hell, she'd never even known our old man.

And I wasn't sure I could handle having someone else to look after. Hadn't it been easier in those days of dust and metal, when I'd been roaming around all on my own?

"I miss my mom," Zee whispered. "I know she wasn't anything much like Alpha, but she still made me feel safer, you know?"

I didn't know. I'd grown up with no mother. And Hina had just seemed strung out and vacant, when I'd traveled with her on the road.

"Even with Frost around," Zee said, "I felt safer with her. And with Crow. He'd look out for me, when he could."

"Right. The watcher."

"It was like all of us against Frost, we just couldn't say it. We just couldn't leave. I mean, my mom tried. At first, anyway. I know she did."

"You don't have to defend her to me."

"If she'd been more like Alpha, things would have been different. So fearless. So sure in what she wanted. I never knew someone like her, Banyan."

"I know. Me, neither."

Zee let her head press at my shoulder, her hair wet and cold against my neck. I tried to get my arm unhooked so I could put it around her, but it felt too awkward.

"I should have saved her," I said.

"You can't think about it."

"Ain't me thinking it that's the problem."

But maybe it was. Because as I sat there, I thought about it all, all over again.

I thought about my mother—so many years trying to make trees for the mainland. All those lives she took, and then, in the end, taking a bullet for me. I thought about Hina. I thought about Sal. I thought of all the strugglers behind us. And I thought about my father. The dead and the gone.

But mostly, I thought about Alpha. Little things that were big things. The way she'd talked to me and how her brown eyes had turned soft when she smiled. Her hips and her warm lips. Goosebumps on her golden skin.

I thought about the way she'd trusted me, and the way I'd felt I could trust her forever. And I remembered the first time I'd held her, on the walls of Old Orleans.

I tried to put myself back inside that city. Tried to relive each moment, making dreams out of memories, but I couldn't do it right. It was like all my dreams had burned down.

"Zee?" I said, but she was sleeping again, and it was Kade's eyes that snapped open.

"What you doing?" I asked him.

"I'd be sleeping. If you could keep your mouth shut."

I listened to the sound of Crow snoring, and the endless beat of the wind, and Kade sank back into the gloom, then let his voice soften. "How are you holding up, anyway?"

"Like you give a damn."

"Of course I do." He let out a sigh. "Who else can I count on? The giant's just dead weight."

"Don't say that."

"He could hardly walk before. Now look at him."

"He's a Soljah," I said.

"Used to be. There are no Soljahs in this wasteland. It's a blank slate out here, my friend. For all of us."

"So what did you used to do?" I asked. "Before you got taken."

I figured if we were stuck with this redhead, I'd better get the lowdown on him, blank slate or no.

"Thought I told you," he said. "I was a scholar. And a drunk. A chaser of women."

"Said you were a poet."

"That, too."

"Ah, you're full of crap. Come on, what did you do? Open book, and all that."

"Bootlegger," he said. "I ran corn all around the southeast, helping out those who couldn't afford GenTech's prices."

"Fine. Don't tell me."

"You can't picture me bootlegging?"

"We can drop it," I said, deciding to act like I didn't give a damn. Figured that might make him more honest. Someone thinks you don't care about their story, they're more likely to start itching to tell it.

"Would you believe me if I said I worked the fields?" he said, after we'd sat in silence for a bit.

"In the corn?" Now this, I could believe.

"Yeah," he said. "I was a picker. A good one, too."

"You ever drive them big dusters?" I asked, but then I wished I hadn't. I remembered me and Alpha trapped inside of that duster's cockpit, when we were escaping the locusts, back in the cornfields. That was the first time she'd really touched me. The first time we'd kissed.

Kade was shaking his head. "A duster comes back, and there are cobs in the blades and under its wheels, bits of corn caught all over. I worked on the crew that picks it clean."

"Your whole life?"

He pulled up his sleeve and examined the stump of his arm. "Until my hand got plucked like a kernel. Snatched off by blades that weren't meant to be moving. Then I was useless to GenTech, and they dispose of any field hand that's unable to work. Some get killed. Some get taken. So I ran before the agents could get ahold of me. I traveled all over after that. Did all sorts of things, like I said."

A cloud of snowflakes blustered in through the open panel, and I glanced outside, listening for the sound of Harvest's commandos, imagining them trudging through the blizzard towards us.

All I could hear was the wind.

"How'd you learn to be good with a gun?" I asked, but it was one question too many.

Kade sank back inside his hood. "What makes you so interested?"

"Just curious how you ended up taken. Ended up on that island." I decided to pry a little further. "Got snatched by Harvest?"

"GenTech agents," he muttered. "Harvest doesn't take field hands."

"What else do you know about him?"

"I know enough."

I faked a yawn, acted like I'd lost all interest.

"And I don't think Harvest snatches anyone anymore," Kade said. "Now he's just after the trees." He was scratching at his arm, fingering the holes GenTech's cables had left behind. "I knew a woman once who said they had to be out there, growing somewhere. Across the ocean, maybe. Somewhere we couldn't get. She said we wouldn't be able to breathe unless there were still trees left. Still, I never believed it."

My old man had always said GenTech's cornfields made it so we had air to breathe. But I kept quiet now. I felt like there was something Kade wasn't telling me, and my silence was the one thing that might get him to speak.

"Come winter, when there were no locusts hatching, we would rove all over the fields," he said, almost whispering now. "Anywhere the agents told us to go. But all summer long, every field hand has to live in the Stacks, right in the heart of the fields. You've heard of them? The Stacks?"

I acted like maybe I was sleeping, though I was trying to picture how any sort of settlement could survive in the cornfields—corn being the one thing locusts can't eat, but the stalks being the one place they can nest.

"The Stacks are made of blood, sweat, and tears," he went on, like he was happy enough just to talk to himself. "The walls are made of woven cornhusks, layered five yards deep. Gets so hot, but no one ventures outside when the locusts are hatching. Unless you're on shift, of course. Agents get rid of the lazy ones faster than you can sit down on the job."

When he paused, I knew there was more.

And I knew he wanted to tell me.

The wind rattled the walls, another gust of snow blew in.

"Better close that panel," Kade said, and he unwound himself so he could reach up and latch the steel back in place. It sealed us inside, making the wind no more than a distant rumble.

I waited for him to speak again. Biding my time.

"There's nothing to do in the Stacks," he said at last. And it was like some part of him had just been unplugged, his voice was so flat. "There's nothing to do in the fields, either. Except watch for the locusts and make sure your work gets done."

"Long days," I said, a little prod to keep him going.

"Every day. It's mindless. There's nothing to think about. Nothing to hope for." He took a deep breath, then blew it out in a big, sad sigh. "So you hit the crystal pipe as soon as your work gets done."

And there it was. The dude was a crystal junky. Or he had been, anyway. And either way, it didn't fit with his smooth talking or his acting like he was so in control.

I remembered Frost, all hopped up on that shit. And being hooked on crystal ain't something you just make go away.

"GenTech turns a blind eye?" I asked.

"A blind eye? They're the ones that made sure we got it. Used to be field hands would smuggle it in, now agents bring it to the fields and deal it direct. Half of them are hooked on it, too, of course. But what they don't smoke, they pass out to the workers."

I wondered if that's how old Frost had reached Promise Island. Had he traded crystal for a way to the trees?

"Where do they get it all?"

"The crystal? Straight from the source, bro." Kade was on a roll now. "The Samurai Five."

I'd heard of them gangsters. A syndicate, is what people say. They're like ghosts in the Steel Cities. You don't see them, you don't know no one who knows them. But they brew the crystal that cripples anyone who touches it. Take one hit, and you'll crave it till the day that you die.

"So you used to smoke it," I said, not a question.

And Kade didn't answer. He was coiled and hunched in the darkness, and I wondered how deep the demons burrowed inside him. They say once you been hit by the crystal, nothing's the same in your head.

"You think any air's getting in here?" I asked, almost worried about him, wanting him to say something to let me know he was all right.

"Wake up, and we can crack the panel again," he muttered.

"What if we don't wake up?"

"You ever wonder if that might be a blessing?"

I thought about all the life this guy had lived already, imagining the pain he'd burned through. And I thought about pain all the way till I slept.

"Banyan," a voice started calling, hours later.

The voice came from behind me. Below me. And the voice kept calling, louder and louder, till finally I busted awake.

It was Crow. His legs were trapped beneath me, and I squirmed around, trying to get free of these bodies I was all jammed up against.

"What is it?" I asked him.

"You were dreaming. Hollering."

"Is it morning?"

Kade was scrambling for the panel. Frantic as he tried to bust the thing loose. And when he got it free, no light poured in.

Everything stayed muffled.

"It's froze solid outside," he said.

We were buried in snow.

CHAPTER FOURTEEN

We punched at the steel walls around us. Rocking and heaving and finally shoving the shelter to one side enough that we could force our way out.

Then we were tumbling into the big white drift.

I shook and scraped, shoveling my way upward. I thrashed at the snow and kicked myself free. Aiming for the sunlight above, high and bright, yellow and gold—and finally I broke loose into it, and I shivered, squinting at the vastness of a clear blue sky.

"Banyan," called Zee, staggering up beside me and coughing. "Help me with Crow."

We reached into the snow and dragged him up, and then we helped Kade dig his way out.

"You can stand?" Zee asked Crow, brushing the white flakes off his purple coat.

"It seems so," he muttered, staring down at his legs, still sounding like a shell of the man we'd known. "For now."

"For now's a start." She smiled up at him, and it was as if her smile could melt even Crow. He took her hand in his, his huge fingers squeezing Zee's through the gloves she wore.

"Thank you, Miss Zee."

"You don't have to thank me."

"But you didn't leave me behind," he said. "And now look at us. Look at all this."

I followed Crow's gaze, and my eyes grew full of what soared up ahead. A new world, now the blizzard and mist had vanished. A world of tall silver cliffs and spires. Rivulets of stone and ice engraved against the sky in an endless uprise, scraping the sun and tugging open the clouds.

Mountains, that's what they were. Mountains that stretched on and upwards. And I could see no way we could cross them. I couldn't even imagine a route through. But beyond those monoliths, far above the etched earthy swell, I saw plumes of ash. Steam and smoke.

"The Rift," Kade said as our eyes scratched the horizon. We couldn't see the lava fields, not yet, but the sky glowed orange out there, as if a terrible fire raged beyond the great peaks.

"I read about mountains," Zee said, her voice small as the view was big. "Never thought I'd see them."

I'd heard about mountains, too. My old man had told me. They were the call and curse of many a tale. And out of their snow had run old world rivers, deep and wide and clean.

I peered back the way we had come, and then scoured every other direction, searching for Harvesters but seeing no sign of life. The snow must have slowed Harvest down. It had even covered our tracks.

As the others gazed up at where the world grew jagged, I waded across to the tank, thinking we had best get moving, knowing Harvest wasn't going to give up, and the trees weren't going to make it south by themselves.

I dug out the tank's wheels as the others talked, pointing up at the peaks and arguing about something. Next, I got the top of the tank loose of snow, and I set to work at breaking off the slabs from the sides. But as the snow crumbled and dusted, my hands quit working.

I backed away from the glass, stumbled smack down on my ass.

And I didn't try to call out or nothing. It was like my voice had been snatched out of my skull.

Thought my mind was gone, too. Like it had given up and run away from me. Because inside that tank was the seven saplings and my father's remains, shrunken and shrubby at the root of them, but next to that mess of green and black, there was now another body, all wrapped in purple.

I spun up off the snow and pounded my fists at the glass, and Alpha's eyes blinked open, then locked on mine. Her head was floating up out of the liquid, her skin slippery and gold.

I heard Zee holler behind me. The others rumbling up. So they could see what I saw. It weren't just the hunger and loss playing tricks on my mind.

Alpha shoved at the glass ceiling above her, and I got my hand under it so we could pry the top back, hoisting it open on stiff hinges. And before there was really space for it, I'd wedged my arms inside the tank and was reaching for her and holding her. The glass still between us. The warm, gluey liquid oozing up my shoulders and neck. Alpha pressed her head against mine, and I breathed in the chemical smells of the tank as I kissed my girl's eyes and her lips, and all of her was so warm and soft but at the same time electric.

I peered down and saw the coiled saplings, and they were close enough I could have reached out and touched them, too. But I didn't touch them. I just squeezed Alpha against me and hauled her out into the snow.

Crow slapped his arms around us, laughing. He leaned on my shoulders, and I could feel his breath blow hot on the top of my head. Then he pulled away. Trying to give us a moment, I reckon.

Zee and Kade just stood there and stared.

"How?" I said, gripping Alpha's shoulders and holding her out before me, like she was a drink and my eyes were blown open with thirst.

"I'd been following your tracks. Then the snow started," she whispered. "The tank was the first thing I saw. Bright and warm through the snowstorm. Even warmer once I managed to get inside."

"I thought you was dead." I was shaking so hard, I started shaking her, too.

"Almost. Got pinned under bodies, stuck in the hull, but when the boat sank, they floated off me. I swam up and out. Swam from one building to another, till I made it to land. Thought I was the only one still heading south, then I saw your tracks just before dark. Figured only one fool would be out on the snow with that tank, hell-bent on nowhere." She turned to Crow. "Maybe two fools, I guess."

"Don't look at me," he said. "They dragged my ass the whole way."

I hugged Alpha so tight against me, we fell back into a big drift of powder. And she was grinning so hard, it was like I'd never really seen her smile before now. I kissed her. Right there, in front of the others. Hell, I might never have stopped if she hadn't finally pulled away from me and pulled us back up off the snow.

She blushed red as she smiled at Zee. But then she frowned at Kade, glancing at the sub gun where it hung from his shoulder, her face turning sour as she turned back to me. "And what's he doing here? We're all still on the same team?"

"Hell-bent on nowhere," Kade said, and he made this stupid salute.

Alpha leaned and spat in the snow. "What happened to your face, Red?"

"Your boyfriend's fists."

She raised an eyebrow.

"It's all right," I said. "A misunderstanding is all."

Kade made an empty laugh.

But we had to trust him, I reckoned. He was the one had let us go, called a truce on the boat, and he could have shot me any time he'd felt like it, once we'd made it to land. He needed us, and we needed him. And I knew now he was as broken as we were—a one-handed field hand, his mind wrecked from crystal. Hell, Kade was damaged, so I figured he fit right in.

"There's no one else?" Alpha glanced about as if a bunch of strugglers might bust out through the snow to join us. "I went into the hull to get the kids out. The little ones." She gazed back in the direction of the lake but couldn't finish her story.

"It ain't your fault," I told her.

"No. It's Harvest's fault. And I'm gonna kill him. I'm gonna kill him or die trying before all this is through."

I peered into the tank, my hands still squeezing Alpha's fingers. Still marveling at the feel of her skin against mine. "I can't believe you climbed in there."

"It saved me. The lights flashing red and gold through the blizzard. I was seizing up, stumbling and shaking something fierce."

"Did you touch them?" Kade peered in at the bundle of green limbs. "The trees?"

"Tried not to. Didn't want to mess with things." Alpha gave me a look as she said it. And I wondered what it'd feel like to hold the tiny saplings in your hand.

Zee blinked back tears as Alpha put her arms around her. My sister surprising me again with how much she cared. But she was already building a new family, I reckoned. New people to stop her from being alone.

"You all right, girl?" Alpha squeezed Zee like she was her own sister, and I envied the way she could show her affection, but there didn't seem to be room in my heart for all of them. I don't know. Maybe your heart gets smaller if you spend too much time just looking out for yourself.

"It was awful," Zee whispered, her voice stifled and choked as Alpha held her. "It was like we lost Banyan, too."

My face burned as Zee started to cough worse than ever. But what the hell? I hadn't abandoned her. And what more did she want from me? Ain't easy, being a brother to a stranger, I tell you that much.

Alpha soothed Zee until she began to breathe easy, and then we all stood there a moment. Crow wavering on the wooden legs he'd anchored in the snow, my heart finally slowing down as I gazed at my pirate girl in all her ragged beauty.

"All right, hon," she said to Zee, letting go of her gently. "I hate to break up the reunion, but we got a long ways to go yet."

"True that." Crow gazed south at the mountains and the orange glow beyond them. "And this new snow will make us easy to track."

"How many rounds you got left?" Alpha asked Kade, and he uncoiled his too-big coat, revealing a belt full of bullets. One strip of ammunition, tied below the bite of his ribs.

"That's it?" Zee said.

"Keep that chin up," Alpha told her. "Some's better than nothing at all."

But I swore then, if I could get back to the dusty world that lay south, I'd leave all the bullets behind me. No more guns. No more fighting. I'd plant those trees and be a builder once more. I'd build that house for Alpha and me in the treetops, surrounded by sweetness and shielded from suffering. And I started to think love is like every tree I ever crafted, taking broken pieces and making something beautiful, something better. Something to believe in. And something to hold onto, when all else is black.

PART TWO

CHAPTER FIFTEEN

We steered the tank towards the mountains, moving as fast as we could, but we sank too deep in the powder to keep up a good speed. We were as hungry as we were exhausted. And we had to keep glancing behind us, searching the frozen landscape to see if Harvest was closing in.

My body felt weak and shriveled close to the bone. But I waded along next to Alpha, shielding my eyes from the sun and studying each part of my girl like I was about to go snow-blind. I even let myself grow hopeful, with our hands once more entwined and our eyes setting fires between us.

But too soon, the fear seeped back like a cold fever sweat. I mean, all I'd wanted was my pirate girl back, and it ain't right how quick you can take things for granted. As the day wore on, the dead spooked at me again, prying open my mind so I could see their faces—my father and mother, Hina and Sal, every struggler I'd seen perish along the way.

"We get back," I said to Alpha as we pushed on ahead of the others, following the plateau to the base of the mountains, "we plant us a forest. And I ain't never letting you out of my sight."

"Can't say that, bud." She squeezed my fingers, but her gaze was fixed on the peaks up ahead. "Can't let me and you make us weak. Not if we're gonna keep fighting."

"Get south," I said. "Somewhere safe. And I'm all done fighting."

"That easy, huh?"

"There ain't been nothing easy about it."

"But you think we're gonna dig down and plant us those trees," she said, "and just sit there watching 'em grow?"

"Sounds real good to me."

"And how do you think GenTech's gonna feel about that?"

"I don't give two damns about GenTech."

"Yeah, you do."

I quit wading through the powder, and Alpha stopped to wait for me, still clutching my hand in hers. Both of us were breathing hard from the effort required to keep moving, and the deep snow sparkled far as the eye could see.

The others were starting to catch up. We'd got the tank boxed up back in its steel cloak, and Crow had the control pad in his hands as he sat up on top, nudging the thing's wheels through the snow. Kade and Zee were stomping along beside him, and I saw Zee was laughing, cracking up at some joke Kade had made.

It bothered me. There weren't no reason to be laughing out here. But I'd decided to trust that redhead,

I reminded myself. So I busied my brain by peering north to see if I could spy Harvest's troops behind us.

"You ain't thought this thing through," Alpha said, letting go of my hand.

"I've thought plenty. I ain't losing you again." I turned back to face her, but she was staring up at the peaks. "We get back, we keep these trees secret. And I keep you safe."

Her face looked all prickly and pissed. "That's what your dad would have wanted?"

"How the hell would I know?" I crossed my arms at my chest, as if it was just the cold I was feeling. "Man did nothing but keep secrets from me."

That night, right at the foot of the mountains, we pulled the steel cloak off the tank so we could settle inside its walls again. I hadn't wanted to, but Zee's cough had got worse as the day wore on, her crusted lungs sounding rougher than ever.

Tired as I was, I didn't feel like turning in yet, so I stood under the stars awhile, watching the numbers count down on the tank.

The red lights pulsed inside the glass as the time ran out, and I tried to picture what would happen when there was no time left. The tank would lose its charge, that had to be the problem. And then the trees would be too cold, I reckoned. Hell, maybe that liquid would freeze, and we'd have nothing but seven icy saplings.

"Take turns keeping watch?" Alpha said, appearing beside me. She'd been ignoring me through the last part of the day—such a waste, when all I'd wanted was to be with her.

I glanced at the blanket of snow that stretched beneath the darkness behind us. And there was still no sign of Harvest's commandos, but it was as if I could feel them out there on the frozen plateau, closing any gap we'd created between them and the trees.

"You can sleep first," I told Alpha.

"With Crow's snoring?"

I turned to face the tank and saw the two of us reflected in the glass, our bodies lost inside thick clothes, our faces peering out from the hoods of our jackets.

"The tank's warm," she said.

"Well, I ain't getting in there for nothing." I stared past my reflection at the twisted limbs of the saplings where they floated in the liquid, still tethered to the knotted remains of my dad.

"I meant we could lean against it," she said, and I sure needed something to lean on, so we sat with our backs against the tank, the glass hot through our chunky coats.

We faced north. Watching for Harvest. Knowing his troops weren't the sort who'd stop and rest someone's broken lungs. One of them replicants needed to stop, the others would have just kept on going.

"I know I ought to be more grateful," Alpha said, after I'd just sat there saying nothing, feeling all closed up. "For you, I mean. For how you feel about me."

"You don't have to thank me."

"But it's like something out of an old world song," she said. "This feeling. Love. The way that you mean it."

"The way I mean it don't belong to the old world."

I watched the tank's lights throw crazy patterns on the snow, making silhouettes of the saplings, as if the trees had already grown tall enough to cast their shadows upon us.

"I know you want to keep me safe," Alpha said. "And I mean to look after you, too."

"Lord knows I could use it." I tried to make her grin, the way I said it, but she was too lost inside what she was trying to say.

"It's just I know you want to keep these trees safe, too. And we both know what that means, Banyan."

"I don't want to talk about it no more." I turned to her. Her face chapped from the cold, but so beautiful, and so damn alive. "Let's just try to get back. I mean, look at us." I pointed out at the white freeze and the big black sky. What was it Kade had called it? A blank slate.

"I wanted you to know I'm grateful is all," she said, her voice small in the vast emptiness of the night.

"I don't want you to be grateful. I want you to feel how I feel."

"I'm working on it," she said, like she was trying to sound easy, but the words came hard. "This is new for me."

"It's new for me, too."

"So we figure it out together?"

"I'll do it any way that you want."

She smiled as she leaned her head against the glass.

"Do what?" Crow's voice crept out of the darkness.

"You should be resting," Alpha told him.

"And so should you." He crawled up beside us. I mean, literally dragging his ass through the snow.

"You gotta try," Alpha said. "You need to try standing. Walking. The more you do it, the better it'll get."

"And how would you know? These things they scienced onto me are tired and useless. I and I is flimsy, all the way through."

"And what?" I said, trying to force some cheer upon him. "You're gonna leave my sister alone in there, sleeping next to that scoundrel?"

"Don't you worry. Crow here's still looking out for Miss Zee. I believe the redhead be all right."

"You sure about that?" Alpha got to her feet. She glanced at Crow, then rolled her eyes at me before heading to the shelter. "Guess I'll take the next watch, bud."

"What's the rush?" Crow called after her. "Don't want to talk story with me?"

He collapsed back so he was propped against the tank beside me, right where Alpha had been. Quite the damn trade.

"You all right, little man?"

"Oh, sure. Just figuring I'd freeze first and starve second."

"Nah. Tough young guy like you." He punched at my leg. Not hard or anything, but there was something painful in the gesture.

We both watched Alpha crank up the side of the shelter, then crouch in beneath it.

"Glad she's back, no?" Crow said.

"Somehow makes it all worth it."

"Aye." Crow bared his teeth, white as the snow, but he weren't really smiling. I'd given up hope I'd ever see him smile again.

"So she talked to you?" he said. "About Old Orleans?"

"What about it?"

"About her plans." Crow picked at the bark on his leg. "For our trees."

"Yeah. We talked about it," I said, though I wasn't really sure that we had. "What she say to you?"

"Girl's got lofty ambitions."

"When were you even talking to her, anyway?"

"On the boat."

"All I remember's you stood at the bow. Silent."

"True that."

"True what?"

"We talked, man," Crow said. "Take it easy. I figured you two been talking also."

"Sure. We talk plenty."

"And not just talking to that sweet thing, I hope." He nudged me, but playful weren't something he was good at no more.

"So what about you, anyway?" I said. "What's your ambitions?"

"Told you, just get me to Waterfall City."

"Didn't you get thrown out of Waterfall City?"

"They'll welcome me back with open arms, if I come bearing fruit trees. You'll see. You born Soljah, then you die part of the tribe."

Crow made another attempt at smiling. Then he pointed to the far edge of sky, where the giant moon was poking its head up, and we sat there for a bit, watching the moonbeams flood the snow. Crow leaned closer to me and dropped his voice. "Rastas know how to keep a secret," he said. "The rivers. The falls. Good places to hide from GenTech."

"Niagara." I nodded. Sure, you could stay out of sight there. If you knew the right place to go.

"Agents keep their distance," Crow said. "Always have."

"The Rastas would let us in? All of us?"

"Course." He tapped the back of his head on the tank. "When they see what we got."

"Nice to know we're all set then." I shook my head at him. "Guess we just have to get over these mountains, huh?"

"Past the Rift."

"Keep away from Harvest."

"And steer clear of GenTech." Crow's eyes glittered, as if they might work up a grin from the rest of his face. "Told you before you should have stuck to building."

"I'll be damned," I said.

"What?"

"Thought for a second you was gonna smile."

After all, he had to know all this talk meant nothing. Except I could see that it mattered to him. Not just securing the trees for his people—it was more than that. He seemed to want my support for something. Because we were friends now, I guess. Because of all we had been through. I mean, I couldn't see why else he would care.

"Alpha's right, you know. Your legs might work better," I said, "if you don't get so down about it."

"You saying it's all in my mind?" Crow stared into the night, and he sure weren't close to smiling no more.

"I never said that."

Tell you the truth, I just reckoned Crow was as tired as I was. I figured one uprising had been enough for him, too.

CHAPTER SIXTEEN

At sunup, there'd still been no sign of Harvesters. I'd taken the first watch, and I'd taken the last. And when I heaved the steel box up onto one side, I found Kade sleeping with his arm around my sister.

"Hey." I kicked him in the back. "What the hell do you think you're doing?"

He wriggled his hand out from under Zee's waist. "She was cold," he said through a mouthful of sleep, swatting his hand at me like I'd just blow away.

"Sure she was." I hauled the box aside so they were out in the open.

Zee coughed herself awake. "It's all right, Banyan. I got the shakes in the night."

"Next time you get the shakes, you can let me know."

"Take it easy." Kade stood up slow, stretching his shoulders.

"Don't tell me to take it easy."

"Then stop being such an ass. She was cold." He cracked his neck. "I don't see why you and your girl get to be the only ones keeping each other warm."

"You're full of it." I leaned in close to him. "You think I don't know what you're up to?"

"Banyan," Zee said, using my own name to scold me. "I can look after myself."

"You're my sister. And I'm supposed to take care of you."

"Then get me somewhere warmer." She pushed past me, her lungs heaving worse than ever. I turned to watch her stumbling through the snow.

"I don't know, bro. She is pretty as a poem." Kade said it so only I could hear him. "And a man has needs, right?"

I spun around with my fists up, but he shook the sub gun in my face.

"You're too easy," he said, laughing.

"What? This all a game to you?"

"Oh, yeah." He blew out a shock of steam. "I'm having a wonderful time."

We began up the mountains, the air growing thinner, and as we got higher, the snow grew stiffer, till soon it was nothing but ice.

It was like scaling a slope made of broken glass, and my feet grew swollen and painful, kicking at each step to try to get some grip with my boots. We held onto each other as the going got steeper. I was panting and sweaty inside my big coat, my skin all scratchy against the GenTech fuzz. And before long, we were struggling to keep the tank upright.

"Time to get down." Kade was leaning hard against the tank to stop it sliding backwards, and he stared up at Crow, who, as usual, was slumped up on top. "You'll have to walk like the rest of us. No more special treatment."

"Don't talk to him like that," Zee said. But Kade was just saying what we already knew. We'd have to practically drag that tank up this mountain, and each of us had to carry their weight.

"It's all right, Miss Zee," Crow said. "Might do me some good. Use it or lose it." He glared at me as he slid down the side of the steel box. "Think positive. Right, man?"

I helped him get steady, but then I let go of him. I mean, I couldn't carry that giant. And I couldn't stand the idea that he might need me to.

"You can do this," I said, hoping it didn't come out like a question.

"Guess we're gonna find out."

He took his first wobbly stride forward. Bits of purple rags were still caught on the brown, knotted bark of his legs, and those rags fluttered like tiny flags in the wind. He took another step. Then another. And when he slipped backwards, there was Zee, stopping him from falling, taking his hand and putting it firm on her shoulder.

"You can lean on me," she said. "As long as I'm standing."

We watched them start up the slope together, Crow with both hands on Zee's shoulders.

"He's gotta learn," Alpha said behind me, keeping her voice down. "He's gonna have to take care of himself."

"The General's right," Kade said, nudging the tank up the slope, the control pad in his hands and his back against the steel. "Dead weight is the worst weight of all."

Only good thing about the ice was our tracks got harder to follow. You could still make them out, though, if you looked close enough. And at midday, when the sun shone highest, we noticed there were other tracks on the slope ahead of us.

"What do you make of these?" Alpha said, kneeling to take a closer look.

Crow was bent over double, still holding onto Zee for support, while he studied the tracks in the ice. "Whatever it is," he muttered, "it's not something I want to meet."

"Must be some kind of pod." Kade scoured the mountainside above with the scope of the sub gun. "GenTech-built."

"It's no pod," Crow said.

"No." Alpha stood back up and shivered beside me. "I don't think so, either."

"So what the hell is it?" I asked her.

"Something that leaves footprints."

"Footprints?" Zee frowned.

"Aye." Crow peered up at the peaks looming craggy overhead. "And if they're footprints, then those are some mighty big feet."

"It's a pod," I said. "Kade's right for once, the tracks must be GenTech. They're the only ones who found their way north to this place. Figured out some route through the Rift."

"Harvest made it up here, too," said Zee.

"Aye." Crow glanced down the slope behind us. "And it doesn't seem like Harvest's working with GenTech. No agents with him. He be freelancing, I'd say. Which means, who else knows the way through the Rift?"

Pretty soon, the wind howled so hard, we quit talking about it. Just cinched our hoods tight to our faces and carried on up the slope.

None of us wanted to follow the tracks to find out what had made them. But we didn't have no other choice. Harvest was bound to still be in pursuit. And we had to get south somehow.

We'd hit a frozen channel that seemed to split the cliffs around it, creating a steep path up to a mountain pass that we reckoned would lead over to the other side. I shuffled up backwards, my aching back pressed against the tank to keep it from falling, and I kept kicking my heels into the ice as the wind blew the high clouds into mist.

Below me, Crow was still using Zee like a bony crutch. But he kept onward and upward, his stiff legs keeping him anchored so long as he moved them real slow. And that was all right. Slow was the only way we could move, anyway. Crawling our way up to the heavens. Everything steep and high pitched.

Just keep on, I told myself. Just keep going up and keep going south until you find someplace safe.

"Come on," I yelled down the slope, calling for Crow and Zee because they'd got stretched out behind us, but my voice got swallowed up by the wind.

"You think we should wait?" Alpha said. Both of us were leaned up against the tank to stop it from sliding.

Seemed we had a mile left to go to the top of the pass, and not an hour of sunlight.

"They can look after each other," I said. Because that's what Zee and Crow been doing, right? Long before I came along.

So we kept pushing at the tank, shoving it up the last frozen stretch, the sun creeping down and painting the white mountains pink.

Then I heard Crow's voice moaning in the distance below. So far away, like he'd been buried inside the earth. And it wasn't until the patches of cloud parted beneath us that I saw what he was moaning about.

The troop of Harvesters. Trudging through the snow. Getting closer to the foot of the mountains.

CHAPTER SEVENTEEN

At the top of the pass, we were tucked out of the wind, and the stars sparkled so close you could taste them. I rested against the tank with Alpha as Kade began heading back down the slope without saying a word.

"Guess he had a change of heart," I said, watching Kade descend, scraping to hold on with his one hand but mostly just sliding along on his ass. Hell, he might never have stopped if he hadn't run right into Crow.

"Red must like Zee even more than I figured," said Alpha. "Least that's my take."

"Well, I don't reckon she's liking him back."

"No?"

"You should warn her," I said. "We both know what he's after."

"And what's that, bud?" Alpha's face was buried in her hood, but I got the feeling she had just winked at me.

"Come on," I said. "She listens to you. You should look out for her."

"I'm looking out for those Harvesters."

The base of the slope had disappeared in the darkness, but I could see lights flashing down there, like torch beams at the bottom of a deep pit.

"How far do you reckon?" I said.

"They're a couple hours behind us. Less, if Crow keeps slowing us down."

I watched as Kade pulled one of Crow's arms over his shoulder. Ten-foot tall, but Crow was stooped so low, he was damn near folded in half. Zee had him by the other arm, and they were dragging him up the mountain between them.

"Should leave me," Crow mumbled when they finally reached us.

"That's no way to talk," Zee said.

"Just holding you back." You never heard such a big voice sound so pathetic. And he kept whining as we dragged him to the other side of the pass.

A valley stretched to the south, the terrain dropping down steep and disappearing under a blanket of night, until it reared up jagged and snowcapped once again in the distance. And beyond those rocky peaks, on the far side of the valley, the Rift glowed red as it flickered and spat.

I'd never felt so numb with cold nor more in awe of the earth and the sky and the battle one waged with the other. The wind had dropped and turned things silent, and the night grew more strange and beautiful because of it. The moon was not yet fully up, but I knew when it rose, it would dwarf even these mountains, just as it could outshine those stars.

And the five of us were like wide-eyed pilgrims, gazing at the soaring peaks and the steamy red sparks beyond them. It felt like standing at the top of the whole damn world.

The lava bloomed across the southern sky, splashing against the wall of mountains that kept it from pouring into the valley below us, and that lava looked alive. Trapped. Like a living thing caught in the rocks.

"How can there be a way through?" Kade said.

Alpha shrugged. "How else did GenTech get us up here?"

She was right. Somewhere there was a path, a passage, a way that the agents had taken us. A way back to the world that we knew.

"So we go down?" Zee peered into the depths of the valley.

"I say we keep to the high ground." Kade pointed. "Follow this spine of rock as far as we can."

The peaks to the west rose tall and crowded, but east of the pass, the ridge ran smoother than anything we'd faced in a while. Hard to see, dark as it had gotten, but it looked like the ridge curved south eventually, and that meant we might avoid dropping into the valley and having to climb back out.

"Problem is," said Crow, still leaning on Zee, "these tracks go east also."

He pointed at the strange marks in the ice. We'd followed them the entire way up the pass.

"Maybe they're heading the same way we are," I said. "Maybe they can lead us on through."

"We take the ridge," Kade said. "None of you has a better idea."

"How about this for an idea?" I grabbed the tank's control pad from the ground, my legs numb and weary. "We all ride on top of this thing."

"We can try," Crow said, and I helped him climb up there, feeling like a sack of shit for not helping him before.

I caught Zee staring at him, her pretty face choked up and wrinkled with worry. She could hardly breathe, but she looked more concerned about Crow.

"Told you," Kade said behind me, real quiet. "Dead weight."

I glanced up at Crow, but he hadn't heard the punk. Or maybe he had and was too gone to care. And it bothered me that Zee hadn't heard Kade, either. What was the redhead playing at? Acting the hero, helping out, but on the inside, just looking out for number one.

Alpha had scrambled back to the other side of the pass, standing atop the edge of the slope we'd just climbed.

"We're not gonna make it," she said when I joined her. We stared down at where the Harvesters' torch beams wavered and spun, splashing higher as the troops moved up quick. "Not with Crow."

"You know we can't leave him."

"Never said nothing about leaving him." She turned to face me, and her eyes were all wet. "But he needs to get his shit together. We've seen him use those legs. It's just in his mind."

"You can't say that." Zee had come up behind us, and Alpha turned away, not letting on she was crying. "You could help him, instead of whispering about him."

"Easy, girl," Alpha said. "We've all seen him use those legs proper, that's all."

"He's trying. You don't know him like I do." Zee went to say more, but then she got choked up, coughed up something dark and spat it out on the ice.

And was it blood? No. Couldn't let myself think that. I'd promised to get trees growing around her. She was going to get a forest just as pretty as she was. A place she could rest easy and breathe the clean air.

"Let's go," Alpha said, steering my sister back towards our busted Soljah and our slippery new friend. "All of us."

"Try to breathe softer," I called to my sister, but it came out wrong. Like I was bossing at her, instead of being a good brother. Like I was faking the feeling, and she was still too much of a stranger.

We squeezed on top of the steel box, Alpha working the controller up front, and Kade stationed in the rear with the sub gun. He wrapped his free arm around Zee, and I watched her nestle against him, leaning away from me as she did.

And as the moon began to rise, we started making good speed. Zipping along the ridge, dodging the steep chutes and boulders. Only time we got off to walk was when the route got too skinny, and then we picked our way along behind the tank till things got wider again.

It was a clear night and colder for it. The huge moon looked as frozen as everything else. But we kept warm enough, being all bundled together. Just our teeth chattering. Our fingers shaking in our fuzzy gloves, and our toes numb in our boots.

Weren't talking at all. Hell, even Kade kept his mouth shut. And I reckon in the end, we moved too quick through the moonbeams. Because we never slowed down to think about how long those tracks had sat in the ice ahead of us. Or how close we might be getting to whoever had made them.

They were waiting for us. Must have heard us coming, or glimpsed us through the dark. And there was no warning.

Just a rush.

A swarm of shadows swept up from both sides of the ridge, appearing before us and behind us, smothering the path.

Our attackers were cloaked and hooded, the clothes they wore shaggy and thick. And they had bows, pulled taught and snapped back with arrows.

Alpha slammed the tank to a halt amid the surge of bodies. And before Kade could open fire, I yanked the gun out of his grasp.

He spun around to glare at me, his eyes on fire.

"Can't shoot our way out of this one," I said, staring down at the hooded strangers, the rows of arrows. There were maybe fifty of them surrounding us.

"Look at their weapons," said Kade. "One bullet would send them running."

It was too risky, and it was too late, anyway—they were pulling the gun from my grip.

"Kade," Zee called, but we soon lost my sister. Alpha grabbed my hand as the strangers pried at her, but then they ripped her away, too.

Crow was gone. Then Kade. But I bolted upright. Out of reach of the fingers, standing in the middle of the top of the tank.

I felt the sharp point of a spear jab the side of my leg. And I watched the cloaked strangers below me, their eyes bright as the moon could make them, their mouths murmuring words I couldn't make out.

But then I heard something else. A heavy, thumping sound, just down one side of the ridge.

Rocks were falling beneath us on the western slope, clattering into the depths of the valley. And then, through the darkness, six figures appeared, struggling up onto the ridge with ropes pulled taut behind them.

The ground shook and scrabbled with a strange stomp and shuffle. And I heard a wailing moan echo out across the mountains. It was the sound of something alive. But no human had made it.

CHAPTER EIGHTEEN

First thing I saw was horns.

They stuck straight up over the ridgeline as the thing climbed towards us, silhouetted against the giant white moon. And those two horns were massive. Each of them as long as Crow stood tall. Set wide apart and curving upward, thick as two skulls mushed together at the bottom, but tapering to sharp points.

And that was just the horns. You should have seen the rest of it. A quick burst of speed, and the thing scrambled towards us, lumbering up to the flat top of the ridge, so it was towering above me, blocking the moonlight. Must have stood more than fifteen feet high.

Its head alone was bigger than I was. Its four legs stood taller than me. And it was buried in fur. All of it shaggy and shaking as it stamped about, making that low, rolling wail.

I gazed up at it. Trying to take it all in. The small eyes and floppy ears and rounded back. The short tail at its rear end, and the long, hairy tail up front where its nose should have been. A snout, I reckon, is what you would call it. Only that don't come near a hundred miles of describing it. I mean, it was a snout that hung right down to the ground.

My body got limp as I stood there, listening to the great beast breathing deep, shadowy sounds. The strangers with spears and arrows stared up at me. Surrounding me. But for the moment, they left me alone.

On top of the tank, I was almost high enough to look into the beast's eyes, and it was so close, I could reach out to touch it—so before my brain knew what the rest of me was doing, I did. I felt the smooth surface of its horns as it curled its shaggy, long snout in my direction and took a sniff at me.

An animal. A living, breathing thing that weren't a human or a locust. Eyes and ears and a big beating heart. You best believe my hands were shaking so hard, they shook up the rest of me.

And then the thing tapped its snout at my head.

The people below waved their arrows and spears as they busted out laughing.

I glanced down at where Crow and Zee were surrounded, separated from Alpha and Kade. Someone had taken the sub gun and dismantled it. But the faces inside the hoods smiled up at me, their fingers pointing at the beast like they wanted me to go on and get close to it again.

It made a chewing sort of sound when I patted its snout. It slapped its tongue around and let out this big sigh. The hair on that thing was coarse, long, packed thick. And up close, I could make out some color. The horns that reared up from either side of its mouth were the pale yellow of old bone. And, no mistaking it, the beast's fur was a deep shade of purple.

"Get down," Alpha called, but our captors just laughed even harder.

"It's alive," I called.

"Yes, yes." A woman patted the beast's giant leg. She tried to tell me something else, but I couldn't understand what she was saying. She clicked and clacked, and I guess she were joking, because the rest of her folks all cracked up again.

Hell, I'd forgotten what it felt like to laugh like that.

"It's an animal," I said, peering down at where Crow was blocking Zee from the arrows and spears. I glanced at Zee as I patted the thing's head. "Like in the stories. It survived."

"It's purple," Kade said. "And so is all the fur they're wearing."

"These people ain't GenTech," I said. "Look at them."

The woman who'd been trying to talk to me pulled off her hood in the moonlight. She had cheekbones like knife edges, and her long, dark hair wound like a rope down her back. She kept on speaking, and though I'd no way to understand her, the look she gave me, and the way she started to jiggle her spear, seemed to mean I was supposed to get down now. And what else could I do standing up there? There weren't no way to fight these people. And there weren't no way to run.

Our captors had a harness rigged to the beast, and we watched as they reconnected the harness to a salvaged flatbed trailer that had been stashed up ahead, out of sight behind a wall of rock.

The trailer formed a giant steel sled for the beast to haul over the ice, loaded up with junk, rubbery nets strapping everything in place—and it soon became clear they aimed to strap us in, too.

They unwound ropes and unclipped hooks, then peeled back the mesh and forced us to climb in with the salvage. The woman that seemed to be in charge messed with the tank's controller until she figured out how to get it moving. Then she had her folk lower a ramp off the trailer so she could wheel the tank up and get it squeezed in with the rest of the things these people had collected, as if the tank full of trees was just one more piece of junk.

The ramp got shoved back in place, and the strangers started wrapping their thick nets back over everything, trapping us with the big chunks of steel and plastic, binding things tight. Then, once they had the nets secure, our captors resumed their march southward, dragging our asses across the ice in a makeshift sled.

I could get my head clear of the nets just enough to watch them in the moonlight. Half a dozen of them rode on the beast's back, perched behind the hump of its shoulders, and the rest of them took turns walking beside the thing, running their hands along its shaggy coat and speaking to it in their strange tongue.

"Praise Jah," Crow whispered, straining through the nets to watch the beast swagger and roll. "Trees in the tank, and a monster on the loose."

"You ever seen something like it?" I said. "I mean, in pictures? Drawings? I never heard one tale about a thing so big."

"It's like an elephant," Zee said, strapped somewhere in the junk behind us. "But with fur on it."

"An elephant?" Sounded vaguely familiar.

"People used to keep them in cages," said Kade.

"You can't keep something that big in a cage," I told him.

"Depends how big your cage is."

"I wonder what it eats," said Alpha, her head jamming up next to mine as she wrestled some scrap metal aside to scoot closer.

"It didn't eat me," I said. "And I was up close to it. I was patting its head."

"The beast itself could be good eating." Kade's shoulder jabbed in my ribs as he fought the nets.

"Will you get off me?" I tried to push him away. "And don't be a fool. You can't eat something like that."

"He's right." Crow's head sank down below the nets. "Too hairy."

"Not underneath," Kade said.

"But you'd have to kill it," I said. "If you wanted to eat it. And you wouldn't ever kill it." I watched the great woolly thing as it lumbered through the night. "It's too beautiful."

"I might have killed it. If you hadn't snatched that gun off me. At least I might have scared these people away."

"Thought you don't like making new enemies. Thought you're all about talking things through."

"And how are we supposed to talk to them," Kade said, "when we can't understand a word they say?"

After a mile or so of staring at the beast and arguing about it, we began to explore what was hooked in the sled all around us. Nothing much. A few old stoves, punched-hole crates, some long coils of chain, and bits of piping. I kicked loose a few rusted old hubcaps.

"What do they want with all this?" Zee asked.

"It don't matter." I knew the look that was on Alpha's face when she said it. "What matters is where they're taking us, and what they aim to do with us when they get there."

"I'm guessing you'd have taken your chances with that gun," Kade said. "Same as me."

"Give it a rest," I told him. "They could have killed us by now if that's what they wanted."

"Don't mean they won't later, bud."

"You're agreeing with him?" I couldn't believe it. "They had arrows pointed at every one of our heads."

I felt Crow arcing up against the nets beside me again, peering out at the night.

"What is it now?" I tried to get so I could see out there with him.

"Moon shadows," he said. "Moving quick behind us."

My eyes followed the frozen ridge as it curled back the way we had come from, a silvery-white slab peeling open the night. And I saw the flicker of shapes advancing. No torch beams needed now. All the Harvesters needed was stealth and speed.

"Harvest's not gonna believe his luck," Kade said. "The trees in a box and the bones of that beast. Nice work, bro. You've put us in a prime slot."

"Harvest ain't getting neither one," I said. "We should warn these folk what's coming."

Kade struggled his arm loose and pointed at the strangers hauling us south. "And what good are their arrows against Harvest's army?"

"Stop it." Alpha grabbed his arm, shoved it back inside the nets. "We have to wait this one out."

"You just want to sit here?" said Kade. "Get caught in the crossfire?"

"We won't." This was Zee. "Not if we stay hidden."

"That's right, hon." Alpha was already working her way under the salvage. "Let the battle bring down the numbers on all sides but ours."

We followed Alpha's lead. Crawling away from the nets, wheedling our way down into the junk. Grabbing at the tin and plastic and old bits of rubber and pulling it around us, all of it sharp and flaky and cold.

The junk clinked and crashed as we scraped our way through it. The smell of damp mingled with a rotten PVC stink. But I kept working my way under the trash until I found the steel-cloaked tank, and I made sure it was good and buried under all that junk.

When the beast stopped moving and the sled quit sliding, everything got so quiet, I could hear the blood in my veins. There's no mistaking that silence before the storm hits. When each second could be an hour, and each moment could be your last.

Then I heard voices. The scrabble of feet. There was a shriek, like a war cry, rising up in one direction. But from the other direction came the sound of guns.

Bullets clanged at the salvage around us, drilling into pieces of junk and shaking things loose. I heard the beast wailing. Its heavy legs stomping the ground. Then the bullets let up for a minute. Our sled must have gotten unhooked, because we were being shoved aside and the sled was toppling, everything spinning and crumpling until we rolled to a stop.

"Banyan," yelled Alpha, somewhere above me now. "There's a split in the nets."

I struggled towards her voice, but I was all the way at the bottom of things, and the salvage was pinning me down.

"The tank," I called. "Get the tank."

I could hear Zee choking, spluttering on the loose rust. I'd thought I couldn't get any lower, but she was further down still.

"Crow?" I shouted. "You see Zee?"

No answer.

"Damn it." I couldn't get up or down or even sideways. "Get this shit off me."

"I'm out." Alpha sounded far off. "They're gone. In the distance. They're chasing the Harvesters back."

I hollered for Kade, hearing Zee wheezing worse with each breath. "Somebody help her."

"I see the tank," Alpha said. "It's up here with me."

The junk shifted, loosening a little. I got an arm out where I wanted it. Tried to claw myself free.

"Zee?" I hollered.

"Relax." Kade's voice came from higher up. "I have her."

Yeah. Of course he did.

"Come on, hotshot," he said as he helped pull me loose. "We're just waiting on you."

CHAPTER NINETEEN

For a moment, we couldn't do a thing but stand there. We'd gotten the tank free of the nets and the salvage, and we needed to head south and be fast about it. But instead, we peered north, watching the troops with guns scatter in the wake of the rampaging beast.

"They can't even make a dent," Alpha said. And she was right—the bullets didn't slow down that thing a damn bit. They couldn't pierce its hide, and it just swung its snout in the air and reared up on its hind legs, then pressed on charging, horns low to the ground.

The cloaked mob sprinted behind the animal, protected by it, leaning out alongside it to let loose with their arrows and spears.

"Let's move," said Kade, and I grabbed the controller from under the tank, untwisting the wires and tapping at it to fire things up.

But nothing happened.

I flipped every switch, hammering the plastic with my fist.

"What's the number?" asked Zee, her choked voice straining. Kade had his arms wrapped around her, muffling her coughs with his chest.

I yanked the panel open, not thinking. And the glass inside was pitch black and cold.

The white number blinked slow now. Nothing but zeros. Everything was switched off and shut down. No golden glow. No flash of red. So dark inside, I couldn't even see the trees.

"What do we do?" I whispered, trying to peer through the glass.

I turned to Alpha. Crow. Kade and Zee.

But all of them stood like I stood. Staring at the tank like it was a thing that had died and snatched away every promise and every last dream.

The tank protects the microclimate. That's what my mother had told me. Keep him safe, she'd said. Those were the last words that came out of her mouth.

And I hadn't even made it to the Rift.

The mob was running back towards us now. Their arrows made a sucking sound as the spiked tips whipped through the air.

And those arrows could have taken down any one of us. They could have ripped us open or sliced us apart. But we hit the ice at the sound of them, taking a dive before the one thing that needed us to keep making a stand. And as the arrows pierced the hard ground around us, I heard one make a cracking sound above me.

Then there was an awful crunch.

That arrow had hit the tank, right where I'd left the steel panel hanging open, and I glanced up just as the glass shattered. The liquid inside exploding outward. Steam and spray like sparks in the night.

A second wave of arrows whistled and thunked. A third wave. A fourth. I staggered to my feet, grabbing for the tank, then shoving it before me. Sliding it. Forcing it to move.

An arrow drilled my lower back, and the pain made me feel forty pounds lighter. I could hear Alpha and the others. Begging me to quit. But I was trying to find cover in the rocks at the top of the cliffs, and I weren't quitting for no one.

I blocked any more arrows from reaching the saplings, plugging up the hole. I felt an arrow pierce my thigh, and my whole body shuddered. I stumbled. Lost my grip for a moment. The next arrow clipped my neck, and a warmth gushed down my shoulder.

Then Kade was there, trying to grab the tank away from me.

"What are you doing?" he screamed, howling through the night.

But it was too late. I was at the cliff's edge, grasping the slippery walls of the box and pulling it closer.

And the ice began cracking beneath me.

All I could see was a tumble and spin. Icy shrapnel. Gravel and spray. I bounced in the air and shot down the slope, arrows snapping off my back and my leg, the bladed tips hammering inside me as I skidded and thumped and my blood squeezed and spilled.

I could hear the squeak of my body on the ice, the whoosh of the world shrieking past me. I kept grabbing for something. Kept finding nothing at all.

And the broken steel box bounced with me. I could feel it. Hear it. As I stared up at the moon and the ridge, all so far above.

I clawed at the ice. Slowed but kept sliding. Dropping inside this funnel from out of the sky, this gaping mouth made of stone that drank up the starlight. And then I was pouring down the throat of the mountains. The way growing steeper. I stretched my arms like they were wings. And damned if that steel box didn't spin right past me, as if my old man was leading the way.

At the base of the slope was a hole, and we slipped quick inside it. Like we'd been snatched and chewed and now faced being swallowed.

No more sting of ice or rubble. Just black and blur and the wind in my lungs. And it was over too quick to even see what was coming. I glimpsed a splash of silver. A smear of gray. And then I slapped and sank, and the busted remains of the tank gouged into the mud, right beside me.

I scraped my face from the sludge. Heard voices coming towards me. I could hear the squelch of footsteps as the mud bubbled and stank and rose up past my shoulders and sucked at my neck.

As I tried to pull free of the slime, the voices groped closer, everything slip-slapping with the stagger of feet.

And the last thing I saw was the broken box sinking. From out of the ruptured steel reached the gnarled bark of Pop's hand, and it was like he was trying to offer me a fistful of flowers. Because sprouting from his stubbled palm, swaying in the half-light, uncurled one of the last seven saplings. Its buds bruised and splattered. Its stem sapped of strength.

CHAPTER TWENTY

Felt like a week I lay dying. Perhaps longer than that. The sound of the world, like the beat of distant drums, rustled and shook until it cracked me open again. And when it did, I came to with a gasp.

Steam filled my nostrils, turning my head sour. I called out, and someone restrained me, fluttering at me and shushing me as the earth cradled my bones.

I felt heat flashing beneath my back and my legs. Rested my skull and let the heat seep into my brain. Then I blinked at the steam that drifted above me, as hazy as everything I held inside.

"Rest," a voice said, drawing out the word like it was sucking it dry. I twisted and turned to see who was speaking. A woman touched my forehead to stop me from moving, shifting her position so her eyes could meet mine.

She looked like she'd been whittled from out of the ground. Her skin was dark brown and wind burned, and her long black hair was shiny as it was straight.

I took in every sight, every detail. Even the bitter stink of the steam felt good on my tongue.

"Where am I?" I murmured.

"Safe," the woman said, again stretching out the word. Her voice was about as pretty as she was.

"The trees," I said, and my own voice sounded foreign to me. Guess that's what happens when you find yourself coming back from the dead.

"Rest," she said again.

"They're safe?" I whispered. She placed a hand over my eyelids, her skin rough, and soon I was rolling in a sleep too deep for remembering, and far too deep for dreams.

No day. No night. No moon and no sun. When I awoke, all I saw was the rock walls and the steam shrouded around me. I pushed at the edges of darkness, forcing my eyes to stay open, but then I'd drift again and wallow in sleep.

Came through in the end, though. Hunger gnawed at my belly. Questions gnawed at my mind. And finally I was able to get my elbows beneath me and lever my head off the ground.

I peered around the cave, and there weren't no one there. I almost called out, then thought better of it. I ran a hand to my lower back, where one of the arrows had pierced me, then to the gash one had left on my neck. Something was wrapped at my throat—a rubbery peel of mud, slimy and twisted. But the wound on my back was packed full of a crusty powder, and I scratched it with my nails.

My stiff legs bent with an uproar. Moving even a little made every little thing hurt. Back of my thigh, where the second arrow had gouged me, had been packed with the same dry dirt as the wound on my back. And the old GenTech rags had been torn off my bones, so I was naked as the forgotten day I was born.

But I was warm. Hot, even. The rocks toasted my feet and baked the cave walls all around me, the steam billowing in waves. I checked the back of my thigh again, scraping further at the caked-dry mud. And beneath the surface, the mud was oozing and silver. The same gray mud I'd fallen into. The mud I'd seen the steel box sinking beneath.

I studied the rest of my frail body. It was stretched out thinner than it ever had been—which is saying something when your whole life's been spent hungry. It was like the cold weeks had eaten away at me. I could see the beat of my heart where it pulsed through my chest.

Slowly, I made my way to a flinty wall and hung there, leaning against the stone. Then I edged my way around the cave, clutching at the rocks and sucking in the steam, until I found an opening to a passage where the air was clearer.

The passage traveled in a straight line but bent upwards, and I felt every inch of the slope, my legs trembling, my hands clutching the walls for support.

Could hear the end of the passage before I could see it. Voices echoed towards me—loud voices, calling out to one another in the foreign tongue I'd heard at the top of the ridge. The same language the woman had used, when she'd been jabbing at me with her spear and I'd been staring at the beautiful beast in the moonlight.

Memories bounced inside my skull and crashed against one another. I pictured that massive animal, thick with purple fur, rampaging through the night amid gunshots and arrows. And I remembered falling. Pop's broken tank beside me, in pieces in the mud.

I'd left them on the peaks—my girl, my sister, and my friend. They'd been surrounded by strangers' arrows and Harvest's guns.

I thought of Kade, trying to wrestle the tank away at the cliff's edge, trying to work his way into Zee's affections, and always trying to weave things the way he wanted, spinning you a part of some yarn with his words.

The voices hit harder as I neared the end of the passage. A pale light smudged the far side of the gloom. And when I reached the light, I leaned against the rock, trying to catch my breath, but the view stole my breath clear away.

The sloppy gray pit I'd landed in was at the base of a crater. Mud belched and smoked in the pit, and above it, rock walls funneled all the way up to daylight. It was like looking at the sky through a chimney, only you never seen a chimney this big. Thing must have been a half-mile wide and a half-mile deep, and curved around the walls was a swirl of steps and stone ledges that spiraled from the top of the crater all the way down.

People were climbing those steps and switchbacks, winding around the ledges within the crater's walls. And it weren't just people—the beasts were up there, too. I spied a whole herd of them four-legged animals, some of them almost black, others close to pink, but all of them some shade of purple. And I watched those shaggy great things, beneath the cold light of the faraway sun, until sweat and steam ran into my eyeballs and quit me from staring. I wiped my face, blinking, then started out along the rock path that rimmed the mud pit.

The path looped around the bottom of the crater all the way from one side of the pit to the other. And off from it, other passages led into the rock. Many of the openings were small, like the one I'd staggered out from, but some of them were huge, as tall and wide as those big purple critters, and a stench bulged out of the larger tunnels, punching inside the sour smell of the steam.

I kept groping along the wall, working my way around the pit, but before I found a tunnel I felt like starting down, my direction got picked for me. A gaggle of bodies came bursting out of the tunnel I'd just passed, and before I could even get turned around, their hands were grabbing at me, lifting me. They weren't being rough about it, though, and I remember that surprised me—the softness in their voices, the gentle way they scooped up my limbs. It was like I was something they were afraid of breaking. As if I might shatter if I got clutched too tight.

CHAPTER TWENTY-ONE

The room was lined with old hollowed-out televisions, and tiny fires flickered behind their glass screens, sending shadows across the walls and puffing smoke at the ceiling. When I coughed from the fumes, my ribs ached and my back pounded and my brain was just a rattle and throb.

I let my eyes get used to the flames as they thawed the darkness, the old world televisions making pretty pictures as they blazed. And I spotted more salvage at the far end of the room. Photographs in shattered glass. A toy piano and a plastic chess set. Everything painted orange by the oily flames. I huddled there, glancing about at the old scrap, the steam and smoke and stone. And I waited on the women to speak.

There were three of them, and the thrones they perched upon had seen much better days. The seats would once have been padded, but now they were just springs and steel. The women looked pretty comfy, though, as they stared down at me. One of them even had her seat wound back so it lifted in the front and stretched her legs out before her, supporting her bare feet on the rusty coils.

They wore purple fur and leather, and their dark skin glistened in the heat. The one who sat in the center with her feet up was a shriveled, pitted thing, her skin crinkled and chapped, eyes that took up half her face. She had to be old as anything. The woman's hair weren't so much white as translucent, and most of it was coming out of her ears.

On either side of that ancient face, the other two women looked shiny and new, but they were weather beat once you looked closer. And one was almost identical to the other—same face and hair, same dark skin—except the one on the right held her mouth stern, while the other's eyes beamed bright. And the bright-eyed woman was the one I'd come awake to. The one who'd whispered to me when I'd first stirred again.

I became aware of how naked and thin I was before them, there on the stony ground. I tried to cover myself, felt my face turn fool red.

The old woman leaned forward a little, clacking and droning at me.

"The Elder welcomes you," said the woman on the right, scowling as she translated. "The Elder is glad you've become awake."

"Who the hell is the Elder?" I said. "And who the hell are you?"

"I am the Speaker. To you and all strangers. My sister is the Healer." She pointed at the bright-eyed woman on the other side of the old crone. "To all who are sick."

"But who are you people? What is this place?"

"Our people have many names." Her accent bent the words in odd places. "You can call us Kalliq."

"And you live here? Above the Rift?"

She frowned.

"The fire," I said. "The lava. It's close, I reckon. Making all this steam."

"It is the Burning Wheel."

I glanced at the Healer, and she just gazed down at me, her eyes full of wonder. Like I was as strange to her as she looked to me.

"And these things," I went on, turning back to the Speaker. "These animals. Where did you find them?"

"Animals." The woman smiled. "We did not find them. The mammoths were already here."

"Mammoths," I whispered, tasting the word on my tongue. "They lived before the Darkness? The twenty years of night?"

It took the woman a moment to understand what I was asking. "They were made here." She pointed down at the stone and bent forward on her metal throne. "They were extinct. Hunted until there was nothing. But before the dark came, your chief brought them back."

"What chief?" My voice cracked. "The Executive Chief?"

I pictured those thready beasts, all covered in purple, and I reckoned GenTech must have brought them back from the dead, all right. Much like they'd been trying to do with the trees. Only they'd brought back the mammoths more than a hundred years ago, before the Darkness. And then, after the twenty years of night, the only mammoths left had been trapped up here, north of the Rift.

"So GenTech made them," I muttered, but at the mention of the name, the old woman began jabbering at the women on each side of her, and she looked all bent out of shape.

"The Elder says the mammoths were created for us." The Speaker thumped her fist to her chest. "For Kalliq. And for Kalliq alone. A gift from your GenTech tribe, before the dark came. A gift to see us through."

"Well, I ain't asking for your gift back. The Elder can relax. GenTech ain't my tribe."

"You were wearing their symbol. Their clothing."

"Me ending up in their clothes is a long story," I said. "But how does the Elder know so damn much, anyway?"

"Because she has been here. Always," said the Speaker. "Born before the skies turned black."

"Since before the Darkness? That was a hundred years ago. Or more. That's impossible."

The Speaker suddenly rose from her seat and prodded a long finger down at where I sat huddled and naked. "So is what you have brought here," she hissed, like she was accusing me of something wicked. "So is the future you bring."

I stood up so I was level with her. Never mind her temper, or her accusations. And never mind that I was naked. I wanted answers.

"If she was alive then, tell me what happened," I said. "What caused the Darkness? The twenty years of night?"

"The stars fell." The Speaker clenched her fists, raised them over her head, then cast them down. "All the world over. A storm of rocks from beyond the sky, big as worlds split in two. They punched the moon closer. Ripped up our lands and the oceans, clouding the world with dust. Blocking the sun."

"Creating the Rift?" I asked. "Your Burning Wheel?"

Yes, I thought. And if it had brought the moon closer, it had created the Surge—the towering, spinning seas that were all that was left of the oceans.

The world had been punctured, made weak and splintered. Left as fragile as the folk left hanging on.

The Healer stood up from her chair, came and checked the wounds on my back and my neck. She probed at the dirt that was packed in my thigh, her fingers reaching inside the wound.

And she reminded me of Alpha. Not the way she looked or the way she looked at me. But I remembered how my pirate girl had tended to me back in Old Orleans, when a fever had spread through my veins. And as I remembered her, the fear swelled inside me. She'd been up on that ridge, the arrows raining down, and I had left her. I'd abandoned her. Again. I'd left them all. Weaponless and stranded in the night.

"There were others," I whispered, staring up at the Speaker. I stuck a thumb at my chest. "My friends."

"Yes." She seemed to smile at my panic. "They are still with the patrol. Last seen near the outer rim."

"Alive?"

The Speaker waited, like she wanted to see how much I might squirm.

"Alive," she said finally. "The patrol will return here. And bring your friends before us."

"When?"

"After hunting."

"Hunting what?"

She pointed at the salvage around the room, and I sank to the ground, breathing hard as the Healer prodded at the dirt she'd stuffed in my wounds.

So my friends had been seen. They were alive.

But they were so far away. And did they even know I was down here? I mean, here I was, stuck inside the earth, no way to know what dangers they faced.

I worried about Zee without me there to look after her, no one to make sure Kade didn't get too damn close. And I'd been a fool to trust him, I reckoned. The redhead with the silver tongue. He'd had it in for me—truce or no truce. He'd just been using me to get in with the others and get to the trees.

Maybe I'd gone soft after I'd beat his face bloody, or after I'd learned he'd been hit by the crystal and lost his hand in the fields. But he was after my saplings, and he was after my sister, and I could now see that clearly. There weren't no room for sympathy. We were all just dead weight to him in the end.

"Where are the trees?" I said, staring up at the Speaker. But the Elder started jabbering on again, and the Healer bundled me out of the room.

I was breathing hard by the time we reached the end of the tunnel. I had to stop and rest, the steam stinging my eyes. But the Healer's bright face kept staring at me, curious and happy. I mean, her mouth never seemed to quit smiling at all. Reckon I was more used to the way her twin had looked at me—all bitter and pissed and full of scorn.

We entered a cave full of folk working at big patches of fur they'd stretched out on the walls. They were beating the stuff flat and shearing it into sections, weaving the purple thread into clothes. The Healer took me to one side to sort through a stack of their handiwork. Threw some pants at me, a pair of leather boots. Then she handed me a bright pink vest like the one Alpha had once worn. I mean, this one was new and clean, but I'd no doubt it was made of the same material. That somehow a little of this fur had made its way south, even if the mammoths themselves never had.

I checked out my new outfit. The vest practically glowed in the dim light of the cave, and I must have looked a right old sight in it. Still, at least I weren't naked no more.

Back in the tunnels, we started to pass more and more of the locals. Steam swirled off their clothes, and their faces lit up when they saw me coming towards them. These people sure seemed friendly—except for the Healer's twin, the one they'd picked to do the speaking.

The next cave we reached was large and well lit, with oil lamps in tin buckets all across the walls. The steam whirled thicker here, and I almost slipped on the rocks, but the Healer put my hands on her hips, making it so I could follow her as she pushed on inside.

Center of the cave, the steam lifted a little, and we reached a small pool, full of mud that looked more like liquid, real silvery in color and bubbling up something fierce. At the edges of the pool, bright against the dark stones, there was a layer of a soft green something. But I didn't kneel down to inspect it. Not right away.

All I could do was stare into the center of the pool, where my seven saplings soaked up the heat. And I felt a bit lighter, just seeing them again, but I also felt heavier. Because there seemed to be so much resting on those little trees. So many people who wanted them. And I knew I could not get them south on my own.

CHAPTER TWENTY-TWO

The trees looked stronger. Thicker. Their stems each as wide as a finger, the buds on their limbs bulging up and swelled out, like the leaves inside couldn't wait to burst free.

I plunged into the hot sludge, scalding myself as I splashed forward. And I felt a jolt when I touched the first sapling—the shock of a memory, because for a second, it was like I was a nipper again and my old man was holding my small hand in his.

I stared down into the pool, and there, floating in the water and all covered in mud, was the last broken bits of Pop's body. So much smaller now, as if he'd been almost all used up. I could still make out the shape of his sunken belly and a swollen knot of bark where his chest had been. And his head still resembled a man's skull, though it had become shriveled and tiny, though roots covered his eyes and nose, and a sapling sealed shut the mouth that had once told me stories and laughed at my jokes. The same mouth that had kept secrets from me and spent so many days hungry and never known nearly enough smiles.

As I held the tree, I felt the loss wash over me once more, and I tried to let it sink in. Pop was the one person who'd known me. My one friend, all those years on the road.

"Safe," the Healer said, her voice at my shoulder. Her eyes staring at the seven trees.

"You did this?" I whispered. "You fixed them?"

She stayed quiet, but I sensed her confusion. I held a sapling in one hand and pointed up with the other, showing how tall it had grown. Then I pointed at the woman. "You," I said.

"No." She put her hand on the sapling, just below mine, and she pointed at the gray, muddy water and rumbling heat. "It is the Burning Wheel."

The soft green something on the rocks was a sort of moss. Algae, the Healer called it. A living thing. Like the trees, and the mammoths. And that meant it was one more miracle, still hanging on.

The algae was soft and slick, and I smeared at it with my fingers as I sat at the edge of the pool and stared at the trees.

"Eat," the Healer said, scooping up some of the moss with her thumb.

I stared at the strange goo. Didn't look like something anyone would go eating, not even in an old world story. But I was so damn hungry that I figured I'd give it a shot. I let her stick her thumb in my mouth, and the green moss fizzled on my tongue. It weren't so much that it tasted good, but it tasted real, if you catch my meaning. It tasted alive, and it sure as shit weren't corn. As I sucked at it and let it slip down my throat, my whole body got ripe off the sparkle.

"It's good," I said, and the woman beamed. Then she tugged off my pink vest and set to working fresh mud into the holes the arrows had left behind.

The mud was warm and foamy in my skin. And I just sat there, letting the Healer work her magic as I scooped up more moss to eat. I'd say it was like something out of a dream, only there weren't no dream I'd come up with that even came close. Guess the insides of the earth can be even stranger than the inside of your head.

But just like the inside of my head, this place was loaded with questions. And the few answers it had given me just made me want to ask something more.

The Speaker told me the mud bubbled in pits and pools all throughout the Kalliq's maze of tunnels and caves. It was because of the Burning Wheel, she said, as if it were something sacred, though I reckoned that was just the name they'd given the Rift.

The ground heated the mud and water and helped brew the moss that collected on the sides of the pools. And so the silvery mud had become these people's medicine, and the moss was their meals. They scraped up enough of that algae to feed the whole tribe, adding meat to their menu when a mammoth stumbled and fell in the mountains, or if one died of old age.

Had been a long time since a mammoth had fallen, and the last dried bits of meat had been chewed off its carcass. But I did wonder what that beast's flesh might taste like. I mean, this algae stuff filled you up, all right, but before long, I was craving some crunch.

One of those mammoths died, the Speaker said, the people used every bit of it, whittling weapons and tools from its bones.

Tusks, she called their horns—made out of ivory. Stronger than bone and sharper than teeth. And that long snout, the Speaker called that a trunk. Said the mammoths used to be able to pick up a blade of grass with it, or pull apart a whole tree. Back when there'd been blades of grass and trees to go pulling at.

Anyway, if a mammoth died, it was like it kept on living, the way these people didn't waste none of it but put it all to good use. They made blankets from the tough hide, burned fires and lamps with the oily fat. And they sheared off fur when they needed it, weaving it into clothes. So a mammoth meant more than just a creature to marvel at or something to ride on. And the Kalliq fed those things the biggest portions of algae in return.

That all being said, you can see why it was a shock when I found them drowning one of those beasts in the big gray pit.

The circle of sky at the top of the crater was pitch black with night, and the mammoth had come back from patrolling with a gash on its side and a limp in its leg. The Elder was overseeing things when I got there, which is to say she was chanting softly as the Kalliq prodded the mammoth into the pit with their spears.

I thought the whole thing was sick. The poor animal trying to scrabble free as they forced it deeper, moaning as the mud rose fast against its busted-up legs.

"What the hell?" I yelled out, my voice lost beneath the wail of the drowning mammoth. I'd only been around a couple days. Still a stranger. And hell, maybe I always would be, but I had to say something.

The Speaker grabbed me, stuffing her hand on my mouth and pulling me away from the action. "For the Burning Wheel," she hissed, sour-looking as ever.

"Are you insane?" I shoved her hands off me. "For the Rift? You're gonna kill this thing?"

"Sacrifice," she whispered, turning back to the pit.

The mammoth moaned even louder as the mud surged up its neck. It flailed its head this way and that, until its trunk was the only thing left, poking up out of the mud, twitching about and still breathing.

Until the poor thing was full spent and done.

Each day, I'd check, but each day, there was no news of my friends. No updates about the patrol they were with or when they'd return. No scouts who might have seen them coming back from what the Kalliq called the outer rim.

I'd just have to be patient, the Speaker said, when I pestered her about it. Then she'd scowl at me until I left her alone.

But it was hard to be patient. And the stronger my body got, the more anxious I grew.

I kept picturing Kade with his arms around my sister. I imagined him telling them all that I was dead and they had best forget me, and somehow Kade always seemed to have the right words to say. Something smart, or kind, or something funny. And what was it he'd said to me, about a man having needs? Well, I had needs of my own and didn't know what to do with them. I yearned for my pirate girl, and it burned me up through the night. I'd fall asleep thinking of her, imagining her body against me, remembering how I'd kissed her when she'd returned to us in the snow. But then I'd wake up from nightmares where it was Kade she was kissing. Her fingers gripping the short red hair on his skull.

Still, it was a break from the nightmares about Hina and my mother and the fields full of locusts. Or the ones where Sal's head kept exploding in flames.

Don't know how I slept a damn wink.

And it went on like this. The waiting. The fear. Some days, I'd follow the ledges that spiraled out of the crater, making my way up that chimney that led to the sky. Trying to clear my head as I watched the cold light of the world get bigger, winding my way upwards, until finally I'd reach the top and stare out at the peaks that towered above.

I could see the Rift glowing in the sky beyond the peaks to the south.

I'd spy groups of Kalliq venturing out across the ice or coming home down the side of the mountains. I'd see riders atop mammoths lumbering through the glistening snow.

But I was starting to be a jangled mess of crazy. Hoping each new day that the patrol would return with my girl and my sister and my broken Soljah. Hoping they would be brought down into the crater, so the Elder could give them to me.

Because she'd hand them over, I reckoned. I pretty much had the run of the place, after all. Though the

Speaker seemed loath to admit it, the Kalliq had a sweet spot for their skinny new guest.

It was obvious I was to be looked after and looked up to. I was to be kept safe and made healthy. These people had mammoths and moss and their mud, and that was worth more than anything I'd left behind in the dusty world that lay south. But I'd given them something the Kalliq had only heard about in tales told by the Elder. I'd given them something they'd only seen in pictures, faded imprints locked inside the salvage they hunted beneath the ice.

The Chief had given them the mammoths, they said. Before the Darkness descended. Yeah, it was some GenTech science that gave them that miracle.

But it was Banyan that gave them the trees.

CHAPTER TWENTY-THREE

I found the Healer knelt in the muddy pool, using copper wire to splint two of the trees together, giving them strength by binding them side by side. They'd grown a little taller since I'd last been down in this cave. They'd gained a good six inches, turned a darker shade of green.

"Looking good," I said, startling her, but even getting spooked made that woman smile. I sat on the rocks, watching as she checked the roots that ran out of the base of the saplings and plugged into Pop's shrunken remains. "Those trees were froze up and broken before you came along."

She could hardly understand a word I was saying, but she got my drift, all right. Someone else would have tried to deny it, or else gobbled up the praise. But not the Healer. She just beamed at me as she tended the saplings, happiness radiating out of her.

And she looked so peaceful and beautiful. Not like Alpha was beautiful. Not in the way that lit a fire in my bones. It was more like I admired her, I reckon. The way she had something to do and gave all her focus to doing it. Because I remembered that feeling, your hands keeping your brain busy, your heart full.

I scavenged up a hammer and chisel, one long strip of wire that was sharp as a razor, a rusty old ladder, and that's about it. Then I threw a fur cloak over my vest and headed up to the top of the crater, where the ice sparkled blue-white and was near hard as a rock.

With the wire in two hands, I could scrape the ice into blocks if I took my time over it, and that's how I started. Worked on that for five whole days. Prep work, really. Making the ice into these thick pillars—a whole section of them, about thirty yards wide, right at the base of the chute I'd slid down with the tank, using the last bits of slope to my advantage, creating some elevation to play with later on. I was at it each morning as the sky grew light, and I worked till the sun disappeared.

And at night, I'd crawl into the warm cave they'd given me, down there amid the slumbering Kalliq, and I'd sleep deep and proper. No more nightmares. Too exhausted from one day of working, too excited about the next.

The fifth day, I went up top with the same tools, along with a couple of old knives folk had gathered up for me. The Speaker wanted to know what I was doing up there, but I just told her she'd have to be patient. And then I pushed on up the steps and switchbacks, spiraling up the rock ledges until I busted out into the cold.

I stopped and stared at the peaks, straining to see if any patrols were returning. Hoping for a glimpse of my friends. I quit breathing and stayed quiet, listening for a sound in the distance, the moan of a mammoth or the click-clack chatter of the Kalliq.

Couldn't see nothing that weren't snow, stone, and sky

Couldn't hear a thing but silence.

I thought about what the Speaker had told me— about stars falling, rocks as big as worlds, shattering the earth and leaving it in darkness. Leaving us with the Rift and the Surge, the huge moon and the swarms of locusts. Leaving the ragged tribes of people who'd hung on after the twenty years of night to stake their claim in the rubble.

And then I did what I'd always done when the world seemed callous and too old and empty.

I started building.

At each wide pillar of ice, I worked with my hammer and chisel. Setting up my ladder for the tall stuff and chipping away at the frozen powder, then etching it with knives.

I worked till noon, then past noon. I worked till I was sweating in my furry clothes. Toiling and crafting. Carving at the ice with my tools, as if revealing what had always been there, making something new by taking something away.

Creating a forest from the frozen landscape.

I built trees I hadn't thought of in ages. Icy leaves like blown glass, shot through with color. Spruce and ash, redwood and oak. I remembered trees me and

Pop had come up with. Made the prettiest Pickle Fir you ever did see. And I even made up some new trees before I was finished, naming them for the people I'd lost, and the folk that were missing.

I built one for Alpha. Made one look like Crow. And almost before I knew it, I'd spent nearly a week working, and I'd gone the last day without eating or drinking or even stopping at all. I was hardly even thinking, just feeling my way, lost in my rhythm, up and down the ladder, back and forth with my tools. And when the sun dropped that day, my forest was tall enough you could walk beneath the canopy, wide enough you could wind through the trees.

And it was then people started to appear on the rim of the crater. As the stars began to twinkle and settle in for the night. A crescent moon rose, splitting the dark sky like a smile, as the Kalliq emerged, cloaked and hooded, clambering up from their tunnels and caves. Their voices were hushed, if they even were speaking, and they walked among the trees in huddled groups of three over here and four over there.

I heard the snuffle and snort and stomp of a mammoth, and turned to watch one scramble out of the crater, the Elder high on its back.

The old woman was helped down from her mount and led into the forest. And I just stood there in the middle of the trees, the hammer and chisel at my feet, the knives in my hands.

The Healer and the Speaker appeared at either side of their ancient leader as the rest of the folk made a wide circle in the forest, surrounding the three women and me.

The Elder gazed into my eyes like she might stretch open my soul to stare deeper inside it. And she spoke straight to me, as her breath steamed and shone amid the crystalline trees.

"The Elder wishes to know why you do this." The Speaker managed to hold onto her usual scowl, but even the ugly way she spoke couldn't put a hole in the moment.

"Just building," I said. My belly was empty and my arms ached, but I could have kept on with the carving and sculpting all through the night, I reckon, it felt so damn good.

"The Elder wishes you tell her why."

"'Cause that's what I do," I said, and I remembered what Jawbone had told me, back inside that pirate city on the plains. She'd said that you either are something or you're not. And it occurred to me that Pop had been right when he'd said I wasn't a fighter. And maybe I wasn't meant to be a lover or a brother or a son, either, in the end.

"I'm a tree builder," I said, and the Speaker translated it for me, but the Elder shook her head, then said something back.

The Speaker made a grim sort of face and stayed silent. But the Healer spoke up. She was a better one for translating it, too.

"Tree King," she said, and all around me, the Kalliq started to cheer.

And I'll be damned, for the first time in my life, I felt like I was home.

CHAPTER TWENTY-FOUR

The patrol entered the far side of my forest. We heard them before we could see them—the sound of something huge shattering my work. And the Elder's beast must have sensed its pal in the distance, because it snorted and wailed, rearing up on its hind legs. And then the Kalliq broke out in voices all around me as we ran through the ice trees.

At the edge of a stand of redwood, we stopped and watched the returning mammoth crush the tall trees beneath it, spraying us with icy shrapnel and slush.

"Alpha?" I called. "Zee?"

I stared at the cloaked figures on either side of the beast. But when words I could understand came back to me, the voices came from up high.

"Where are you?" Alpha called, sounding nearly as stunned as I was. "Banyan?"

"I'm here," I yelled, running to the mammoth. Bodies rushed around me, the tribe reuniting. And one by one, the riders atop the mammoth tugged down their thick hoods and shook their heads at the stars.

There were six of them up there. Two strangers.

And four that I knew.

"I told you he'd be here," Kade called to the others. He waved his stump at me. "You can't get far without your right-hand man."

Alpha was already swinging herself down from the mammoth's shoulders. She dropped off the side of the beast, and we each broke through the crowd until we were wrapped up together, holding one another in the sparkling night.

Both mammoths roared, making a sound like a victory blast. And the Kalliq bustled around us as their friends came back from the cold.

"Let me look at you," I whispered to Alpha, and I took her in. All of her. The golden-white skin, her golden-brown eyes and her busted nose. The beautiful face you'd never be able to draw right but you'd always remember.

"We got word you'd be here," she said, glancing past me at the ice-sculpted trees. "But I was almost afraid to believe."

"They healed me," I told her. "Pop, too."

"You mean the saplings?"

"Yeah. Of course."

She quit smiling, then shoved at me like she was supposed to be angry. Only then she busted out grinning again. "Thought you weren't gonna leave me, bud?"

"Guess you should have come on down the mountain."

That made her smile even bigger. She stuck her thumb over her shoulder, pointing at the mammoth. "And miss out on all this?"

Crow appeared beside us. Wobbling ten feet in the air. "Good to see you, little man," he said, putting his hands on my shoulders to keep himself steady. Or maybe it was to show that he cared.

"You, too." I stared up at him, then I stared at his legs. "You been walking?"

"Nah. Too busy riding." He nodded his head at the mammoth, and I saw Zee make her way through the crowd to join us. Her face wind burned, her long hair a tangled twist.

"You okay?" I said to my sister. It seemed like she'd maybe quit wheezing so bad.

"Barely," Kade answered for her, because suddenly he was right there beside me. His face had healed from when I'd busted it up for him, and he made that handsome smirk of his as he put his arm around my shoulders. "We've been all over these mountains."

Kade took his other arm and slid it around Alpha's waist.

I tensed up. Saw Kade's eyes twinkling.

"You gonna tell him, compadre?" he said to Alpha. "Or shall I?"

"Tell me what?"

Alpha's face turned grim. She took my hand in hers, squeezed my fingers. "We've seen them."

"Harvest?"

"Oh, plenty of him." Kade glanced about at my forest. Then he shrugged with the sub gun on his shoulder. "These people were supposed to be hunting for salvage, but we ended up fighting one Harvest after another, while you've been building your little trees."

"Not just Harvest, bud." Alpha shoved Kade in the gut, but not hard. Just in a way that was friendly. "We went south once this lot figured we seemed to be on the same sort of team, and they could use us in a battle. They showed us the route through the lava. The way through the Rift."

"Aye," Crow rumbled. "Channel of black rock, half a mile wide. But what about the trees, man? They all right?"

"Yeah." I moved away, shrugging Kade's arm off my back. "They're here. With me."

"That's what we heard," Zee said. "Though talking to these people hasn't exactly been easy."

"Well, you heard right. And the trees are safe. They're growing."

"Growing?" Kade laughed. "That's better news than we bring."

"The route south is blocked," Crow said. "The way back be full of agents. Hundreds of them."

"An army." Alpha pointed up out of the rocky basin, where the fiery glow of the Rift flickered behind the peaks to the south. "The Army of the Purple Hand."

"Yeah." Kade nudged her. "Even this pirate's not crazy enough to take them on."

"Don't tempt me." She finally pulled his arm off her, grinning at him the whole time. But then she gave her smile back to me and pulled me close, resting her head on my shoulder.

I stared up at the mammoth they'd ridden in on, and its sad old eyes met mine.

"Don't matter," I said. "I don't need a way back, anyway."

"How's that?" Kade couldn't help but sound serious.

"Right here is Zion," I told them. "And I ain't leaving for no place at all."

When both mammoths raised their trunks to the moon and let out a wail, the Kalliq quit chattering and shuffling around, and they all stared up at the sky.

And folk weren't looking south, where the red globs of the Rift glowed along the tops of the mountains. Instead, they were looking north, where a new set of colors had begun burning the night.

Green waves of light came cresting and spinning out of the heavens, sketching patterns against the blackness and turning blue as the patterns stretched and ebbed.

Looked like clouds of color, swirled quick on invisible winds.

Damn right, this is Zion, I thought. Mammoths and moss. Saplings growing in the mud below, and now a kaleidoscope above. I had my girl, and my sister, and Crow at my side. Place was beautiful.

The Elder's voice rose as the lights turned pink and white above us. And when she quit speaking, there was silence. Everyone just gazing at the billowy flashes of light.

The Healer found me in the crowd. "Friends?" she whispered, nodding at Alpha. She stared up at Crow, smiled at Zee and at Kade.

"Most of them," I said, but I pointed to the strange lights that splashed in the heavens. "What is this?"

"The North Lights," she said, peering upwards, and I watched the glow as it danced in her eyes. "Lamplight of Kalliq."

"It's amazing."

"Elder says for you. Says the Burning Wheel shines for the Tree King."

Kade had overheard, and he busted out laughing. "Tree King? Well, aren't you special?"

He laughed so hard, the Kalliq around us joined in with the laughing. I saw Alpha bust a smile, too. "Like your new duds," she said, smirking as she tugged at my shaggy pink vest.

And I mean, what the hell? Were they even happy to see me? Because I sure weren't in the mood to be the butt of some joke.

"We need to talk, Banyan." Crow's voice boomed above me.

"What about?" I snapped, trying to pull away through the crowd. Alpha grabbed me, though. Kept me beside her.

"About you talking about Zion," Crow said.

"Oh, right. You gonna say I'm crazy cool?" I made my voice deep as his was, scowling up at him.

"More I'm thinking you just be crazy."

But I didn't have to answer him. Because behind us, rising up out of the crater, came the banging of drums.

The Festival of Lights, they called it. And a big old party is what it was. Right inside that big chimney crater, everyone lining up on the ledges and steps, from the mud-pit bottom to the star-filled sky. The North Lights bloomed overhead and lit the insides of the earth, their colors flashing and surging as the Kalliq let loose.

Steel drums chimed and pounded, each beat ringing out all the way to the moon. And it weren't just drums these people had crafted. Folk banged and clattered on old hubcaps, oven doors, and copper pipes. They blew down glass-bottle flutes, struck mallets on racks of tin cans. And the night came undone as the music untwisted, reverberating into the mountains and making everything sing. It was beautiful. Music like nothing I'd heard. Chants and tunes tumbling from the lips of all the Kalliq around me.

I was stood on the steps with Alpha, midway down the crater, staring up at the luminous sky. The air was thick, and the steam was sour. The whole night seemed to be rolling and sinking, the songs shattering like fireworks.

Alpha grabbed my hand and pulled me to the edge so we could see the bodies moving above and below us. Everyone dancing and jumping. Shaking their butts and waving their hands in the air.

There was a girl on a high ledge spinning a hoop made of fire. Dudes swinging ropes they'd turned into flames. I pointed up at the girl with the hoop, nudging Alpha.

But Alpha had started to bounce herself free.

She moved like she was at the very center of the music, all the light and all of the faces, like it was all part of the same tapestry. And as my pirate girl shook and danced and started to move even faster, it was like nothing bad could ever touch her again. As if she'd slipped out of this world, moving too fast for its dirty fingers and the grip of decay. She moved like a twister on the dustlands. Her arms pulsing with the music and her skin glistening, each drop of sweat vibrating with the thunderous steel drum boom.

And I reckon she wanted me to move with her, but I didn't have it in me. I couldn't figure out how to let myself go. And before I knew it, Kade was pushing past me and dancing beside her. He was shirtless, shaking the ugly stump at the end of his arm above his head and grinning at my girl.

I started to slip away through the crowd on the steps, suddenly wanting to find Crow. My old, broken friend. Hell, I knew he wouldn't be dancing.

I found Zee before I found Crow. She was crouched at the edge of the silver mud pit, staring up at the dancers and the circle of sky.

"Kade was looking for you," she said when I squatted beside her.

"Don't reckon it was me he wanted." I watched the steam swirl about us, tinged by the blue lights of the cosmos. And then I peered up at where Kade and Alpha were still dancing away. "You seen Crow?"

"He was talking with the old woman. Then he went off with one of the twins."

"The one that looks like this?" I made my face full of misery.

"No." Zee grinned. "The one who doesn't speak so good."

Already had a pretty good idea where I'd find Crow and the Healer, but I had Zee point out which passage they'd taken before I started to go.

"Banyan," she called, putting a hand on my leg and tugging me back towards her.

"What's up, sister?"

I tell you, just me saying the word made that lass smile.

"What did you mean?" she asked. "About not wanting to leave here?"

"Look around you. No GenTech. No dust. There's food growing, and it belongs to everyone. And the mammoths." I pointed to one, bopping its head out of one of the tunnels as if it was enjoying the tunes. "Hell, this place has it all."

"But we can't stay here. We don't belong with these people."

"I don't belong nowhere else."

She shook her head at me like I was being ridiculous. "You ever even heard of a place like this?"

"Sure. You used to talk all about it. Called it the Promised Land."

Zee rolled her eyes.

"What? Looks more like it than that island we found."

"This ain't the Promised Land, Banyan."

"Well, stories only get you so far, I reckon."

"And you think the trees are safe here?"

"That's the best part of all," I said. "They're safe and healthy."

"So you just want to keep them hidden away." Zee made this face, like she was all disappointed in me.

"Last I heard, you wanted to give them to GenTech. Or Harvest. Anything to make sure they survive."

"I never said I wanted to hide them from people."

"Well, maybe I don't give a damn what you want."

"That figures." She frowned. "We've been talking it through, you know."

"Who?"

"It was something Alpha said. And Kade."

"What the hell's he got to do with it?"

"I don't know why you get like that about him."

"Yes, you do," I said. "Guy's a punk."

"He never did a thing wrong to you."

"No? And what else did he tell you?"

"Don't be like that."

"Used to be hooked on the crystal. He tell you that?"

"Yes. He did."

"Just like Frost," I said.

"Not like Frost. Come on, Banyan. Stop."

"Then quit talking about him."

"I like him."

"You can quit liking him, too."

"Why?"

"Because you're supposed to be my sister," I said, letting myself get as pissed as I wanted. I pointed up at Alpha, dancing without me. Kade spinning her around like a fool. "And that's supposed to be my girl."

"You can be such an idiot." Zee stared up the side of the crater, watching Alpha and Kade vibrate with the music. "Why aren't you dancing with her, anyway?"

I listened as the drums crashed and looped. "Guess I ain't the dancing type."

"I would be, if that was my girlfriend."

"So maybe you should go dance with Stumpy."

"Who says I won't dance with him?"

"You say it like I give a damn if you do."

As I started to leave her, I wondered if she could really be sweet on that punk. And I wondered what else had happened since we'd all been apart.

CHAPTER TWENTY-FIVE

I came to a junction full of steam, then cut in the direction the steam blew thickest. It led me to the cave full of mud and algae and the saplings. The place the Healer worked her magic best.

I slipped inside the cave, my feet shuffling on the wet rocks. Had to wait till the hot mist cleared, but then I spotted them. They were deep in the wet gray mud, up close to the saplings, and the Healer was helping Crow get low in the pool. His bottom half was submerged by the time I reached them. The mud boiled and spat at his chest.

"What you looking at?" Crow grumbled, seeing me over the Healer's shoulder.

"How's it feel?" I said.

"Burns like fire." He winced as he sank further into the slime.

"No pain, no gain."

"Them the words you live by, little man?"

"Little man," I muttered. Why couldn't he just use my damn name?

"Maybe I should call you Tree King, eh? I seen you, top of that ridge. Took a big old leap of faith, no? Dropping off the mountain to take care of your trees."

"Can't say I planned on it." I couldn't tell if he was being serious. "But I guess you think that was stupid."

"Nah. Give yourself a break," he said. "You can't be brave without being a fool."

I glanced at the Healer, and she was beaming away like she usually did, though there wasn't much hope she could understand a word me and Crow were saying.

"Fix him?" I pointed at Crow.

"Rest," the woman said, helping him lie back so his body was floating in the mud but his head was supported.

"Better follow the doctor's orders," I told him, sitting on the rocks beside Crow as the Healer splashed out of the pool. "Though you are missing one hell of a shindig."

"Shindig?" Crow closed his eyes. "You ain't seen a thing till you seen Waterfall City."

"I been there, remember? We built for those Rastas, my old man and me."

"You might have been to Niagara. But there's no chance you been in Waterfall City, not all the way. The ground in there's too sacred. Crow will take you, though. He'll get you inside. Before all this is through."

"Except I ain't going nowhere, remember?"

"The parties," he mumbled. "You never seen nothing like it. And the women." He opened his eyes for a second. "You never knew something could look so good."

"I seen your Soljah women."

"Not the one I'm talking about." He was drifting off. Heading for sleep. "I'll take you there, though. Someday. You and me. And the trees."

"Told you," I said, loud enough to keep him awake. "I ain't leaving here."

"Oh, I know what you said." Crow pried one eye open and fixed it on me. "Some foolishness about this hole in the ground being Zion."

"Let me see—it's safe, plenty of food and water. No one starving. No one trying to kill us."

"Not yet."

"Look at this." I scooped up a handful of algae. "Down in these caves, they got wild things still growing. What? You don't like the smell?"

"I like the mammoths."

"There you go."

"Riding on its back, felt like I had real legs again."

I wondered if that's what had gotten his spirits up. Because Crow had been holding us back on the way up the mountains, slowing us down in the snow and ready to quit, but now he sure seemed fired up to keep moving south.

"They can heal you." I pointed at the Healer as she tended the saplings. "She can work magic."

"Maybe. But that's no reason to stay here. There's a whole world be needing those trees."

"You mean Niagara needs them. Your world." I stood up. "Not mine."

I felt the Healer's hands on me as I pushed through the steam and made for the exit. When I spun around, she was right there at my side. Hard to look in her eyes, though, all of a sudden, as if she was building some sort of wall to keep something from me.

"Must come," she whispered, tugging at my vest. "You must see."

"What about him?" I shrugged back at Crow.

"He rests."

I lowered my voice. "But you can make him better. Right?"

"Come," she said again, and I realized she'd lost all trace of her smile.

The Healer led me inside some sort of vault full of old world salvage. Cave stuffed with junk the Kalliq had rustled up from the depths or pried out of the ice. Hell if I know where they'd found all of it, or what they wanted it for. It was good scrap for tree building, but not worth burying in the ground.

The Healer found a flashlight on the floor and poked it around the place, illuminating the wreckage of a forgotten world. I couldn't figure the rhyme or reason to what it was they'd collected. Some stuff was so rusty, I couldn't even tell what lay underneath. There were old game machines and speakers, a fleet of motorcycles. Engines without cars, and cars without engines.

"What is all this?" I said, feeling the Healer's eyes upon me. "What is it you want me to see?"

She took my hand and led me deeper into the tomb, following the beam of her flashlight as it danced upon the iron and copper, the steel and chrome. Damn fine salvage, some of it. Pop would have rubbed his hands together and called it the jackpot. Was a time I'd have done the same thing myself.

The vault was wider than I could see, and many times longer. We walked all the way down to the deepest-dark end. Then the Healer had me stop in front of what looked like a makeshift coffin, a box nailed together out of corrugated tin.

"Hold," she said, handing me the flashlight. She got down on her knees, unfastening the hinges that latched the box shut, and when she peeled back the lid of that coffin, I damn near dropped her flashlight.

There was a woman in there. I could see the whole body. Her shoulders, her hips, and her legs. I could see her belly and face, her hands at her sides. All of it preserved, and solid as stone.

But it weren't stone. It was wood. Knobby and thick and channeled, everything covered in scaly bark.

I sank down to my knees, slowly illuminating the dead woman with the beam of the flashlight, one piece of her at a time. And she was dead, all right. All the way through. There weren't nothing growing. Nothing green or breathing.

"Who is she?" I whispered, glancing at the Healer.

"She is poison." The voice came from behind me. I spun around with the flashlight and found the Speaker, scowling amid the junk. The woman turned to her sister and spat words in her own language. But the Healer just stayed crouching beside me, still staring down at the dead thing in the box.

"It is disease," said the Speaker.

"No." The Healer got to her feet and fastened the lid to the coffin back in place.

"It killed her." The Speaker stepped closer, her eyes drilling holes into mine. "It is death."

"Where did she come from?"

"She arrived here. Starving and injured. Wearing this." The Speaker strode past the coffin and rummaged at the stacks of old scrap behind it until she found a fuzzy GenTech suit. Then she pulled out a long piece of plastic—a crappy white sheet, just like the ones GenTech had thrown over us when they'd dragged us to Promise Island.

"So she escaped," I murmured, staring down at the closed-up tin box full of GenTech meddling.

I tried to imagine what the woman had once looked like, where she'd been from, who she had been. Now she was just a relic. A refugee of a warped experiment.

"When?" I said. "When did she get here?"

"Almost all seasons have passed. She came like you, in winter. Before the world melted last spring."

Had she been one of the people my father had saved? Had she been set free by my old man before he got wrapped up in chains? Must have been. Hell, maybe she'd been one of the first to flee Promise Island after Pop's uprising got started. Maybe she'd escaped with that old Rasta, the one me and Zee had stumbled upon all the way back at the Surge.

I thought about that old Rasta, the bark stitched on his belly.

"How'd this happen?" I asked, staring at the coffin, picturing the dead body inside.

"She was normal." The Speaker tapped at her face. "Same. Here." She pointed at her belly, then her arms and her legs. "Here. And here."

"No bark?"

The woman turned around. Jabbed a hand at her mid-back, right near her spine. "Disease," she said, turning back to face me.

185

So she'd been patched up. Patched with bark, like the old Rasta near the Surge had been. Fixed with GenTech science. Like Crow.

Like Alpha.

"Then what happened?"

"It spread." The Speaker glared at me like the whole thing had been my fault. "In the spring."

"Spread?" I said. "The bark spread?"

"Yes," the Healer said softly.

The Speaker drew a line from her mid-back till it wrapped around her hips. She traced her fingers over her torso until her hands found her neck and her face. And then she made a strangling motion, covering her mouth and gouging at her eyeballs, squeezing her nose shut and plugging her ears. When she let her hands drop to her side, her face had turned brittle and breathless.

Just like drowning, I thought.

The bark would spread and pinch and seal you inside it. Then you'd drown, surrounded by the air you could no longer breathe. And the people you could no longer touch.

CHAPTER TWENTY-SIX

I ran out of that vault and sprinted blind through the steaming black tunnels.

The spring, they'd said. The woman had come, wrapped in purple fuzz and white plastic, and when the world began to melt, the small patch of bark on her back had spread. Like a disease.

I tried not to picture it. But I couldn't stop the vision putting its claws in my heart. I grew thick inside, like the bark on that dead woman's body, and the image stiffened inside me. Choking me as it poured down my throat.

I imagined Crow stood tall in the springtime, the bark from his legs wrapping up his waist and then strapping itself to his chest. It would coil around his lungs and fuse itself together, stitching his mouth shut as his arms fell like heavy branches.

No idea where I was running now. I just pounded on through the tunnels, shoving aside the merry Kalliq who bounced along and got in my way. The steam in my eyes. The stench of mammoth shit wafting up to greet me. It all made me feel so useless and sick.

I reached a junction I recognized, but I couldn't go that way. Couldn't face Crow.

And I couldn't even think about Alpha.

I knew what it'd be like—the drowning. I knew that feeling all too well. Something clogging you up and cramming your insides. There could be nothing more wicked and no worse way to die.

Suddenly, I was crashing out of the tunnels and back into the bottom of the crater. The party had ended. The Festival of Lights all but burned out. Folks were fading into the holes in the rock, done for the night, and I glanced at the ledges that wound out of the earth above me. I saw stars, but no sky lights flashing. And too late, I turned back to the mud. Too late, because she'd seen me. I heard her hoot and holler, and then my pirate girl was running down the rock ledges towards me. Until she ran straight into my arms.

"Where'd you go?" she yelled. The music had stopped, but Alpha still seemed to be dancing. She reached her hands towards the sky, and she beamed and rolled her head back as she brought her arms down around me. I could feel her breasts shaking through the fur she wore. Her flesh warm and wet. She kissed me, and she tasted so smoky and sweet.

But I was numb. Cold. Like I was the one who'd turned solid.

Alpha pulled at me, easing us together.

"What's wrong, bud?" she said.

I shook my head.

"This about Kade?"

Guess my head shook some more. Hell, I don't even know.

"He's all right, and that's all. You don't need to be jealous."

"I ain't jealous," I whispered. I glanced around at the stragglers who had yet to retire. Too-tired angels. Eyes half closed and dreaming.

"So you want some privacy?" she asked, a sly look on her beautiful face. And her skin was so radiant. So perfect. And so precious to me.

She was too juiced up to see the panic eating at my insides. "Come on," she whispered. "I know just the place."

As we walked, Alpha tugged off her furry jacket and made me swap it for the shaggy pink vest they'd given me.

"That's more like it," she said, pulling the vest on, and she looked so much like she used to. Like she had when we very first met. And that crazy vest looked gorgeous on her. It killed me. I mean, I should have laughed. Should have laughed so loud that I howled at the moon.

Couldn't even force a smile.

She led me upwards. Higher. Around and around the inside of the crater. We walked without speaking. Her hand in mine. Alpha hummed the tunes that the steel drums had been playing, and her voice sounded so pretty, it smashed a hole in my heart. I wondered how much longer she'd be able to sing and talk to me. How much time did we have left? Months? Weeks?

Till the spring, I thought. Just like before, when I'd been searching for Pop. I'd had until springtime. Only I'd found Pop early, and had still been too late.

When we climbed out of the crater and into the night, the strange world greeted us in silence. I stared up at the black sky and the distant stars, and I glanced at the frozen trees I had made. The branches had lost their sparkle and were so easily broken, and I knew they were just faking at something. Just holding on to what was not meant to last. Because in the spring, these trees would melt and they'd vanish, and just be a tale to be told.

But I remembered how this place made things whole again—the silvery mud had fixed me and Pop, flesh wounds and saplings. It had healed us, this Burning Wheel medicine straight from the earth.

The Healer could figure it out, I thought. Clutching for some hope to hold onto.

Yeah. She'd work it out. We just had to give her enough time.

Alpha pulled me into the trees, and we huddled beneath the canopy of a shimmering oak. Our breath puffed white, the air coarse and cold, but I was sweating against the thick fur on my skin.

"They're stunning," she said, staring up at the brittle limbs of the ice-carved trees. "Every one of them. Metal forests, ice forests. And next, it'll be the real thing, right?"

She turned to a tall spruce, ran her hand at its frozen needles. "What kind's this?"

"Evergreen," I said. "Means it stayed the same through the seasons."

"You build any fruit trees? Apples?"

I shook my head, and she turned to me, her hand finding mine. "I don't want you to stop building, you know, even if there are real trees all over someday. You can't ever stop."

"Like anyone would give a damn if I quit."

"I would. I couldn't stand it—it's a part of you, Banyan. A part that's so special to me." She leaned in close, shutting her eyes and lifting her face to the thin light of the moon, and the rays caressed her cheekbones and the tops of her shoulders, and I knew she was nearly as beautiful as the world was cruel.

"Aren't you gonna kiss me?" she whispered.

When I opened my mouth, no words came. Our lips touched instead, sealing the words inside me, and as I kissed her, the words seemed to writhe in my gut. Because I'd meant to tell her. That had been my first instinct. But then I reckoned this was my burden, an ugly cross I should bear by myself. It was the least I could do, to protect her from knowing. I would keep her close by me, and try my best to snatch us ahold of some cure.

She pulled me towards her. Tighter. Pressing her body against me. She was so soft and so warm in the cold sharp night. And when she tugged open her vest, the moonlight slipped down her body.

It should have been everything. It should have felt like every dream I ever had, coming true. The huge moon and bright stars, the trees and mountains. Two hearts beating, and two bodies moving as one. My hands on her hips. Suddenly knowing what I was supposed to be doing, feeling such purpose. It should have been perfect. But it was ruined. Twisted and tainted. As if the purple fist of GenTech probed in my belly, snatching out all my goodness and switching it for spite. GenTech and their backwards science. Their power to give life and then steal life away. This was their fault. All of it. And I should never have hunted them trees to begin with. I should have stayed in Old Orleans and just been happy only ever wanting this girl.

I kept kissing Alpha until I was drunk on her kisses. Until my brain quit hurting and my heart slowed down. And my mind grabbed hold at that one thought before it drowned in all of them. The one thought that just might keep me afloat.

I thought of the Healer and her moss and mud potions. There would be a cure, and she'd find it. It had to be so. If this was a disease, we'd make a remedy. And I'd not lose Alpha. I swore that inside me, right next to the secret that made me so heavy.

CHAPTER TWENTY-SEVEN

I woke up the next morning to a kick in the shins.

"Come on, hotshot," Kade said. He was standing above me, and Zee was stood right beside him. "They're waiting."

"Who's waiting?"

"Your friends," he said. "The old fossil and the rest."

I stood up, uncoiling my limbs from Alpha's. The two of us had been sleeping in the cave I'd started to call my own, and I stared down through the steam at her, wishing I could shut down and start over.

But this nightmare weren't one that let you wake up.

"What do they want?" I said.

"Called a meeting."

"Who? The Elder?"

"Not the Elder." Kade stuck his thumb at his chest. "Me."

"Well, you can go on without me. I got nothing to say to you."

"It isn't me that wants you there. It's them."

I spotted Crow in the corner, leaning on the wall.

"You in on this, too?" I asked him.

"We just been talking to them," Crow said.

"Sure you were. Without me."

"What's going on?" Alpha stumbled up, all bleary-eyed as she got to her feet.

"I don't know," I said. "No one's telling me a damn thing."

Folk were bunched around the mud pit and had started to line up along the rocky steps and ledges. Reminded me of the party for the North Lights, the whole tribe crowded inside the crater, except last night, everything was music and dancing, and now the place was silent and still.

The five of us stood huddled together, half blending in on account of our shaggy fur clothes, and half sticking out like the sorest of thumbs. I mean, every eye in the place was upon us, everyone wanting to see what was about to go down.

I was mighty curious myself.

The Elder entered from one of the side tunnels. She was flanked by the twin sisters, and all the Kalliq got clear out of their way.

It weren't just those three women that got folk moving, it was what the Healer held in her hands—the seven saplings, bundled and wrapped with thin copper wire. And the clump of Pop's remains at the base of them was all plastered in mud, shrunken to the size of a child now, deformed and fibrous and tiny.

I found the Healer's eyes, and she smiled at me, her gaze soft and warm as a sunbeam. Them saplings were really looking like trees now, I thought. Young trees, still little, but nearly three feet high.

When the three women were stood before us, the Elder began speaking, slowly clicking and tutting in her strange native tongue.

"Earth is living," the Speaker translated. "Living thing, like a mammoth. Like human or tree. It breathes and suffers, shivers and screams."

The Elder stooped to the rocks and pounded the stone with her gnarled old fist.

"It has been shorn and beaten." The old woman smoothed the stone with her wrinkled palm as the Speaker continued. "Yet still, it breathes. And so the Wheel turns."

The Healer stepped forward and carefully placed the bundle of skinny trees at my feet.

"The Elder wishes you speed on this journey," said the Speaker, as the old crone straightened up her crumpled body and looked me straight in the eyes. "She asks the Lamplight to shine on your quest."

"Quest?" I said. "Hell, I'm all done questing."

I'd thought the place couldn't get more quiet.

Crow started to say something, but I cut him right off.

"The way south is blocked," I said, spinning around to face him. "You all said so."

"But there's another way." Kade stepped in front of the others, like he was shielding them from me. He pointed at the Elder and the twins. "Your ladies here told me all about it last night."

"And where was I?"

Kade glanced at Alpha, then winked at me. "You were busy, bro."

I turned to look at her. "That's what it was all about? Keep me busy so Kade could talk you a way out of here?"

Alpha pushed past Kade and walloped me, smack in the mouth. "How can you say that?"

"You all tricked me." I wiped a little blood off my lip.

"No, we didn't," she said.

"Come on," Zee whined. "Banyan. It's time to go home."

"Home?" My voice echoed back at me, but I yelled even louder. "I ain't got nowhere to go back to. And neither do you."

Crow shook his head. "Other people need those trees, man. Just as much as you do."

"Don't tell me what people need." I glared at him. "You'd all be dead if it weren't for me."

"Easy, bro," said Kade.

"Shut up, you stumped junky bastard." I turned to him. "I'm sick and tired of you getting your digs in. And I don't give a damn if you think you're better than me."

"Don't call me that," he whispered, his eyes turning to tight little holes.

"We all just damaged goods? That it, Banyan?" bellowed Crow. "And now you got yourself a new family?"

"Family? That's a joke. Hell, I'm the one made sure this lot didn't leave your ass in the snow."

"That ain't true," snapped Alpha. "You know that ain't true."

"And maybe we should have left you," I told Crow. "You were the one wanting to quit, after all."

"Pull yourself together," Alpha said.

I wanted to tell her about that piece of bark on her belly. The disease that would spread in the spring. But I couldn't say it. I had to keep her from knowing. I had to keep her safe, and to do that, I had to keep her right here.

"I'm tired," I said. "So tired. Killing and dying and nothing but trouble."

Kade's disdain flashed in his eyes, and he turned to the others. "Then let him stay here, if that's what he wants."

I took a step towards him. "And what? You think I'm gonna let you take the trees?"

"Not all of them. Hasn't your big brain worked it out yet?" He nodded at the Elder. "We're leaving one with them. Trading them. A mammoth for a tree."

My feet froze solid on the stone. "You got no right."

"And what gives you all the rights?"

I glanced behind me at the Healer. Then I turned to Alpha, took her hands in mine.

"But you gotta stay here," I pleaded. "You have to stay here with me."

"No, bud. Please don't."

"I need you."

"I can't."

"You'll die," I said, then I stared at Crow. "You will, too. You gotta stay here with me now."

"What is this?" said Kade. "Come on, leave them alone."

"I promise." I turned back to Alpha. "You'll not make it."

Kade tried to push past me, reaching for the trees, but I shoved my shoulder into his chest, driving him backwards.

"Why won't you stay?" My eyes begged Alpha's.

"Why won't you leave?"

"I love you. You know that."

"Then come with me," she said.

"No." I punched Kade in the gut, getting him away from me. "You have to trust me, Alpha. You have to let me take care of you."

For a long moment, her eyes dug inside mine, like she was sorting through each thought in my head.

"All right, bud," she said. "If that's what it takes."

They all looked as surprised as I was. Even Kade was taken aback. And I just stood there, breathing hard, my face flushed, with Alpha stood right beside me, taking my hand in hers.

But what about my sister? I'd said I'd keep her safe. Get trees growing around her. And what about Crow?

I stared up at him, but he shook his head at me, and then looked away.

"Sorry, man," he said. "Guess I be seeing you in the next one."

"You think you can walk out of here? You should stay, and you know it. They can heal you."

"I don't need to walk out of here," he said, making a sad smile. "We get a mammoth, no?"

"That's right." Kade straightened himself up, his eyes like poison. "And let's get on with it, shall we?"

I glanced at Zee, but she wouldn't look at me. She just shuffled closer to Crow, leaning against those tree-legs of his as he reached down and put his hand on her shoulder.

So that was it. They were leaving. They were going to keep on without me, and keep on with Kade. Hell, I wasn't the one who'd found a new family—they were the ones replacing me, and they'd probably never look back.

"We trade?" said the Speaker, and I spun around to face her.

"There's a way for them to go?" Screw them, I thought. Screw both of them for selling me out to some junky. "They can head south?"

"We show you." She nodded. "After we trade."

I stared down at the clump of trees on the warm rocks before me. Then I glanced at the Elder's huge eyes, the map of lines on her face.

"Kalliq will trade you one mammoth." The Speaker held up a single finger and pointed across the mud pit at a half-dozen of the critters. They were lined up in a corner, their purple fur bright in the shadows. Then the Speaker held up her other hand and pointed at me. "You will trade us one tree."

I stared down at the saplings. I swear the quiet in that crater rippled across the stone walls.

"Safe," the Healer said. But I couldn't look at her.

I turned to Alpha, then Zee. I glanced up at Crow.

"There's seven," he said. "You got more than you need."

I scowled. "How do you know how many I need?"

"It's a trade," said Zee. "We give up a tree, and we get a mammoth. And then we'll be on our way."

Just like that. I mean, there you have it. I was the sort of brother you just leave behind you, no problem at all.

"How about you take the one tree?" I said. "And I keep the rest here."

"Come on, man." This was Kade. "Don't be greedy. You have your girl. You have what you want."

"Give us four, Banyan," said Crow. "And you can keep three."

"No. You can have three. One for each of you backstabbers. And that's the last damn offer I'll make."

"But what puts you in charge?" The words sounded like they were acid on Kade's tongue.

"You want to ask these people what they think? They could keep them all and not show you the way. All I have to do is say the word, and that's how it goes down."

"So why don't you?" Kade said.

"Because I'll be glad to get rid of you."

"Fine." Crow's voice boomed. "We take three."

I turned back to the clump of saplings.

My mother had told me they'd spread once they got going. Four of them, here with the silver mud, they'd multiply and grow up real good. And I had Alpha beside me. We just needed the Healer, needed her to find a cure for my girl.

I stepped towards the tiny bundle of trees. But my guts gripped tight. "I don't know," I whispered, my back still to the others. "I don't think I can do it."

"Do what?" asked Kade. Snarled up and impatient.

I stared down at the twiggy mess of limbs and the muddy, used-up chunk at the base of them.

"I can't break up the bones of my own father."

I tried not to think about it, but how could I not? Where was Pop's guts? His heart? Had it all shriveled inside him and disappeared?

"It's trees, bud," Alpha whispered, sounding about as sick and tired of me as she could. "You can't think of it like a person. It ain't your dad anymore."

"Then you do it," I said, turning to her. "You break off three of those saplings and give them away."

"Fine." She strode forward, cracking her knuckles. And I started to get sick. Tears blurred up my eyeballs. My chest thumped with each hollow beat of my heart.

She was right, though. It was trees now. Not a man any longer. Not Pop.

I tried to stare at the mud pit, but I couldn't. Just kept thinking of how what was left of my old man's hand had stretched out of that mud, holding a busted tree towards me.

Alpha was on her knees now. Her hands separating the saplings, uncoiling them from the copper wire and rooting through the limbs, trying to find which ones to spare.

"Stop," I called as she went to twist-snap a sapling.

Everything hung suspended.

Alpha turned to me, her fingers still deep in the thick of things. Her hands all covered in mud.

"I should do it," I said, taking a step forward.

"It's all right, bud."

"No," I said. "No, it's not. But it should fall to me."

I waited till she'd stepped aside, then knelt down to that stump with the shrubby crown. I glanced back at Crow, and his eyes were hard to read. Then I found Zee, and there were tears streaming all down her face.

I looked to the Speaker and her beautiful sister. I studied the Elder, her face like the earth, all cracked and riddled with unspeakable age. And then I stared up, high up out of the crater. I stared out of the earth and kept my eyes on the sky. I never looked down the whole time I did it. I just felt for the first weak spot, a place where there had once been a hip and a socket, but now the muscles were puny and withered and stubbled with bark. I felt up to the base of the sapling. The thin roots of the limb that had sprouted from Pop's leg. I kept my eyes skyward. Yanked hard and twisted.

And then I pulled the tree free from the rest.

The Kalliq gasped in unison, making one big whisper as I broke the tree free of my father, and the blood spurted six feet in the air. The blood sprinkled and splattered, and I felt it upon me. Hot and red. Pop's blood, and my blood—the same blood that flowed in my veins.

But I didn't falter. Didn't stumble. Still staring up at the top of the crater as the blood ran warm down my face. And when finally I could make a sound, my scream wasn't of anguish. It was fear, through and through.

Because here they came. Descending into the crater and trapping every one of us. A hundred King Harvests. Goggled faces and gray rubber suits. Guns glued to their fingers and opening fire. Coming to shatter the one place on earth I'd wanted to be.

CHAPTER TWENTY-EIGHT

There were so many of them. It was like Harvest had an endless supply. And here they were, marching behind bullets, all black boots and dead eyes. Never slowing. Just twisting around the inside of the walls as they descended, like greedy arms reaching down towards us.

There was a rush and a riot. Half the Kalliq stormed up the steps to face the onslaught, charging mammoths before them, and the rest of the tribe ebbed inside the passages, hunkering down for the fight.

The Elder took the lonely sapling from my hand, easing it from my fingers as bullets swarmed and drilled the walls around us. And the Healer knelt beside me, bundling the remaining clump of trees in an old plastic pack, winding the saplings into a thin coil, ladling gray mud inside the bag, then drawing it shut.

There was a moment when our eyes met. Me and the Healer. Just this moment, no longer than two beats of my heart. Then I smeared Pop's blood from my face, my hand blocking my vision for a second, and when I saw her again, the bullets were pounding into her body and making her quake.

I called out. Tried to grab her. But she slipped on the rocks and away from me, just as her smile had slipped from her lips and smashed all hope on the way down.

I grabbed the trees and swung the pack onto my shoulders. The Kalliq were surging up the great spiraled ledges, rushing to meet the battle. More than fifty mammoth riders. Then more like a hundred. The beasts pouring out of the side tunnels, stampeding upwards. Purple fur flying towards that army of gray rubber suits.

I stumbled to the rock wall. Ducking for cover. Then I felt Crow's hands on me, pulling me close. And as I fell against him, I watched Alpha swoop up a bow and a sheath full of arrows from one of the Kalliq who'd fallen.

She aimed and fired high at Harvest's troops on the ledges. Still breathing. Still fighting.

But if the Healer was gone, there'd be no hope of a cure for my girl.

The Kalliq were trying to stem the flow of Harvesters. There were so many pale gray troops, with so many guns, but the mammoth hide was too thick for their bullets. And the beautiful beasts reared up on their hind legs and charged up the rock ledges, their tusks bent low, trumpeting and trampling and shaking the walls.

Stones rained down and smashed into clouds of dust as the havoc unfolded, the battle raging on and pinning us beside the pit.

"Where's Kade?" Crow called above the bullets and battle cries. I glanced about but couldn't see that redhead bastard anywhere. And where the hell was Zee?

"We gotta get out of here," shouted Alpha, down to her last dozen arrows.

But where? Which tunnel? Which way was the right way to go?

Because that's what it had to come to. I was hell-bent on nowhere, all over again.

Damn rocks kept tumbling down all around us. But I got low and crawled out through the rubble, bullets thudding into the mud pit beyond, arrows whipping high into the warring abyss.

I scrambled through the rocks till my hands were on the Healer. Then I held her in my arms, pulling her against me, shuffling her limp body back to the wall.

She beamed at me. Blood on her lips. She took my hand and pushed it into her chest. "Etsa," she whispered.

"Your name?"

She nodded, then said, "Healer."

"Banyan." I pointed to myself. Tears welling up. My nose snotty.

"Banyan." Her voice was like cut glass. "Tree King."

She put her hand on my face, then went limp in my arms. Her tongue curled down her chin as her eyes rolled back. And another woman was dead on account of those trees.

"Bring her here," the Speaker called from one of the tunnels. I saw her face through the cascading rocks.

"Cover me," I hollered as I shot up and ran, the trees in the pack on my back and the Healer in my arms.

I reached the entrance to the tunnel as a pillar of rock crashed behind me, cutting me off from Alpha and

Crow. I stumbled. Fell. Landed at the Speaker's feet with the Healer held out before me.

"You must leave," she hissed as she snatched up her sister. "Take your death, and go."

"Tell me which way, and we're gone," I said. There weren't nothing for me here now. No safe haven. No remedy.

The Speaker pointed behind me. Into the open. Right at the center of the mud pit. "You go down," she said. "You hold on and hold your breath. Until you fall through."

"Fall through to where?"

"Catacombs. Rivers of fire."

"And then what the hell do we do?"

I heard a great howling moan and spun around to see a mammoth stumbling blind towards us, its eyes shot and bleeding, its body bouncing and shaking and ready to fall. And I remembered that beast I'd seen sacrificed. The mammoth with the messed up leg.

"Follow the heat," the Speaker said, clutching my arm and pulling me to her. "Then you follow the howl."

As I glanced back at the mud pit, it squelched and steamed. We had to go into it, down inside it. But for how damn long?

"You ever gone down there?" I asked her.

"You will travel beneath the Speak It Mountains." The Speaker's face was pure sorrow. "There it is I learned. And there, you will learn also."

"Learn what?" I shouted over the sounds of terror descending from above.

The Speaker scooped her twin tighter, cradling her dead sister to her breast. "Long have I seen this. Long I have feared."

I stared at the pit again, wondering how much slime we had to go through before we found the far side.

"The furthest peak you see," she said. "Will point to your home."

"Mountains? You sure? Under the ground?"

I heard Alpha screaming. She was somewhere on the other side of the rocks. Calling my name.

The Speaker clutched my wrist. "You will see. And learn. Speak your question to the winds."

I took one last look at those twin sisters. The long, sweeping mane of the Speaker flowed into the Healer's and forged a dark sky between them.

Then I stood, cinching the pack to my spine. And I turned and dashed through the blitz.

The walls were splintering into boulders around me, sealing shut the tunnels and sizzling the mud. I clambered up till I reached the top of a stony pile, and I spotted Alpha and Crow, not thirty yards from me.

But they were surrounded by Harvesters.

I slipped on top of the rocks, trying to hold steady and see what was happening. Trying to figure out something I could do. And as I toppled, I froze up on the inside—one of the troops was pulling off his mask and revealing the scars on his horrible face.

It was him. The original King Bastard. And I could see him talking to Alpha. Looked like he knew her. Like he recognized her from Old Orleans.

It seemed to happen in slow motion, him shoving his gun up into her chest. She had the bow in her hands. But no arrows. Nothing left to fight back with.

Crow tried to take a step forward, but Harvest shoved him in the gut, and he went down so easy. And then Harvest turned back to Alpha, jabbing his gun at her as he stroked a gloved hand on her cheek.

"No," I screamed. I pulled the pack off my shoulders, held it high in the air. "This is what you want," I called as Harvest spun around and saw me. "The trees. They're here. Just you let her go."

"You fool." His voice was so loud, it seemed to blister at the edges. "You think you're in a position to bargain with me?"

"I'll give you what you want," I shouted.

"I don't need you to give it to me, boy. It's mine already." The tip of his gun stabbed Alpha's ribs. His free hand grabbed at her throat. "I'll take the trees and leave you all dead in this hole."

"Let her go." The words tore my voice open. "You owe us that much."

"I owe you nothing," he screamed, rage breaking across his twisted features. "And your suffering shall be severe."

The fighting seemed to grow quiet above us. Like distant thunder. But the rocks still splintered and crashed, shattering and smoking the air.

"Hey, Harvest." It was Kade's voice ringing out. "I've got a sub gun ready to blow your brains out, you piece of shit."

I spotted him crouched in the rocks below me, keeping his head down. His red hair coated in dust, and the sub gun poking through the debris.

Harvest pulled his gun off Alpha, his ugly eyes searching the broken stacks.

"That's right," Kade called. "Keep backing up."

"You can't win." Harvest glanced up at me. "How do you plan to keep GenTech from their prize? They will hunt you down. They will find you and kill you. They'll take back the trees, and you'll have changed nothing."

"And what would you do?" I yelled.

"I have an army. I can protect them." He pointed at Crow on the ground. Waved his gun in the air. "Your friends are nothing. Savages and pirates. And you? You're just a boy."

"And you're a dead man," Kade shouted. "Unless you call this thing off."

"Wait." This was Zee. Her voice seemed to come out of nowhere. But then I saw her crawling through the landslide towards Harvest. And what the hell was she doing?

"We have to stop this," she shouted. "We can't just keep running."

"No, no." Kade's voice got panicked. She was moving into the middle. Coming right between him and his man. "Move, sweetheart. Get out of the way."

But she was blocking him. Blocking his angle. I watched the whole thing happen right in front of my eyes.

"We could work together." Zee glanced up at me as she said it. Then she turned to Harvest, her hands held out before her. Her long, dark hair painted gray by the earth. As if she were suddenly old and frail as the falling rocks, and her eyes were the last thing young and pretty at all.

"Please," she called, blinking at Harvest. "Make the killing stop. And we'll join you. We'll make a stand against GenTech together. The few can't control the many, not now. Not if everyone—"

Her voice got cut before she could finish. Her pretty eyes got squeezed ugly as they bulged out of her head.

And Harvest kept emptying his bullets into her.

"No," Kade screamed as he leapt out from the rocks and rushed towards Zee, unleashing his sub gun over her collapsing body, aiming right at Harvest. But the replicants were falling in front of their master, shielding his body with theirs.

And I stood there on the pile of rocks like I was floating above everything. My stomach churning and my lungs forgetting to breathe. The trees held high over my head. My sister dying on the ground below me.

My father, my mother, and now Zee. I'd lost all the family I'd been given.

But through the carnage, I saw Kade standing over Zee's body, still working the sub gun. Still screaming and fighting. I saw Alpha dragging Crow away from the battle. Still running. Still trying.

And I knew the closer you get to nothing, the more you have to lose.

I shouldered the pack as I rushed down into the battle. But before I could reach the fight, a mass of rock fell and detonated into a thousand screaming pieces, wiping everything out.

I fell back, blind in the dust, rock shrapnel piercing my skin. And as things cleared, the break in the bullets persisted—so I kept low, fumbling forward. I spotted shadows in the blur and crawled towards them.

"Where's Zee?" I said, finding Kade and pulling him upright. He lifted his one hand, and Zee's fingers were clasped tight in his.

I leaned over her. Could hear her chest wheezing and gurgling on some whole new level. She was coughing up blood, her eyes fluttering in a silent howl.

"Can you stand?" I asked Kade.

"I don't know."

"Where's the gun?" I scrabbled around for it. The dust was starting to clear, and pretty soon we'd be out in the open, and the bullets would be flying once more.

"Alpha," I called out, though it meant giving away our position. Reckon I just needed to know she was there.

No answer came back.

Beneath the debris, I felt the tip of the gun, warm on my fingers. I started to grab at it, but then I felt something thumping my back.

I glanced up. Behind me. Peering through the haze. And damned if it weren't a mammoth, swinging its shaggy trunk at my head.

It was the one we'd first seen, the one I'd patted, high on that ridge in the starlight. I'd have recognized that thing anywhere, and now it kept shoving at me, getting me to move out of the way.

Then it reached its trunk around Zee and lifted her real gentle, putting her up on its back.

"Holy shit," I said. "It's helping."

But Kade weren't listening. He was already climbing up there, too.

"Come on," he said, straddling the mammoth's hump and yanking a fistful of fur till the thing turned and trotted in a circle around me.

I snatched up the sub gun, then leapt for the side of the beast and clambered my way up.

And before I'd got used to sitting on the thing, it was charging through the rubble in an all out stampede.

"There." I pointed as we emerged from the dust. Alpha was wrestling a Harvester for his gun, and Crow was pulling himself out from under the rocks beside them.

I aimed the sub gun at the back of the Harvester's head. Had been awhile since I'd killed a man. Not near long enough.

I squeezed the trigger, took him out. And Alpha's eyes grew wide when she saw us. She pulled up Crow as we charged towards them, and together they jumped for the mammoth, then wrestled their way to the top.

I pulled them close, had Alpha help hold Zee in place. Kade was aiming the mammoth for one of the wide tunnel entrances, a passage that hadn't yet been blocked by the crumbling walls.

"Hold up," I hollered. "That ain't the right way."

"And where do you think we're going?" he yelled back.

"We gotta go down." I pointed at the mud pit. "In there."

"Through the pit?" Alpha screamed.

"It's the only way. The Speaker told me. It's the way south."

The Harvesters had us surrounded, closing in, their bullets shrieking through the air.

"Let's do it," Crow said, and Kade turned the mammoth around just as the crater began to collapse all around us.

We plunged on through the hail of bullets, the spinning slabs and the steam.

"Hold on," Kade yelled. And for a second, it felt like we were flying.

But then we dropped and splattered, and the world turned quiet as we sank down inside the mud.

PART THREE

CHAPTER TWENTY-NINE

The hot silver mud seized us and squeezed us and shut down every scream. My flesh pressed flat against my bones, slime oozing into my ears and under my eyelids, jamming up into my nose.

I gripped at the mammoth's fur as the beast drifted lower, pulling us deeper into the earth, as if sucking us inside a wound.

And I felt weightless, as the mud turned even heavier and sealed up around me, but I kept my grip on the mammoth, still dropping with it, lower and lower, until we weren't drowning, we were falling.

I was out in the air.

I let go of the mammoth and braced myself, then landed in a heap, splashing into a puddle and cracking my shoulder on hard stone. I rolled onto my side, smearing the mud off my face and feeling at the pack full of saplings, still bundled and coiled and strapped to my back.

The mammoth staggered to its feet and towered there, eyes blinking from muddy sockets, its long fur matted and dripping with filth. And I pictured the mammoth I'd seen sacrificed, the beast of burden I'd seen drown. Only it hadn't drowned at all. Not if it had ended up down here.

As my eyes got used to the dim light, I realized how much I could see. The walls were covered with the green algae I'd become accustomed to in the Kalliq's caves, but down here, that moss glowed as bright as the North Lights had shone in the sky. I stared up at the thick gray mud we'd pushed through, and it was sealing back in on itself with a squelch, big globs splattering around us, patches of moss crusted across the mud like tiny hands trying to hold it in place.

"Zee," I called, spitting the muck from my teeth. The others groaned and cursed in the gloom, and Alpha crawled up beside me, coated in slime.

"Where's my sister?" I whispered.

"She's here," Kade said, and I followed the broken sound of his voice.

When I found him, I put my hand on his shoulder, and he was shuddering so fierce, I could barely hold on. As he pulled away from Zee, I knelt down beside her. The mud had mingled with the blood on her skin, silver and red, swirling in the mossy green glow of the walls. Zee's eyes were wide open and so white and twitchy, and they somehow reminded me of that old world camera she'd once had, as if she were snapping pictures of me with her eyeballs, freezing these moments in the back of her brain.

"He did good, didn't he?" she said, her voice like rusty metal, and I realized she was staring at the mammoth, behind me.

"Yeah," I said. "So did you."

Kade let out a sob, and I gripped tighter on his shoulder, trying to quit my own tears from falling, because I didn't want this to be the last way Zee saw me. I reckoned I'd already let the girl down too many times.

"I was wrong," Zee croaked.

"You were brave."

"Where's Crow?" she asked.

"I'll find him," Alpha said, and I heard her shuffle away.

Zee closed her eyes, and now Kade was howling beside her, just letting all the pain inside of him loose. It was such a wretched sound. Wild and fierce, but fragile. Like his insides were caught on fire, his spine full of smoke.

"You can make it," I said to Zee when Kade's cry had become a whimper, and my own words got frothy as the tears streamed down my face. "Look at this mud all around you. It'll heal you."

"I can feel it," she whispered. "Prickles."

"It healed me up," I said, but I'd been gouged by a couple of arrows, and Zee had been drilled full of lead.

Crow crawled up on his belly, Alpha helping him claw his way close. And Zee reached her hand to Crow's face, her fingers shaking. She wiped at the mud on his cheeks, tracing the edge of a faint scar.

"I'll miss you," she whispered.

"I shouldn't have let Frost take you out of that house," Crow said, and it was as if I'd never before heard his real voice at all.

"But I've seen so much." Zee turned to me, choking up blood, and I lifted her, holding her gently against me as Kade rolled up in a ball beside us.

"You have to promise," she said, as if scraping the words from the roof of her mouth. "Promise you'll take care of them."

Her lungs were gurgling, swollen and shut.

"You know that I will," I told her.

"But you'll have to give them up," she said. "In the end."

I squeezed her little body.

"Promise me, Banyan. You can't keep them. You have to use them to bind folk together."

"You're coming with us," I said.

"No." She pulled her head back so she could see me. And she made a smile so sad that it shredded my heart. "I have loved you, my brother."

"Please."

"Even if you didn't know."

"Please don't go."

"I'm sorry we weren't small together," she whispered.

"Don't leave me."

"And I'm sorry I won't see you grow old."

"But Zee. I'm already so alone."

"No," she croaked. "No, you're not."

She coughed up more blood, and I felt it warm on my chest.

"Promise me," she whispered. "That you won't keep them hidden." She was sinking against me now. "You have to trust people, Banyan."

"I promise," I told her.

Zee's eyes darted to Alpha. Then she rolled her head towards Kade.

And then her body turned crooked and crumpled.

Her bones were just a shell. Something that would rot. This sister I'd kept a stranger and never loved like I should.

And what had I done to deserve her saying she loved me? I'd never been there. Never known her. Hell, I didn't even deserve to make her a promise. I'd been all set to say goodbye and hunker down in that crater, and she'd been ready to head south without me, and I would have just stood back and watched her go.

But now there'd be no more leaving and no more loving, no more her wishing I was wiser or rolling her eyes at me being foolish, no more the feeling of her head on my shoulder, or the sight of her long hair dancing in the wind.

"We should have gone," Kade said, his voice full of anger as he uncoiled himself from the ground. "We should have gone, instead of arguing. Instead of you wasting our time."

"Stop," I said.

"She'd still be here."

"You can't do that."

"If you had just come along and not been so selfish."

I let his words hang in the air, like I was letting them be true.

"Leave it, Kade," Alpha said. "Think about what she was saying. The four of us have to work together, or it'll all be for nothing."

"It's already for nothing." He slammed his stumped arm against the wall.

"Not if we loved her," I whispered.

He spun around, glaring down at me. "What do you know about love?"

"Go easy," said Crow.

"Your love is selfish. It's just as selfish as you."

"Let him be," Crow said louder. "Miss Zee was his sister."

"But he never acted like it. And what sort of plan is this now?" Kade grabbed his sub gun, shaking the mud out of the barrel, then feeding in the last of his ammo, uncoiling the half-empty belt of bullets from around his waist.

"The Speaker said it's the way," I said quietly.

"You messed up, man. You messed it up. All of it. And she's dead because of you."

I bolted up and grabbed him by his shoulders. Pressed him hard against the wall. "And what was she to you?"

"Someone I chose. Not someone that got forced on me."

Chunks of mud dripped onto us, smacking on the ground and spraying across the walls.

I let go of Kade's shoulders.

He was right. I never chose Zee for my sister. And loving her might have meant even more on account of that.

Yet all I could do now was bury her, and remember her. Or try to forget. But I would not accept the blame for her death.

"You did this," I said to Kade. "You were the ones called that meeting. Distracting the whole tribe. Getting them all in one place."

"Leave it," Alpha said, coming between us. "Both of you. She died because of Harvest. And because of something she believed."

"What?" I said. "That we all have to work together?"

"It's people like Harvest that prove her wrong. Not people like you. And not people like Kade."

He pushed past me and stumbled down the tunnel. I peered after him, toward the waves of heat that waited through the catacombs beyond.

"Please, Banyan." Alpha put her arms around me. "You have to stay strong. I know it's hard. I know it hurts like it won't ever stop. I had a sister of my own, remember? So I know it. The feeling. Having Zee around reminded me what that was like."

"She didn't remind me of anyone."

"I didn't mean it like that."

"We can't let her just sit here."

"I know."

"I don't want her to die for nothing."

"We'll find Harvest," Alpha said. "If he's still alive, we'll find him."

"I don't care about Harvest."

"We'll kill him."

I shook my head. "I want the killing to stop."

"But we gotta fight for that to happen. Can't just run and hide and hope to stay hidden. We'll have to make a stand in the end."

"In the end." My legs gave out as my voice cracked, and I sank down onto my knees, peering up at Alpha. "Maybe when it's all over, you and me could settle down someplace, and I could build something for her. A statue. Something Zee would have liked."

"Course you will." Alpha held my face to her belly, and I felt the cool piece of bark that was stitched on her skin. "We'll do it together."

But you'll die, too, I thought. In the spring.

And I reckoned there was only one way to stop the people I loved dying for nothing. "Me and you get south, we head to Old Orleans," I whispered. "We start the trees growing, make all this death mean something. Then we gather your pirates to protect our trees from GenTech and people like Harvest. We gather all the pirates, from all over the plains."

"What about these two?" Alpha glanced down the tunnel at Kade, where he leaned against the wall, sobbing. Then she looked at Crow, splayed out on the ground beside Zee.

"They were gonna walk away from me," I said. "Why should I care what they do?"

CHAPTER THIRTY

I watched Crow through the shadows, mangled up and twisted. His tree-legs were splintered beneath him, looking less like legs than ever. They just looked like a sloppy old mess.

"Ready to move?" Alpha said, kneeling beside him.

I sat against the glowing walls, peering up at the mud and moss, half wondering if someone might shove their way down here to join us. But the other half of me wondered if that crater had tumbled in on itself entirely, leaving everyone in my Zion dead.

"Can you walk?" Alpha asked, and Crow let out a breath as if he'd been saving it up because it might be his last.

"I can't even stand," he whimpered. And I knew there weren't no way he could. His legs were just busted up bits of bark. The shards all mashed and dangled, revealing tan bits of cracked wood. Any good the Healer had done for him, it weren't doing no good anymore.

I watched as Alpha tried to work a jagged piece of rock from the ground, and when she finally got it loose, she took the rock over to the flank of the mammoth.

"Can you keep him still?" she asked me.

I pushed myself up, my body like one big bruise, and went over to join her, glancing at the mammoth's face. I wondered if he already missed the rest of his kin. Did he realize he was stuck with us now, trapped in the bowels of the earth?

"What you gonna do?" I said, watching Alpha get close to him with the rock gripped in her fist. "I don't want this thing kicking at me."

"He's got a name," she said. "They called him Namo."

"All right, then. I don't want Namo kicking at me." I stared into the beast's strange, small eyes, trying not to pay too much attention to those big tusks of his. I listened to the sound of his breathing. "The ones that named you are most likely dead," I said quietly. "I guess we got that in common."

"He's not gonna kick you," Alpha said. "Just hold him steady."

I kept looking him in the eyes and patting the side of his leg as Alpha wiped the gray mud from his belly and cut off a long swatch of fur. He let out a little rumbling moan.

"Weren't so bad, was it?" she said. Then she took the thick purple threads over to Crow and bound up his legs, splinting them back together and tying the coarse strands in knots. So now Crow's legs were all-GenTech, I reckoned. Bits of tree and bits of mammoth, all wound up as one.

"They'll heal up," Alpha said to him. "Be good as new."

"And what do I do now? Just wait in this hole to get better?"

"You get your ass up there." She pointed at the top of the mammoth. "We're bringing him with us. Made ourselves a trade, didn't we?"

So we started south again. Heading for the heat, just like the Speaker had told me. And it was hot, all right. Got hotter every twist we made through the tunnels. Felt like we were heading straight into hell.

We had Zee's body on top of the mammoth, all tied up in its fur. And Crow had to ride up there beside my dead sister. I don't know how he faced it. I'd barely been able to help get her lifted off the ground.

Just four of us now. Five, if you counted Namo. Five pairs of eyes in the shadows. And six saplings stuffed in a pack.

The straps of that pack cut me like a knife, as if I carried more than the weight of the trees on my shoulders. As if I carried all those who'd already died for them, too. All the strugglers GenTech had taken and killed in Vega or on Promise Island, all the survivors from the boat who had drowned in the lake. And how many Kalliq lives had been lost, on account of these saplings and the forest they might one day become?

I remembered the Healer's face turning lifeless. Etsa, she'd said her name was. As if that was important. As if I needed the name of every woman who died in my arms. I thought of my mother, and Hina. And over and over, I thought about Zee.

They'd all died for the same reason.

Because of the last trees on earth.

And because of me?

No. I might have set things in motion, busting the trees off that island, but it weren't my fault my sister was dead. It was more Crow's fault, and Kade's. They'd been the ones gathering everyone together, making tricks and bargains, desperate to race off once again.

Well, they got what they wanted. Here we were, groping our way south.

I tried to figure out exactly what it was I had promised my sister. Because I'd never been much of a brother to her. Never took care of her the way that I should. So I could at least try to make amends, I reckoned. As if you can do right by someone after they're dead and gone.

And what was it she'd told me? That we all had to stick together. Yeah. That was her angle. Problem was, there was only one person I could trust.

Alpha staggered before me, leading the way through the catacombs, her skin tinted a pale green by the moss on the walls. She was the only one who'd stood by me. And the other two could rot down here, for all I cared. They'd both betrayed me. The one-handed field hand and the legless warrior. They'd made me break off that sapling, and for all we knew, Harvest had his hands on that tree I'd torn loose.

I relived the shock of when Pop's blood had sprayed out, and wondered for a moment if his blood had been feeding the trees in some way, helping them get started. But I somehow knew that the blood had just been the last drops of my old man being human.

And that blood being spilled had been inevitable, thanks to Kade and Crow. They'd ruined everything— them and that parasite Harvest with his army of copies. They'd destroyed the one place I'd ever wanted to stay.

So what promise did I have to keep above all others? What was my purpose? To take care of the last trees. I'd sworn it to my mother. I'd sworn it to Zee.

But I also had a cure to find now. A remedy to save Alpha.

The tunnels we traveled down were high and wide enough that Namo could just make it through. But apart from their size, there weren't nothing good I could say about them.

Spiked rocks hung from the ceiling, the ground was steaming and sharp, and it got hotter with every damn step. Not like the blistering sun or the scorching winds on the plains. This was some new kind of heat I'd not known before. You could feel it on your insides. Couldn't help but breathe it in and cough it back up.

The algae on the walls glimmered. Giving off just enough light to see the emptiness and ugliness and the distance ahead. I scraped up fistfuls of the moss and shoved it in the pack with the saplings, checking the thin little trees were still coiled up snug, damp with the healing mud. Figured the moss was the only thing we'd see to eat for a while, but I didn't eat none of it just then. God help the man who's hungry when he has to bury his own flesh and blood.

"Never thought I'd miss snow," said Alpha as we stumbled and sweated.

"The Speaker said there's mountains down here." I tried to remember the icy white world we'd left behind us, as if the memory might cool me down.

"Under the ground?" She was too worn out to sound too surprised.

"Said follow the heat, then follow the howl, and then the furthest peak points us home."

"Home?" Kade said the word like it made his teeth ache. But then he quickened his pace, shoving past us and pushing ahead.

"Got some nerve," I muttered. "Acting like he's the only one gets to mourn her."

"He was sweet on her," Alpha said. "She was sweet on him, too."

"'Cause he tricked her."

"Guy has a big heart, bud. Like you."

"Just a smooth talker."

"You can be pretty smooth on occasion."

"I don't want you comparing me to him."

"Forget it," she said.

"He turned them against me."

"I don't know."

"She'd have wanted to stay. If it weren't for his meddling. That place was what she always wanted to find."

"But she cared for him. Maybe that can change what you think is important."

"He just used her. I'm telling you. He just knows the right things to say."

I quit talking. The air had got even hotter and even harder to breathe, and Alpha peeled back her dirty vest, rubbing at the old wound GenTech had sealed up, the bit of bark that had saved her life when they'd stitched it into her.

"You all right?" I said, my heart thumping hard at the memory of the dead woman in that tin coffin. The woman who'd been all sealed up and solid wood.

"Stings a little. It's like the mud makes it itchy."

I tried to wipe my hand across her belly, thinking maybe the Kalliq mud weren't doing her no favors at all. I feared it might speed things up, help the bark get growing. A disease, the Speaker had called it. A disease that spread in the spring.

"What are you doing?" Alpha said, shoving me away as I staggered against her.

"Should clean it," I said.

"It's fine."

"Should keep it clean."

"How the hell would you know what to do? I told you before," she said. "Just act like it ain't there."

"You should keep the mud off it."

"Why?"

"Don't ask me."

"And what was all that before about me dying if I kept heading south?"

"Just a feeling," I lied. "In my gut."

"What's wrong with you?"

"Everything."

"Why can't you look at me?"

"I don't want to lose you."

"You're not gonna lose me," she said. "I'm right here."

She kissed me then, and I got no recollection of that kiss ending. I mean, I can't remember my lips leaving hers. So it's like in some part of my brain, I'm still kissing her. Like there's a place where the kiss never stopped.

But I remember Alpha smiling at me after. Her face shy, flushed and breathless.

"Will you keep the mud off it?" I pleaded.

Namo came bumping up behind us, his breath all noisy and warm as he prodded his trunk at my head.

"All right, babe," Alpha said, her eyes fixed on mine as she reached down to wipe her belly clean. "If that's what you want."

We were blackened and baked. Blown out by exhaustion. Alpha and Kade helped Crow down to the ground, and then we collapsed against the rocks. Hard enough work just to keep on breathing. Even Namo slumped down on his belly, squeezing his great frame between the rough walls, and Zee's limp body kept rising and falling as the mammoth sucked at the heat.

We'd ditched most of our clothes. Padded some of them inside the pack with the trees, which I used as a pillow. Alpha had ripped up her vest and wore it in pieces, just a few tight rags tied to her body as we lay there, trying not to touch one another in the heat, our skin sticky against the patches of moss.

"Gotta keep moving," Alpha said, but she didn't move a muscle.

Follow the heat, the Speaker had told me.

But how much heat could we handle?

"Fall asleep," Crow mumbled beside me. "Might not wake up again."

"Don't worry. I'm sure your buddy Kade won't want to leave you behind."

"Can't you let him be?" Kade called from the other side of the tunnel.

"That's touching. It really is." I dug an elbow at Crow. "Said you were dead weight once. Now look at him. One cripple standing up for the other."

"Stop it," Alpha said. "Crow's supposed to be your friend."

"Supposed to be."

"This ain't what Zee would have wanted, bud. You acting like this."

I glanced at my sister's thin, flopping body. All the feeling drained out of her. No pain in her bones. No regret. Just a bloodless hollow, filled with the fear and sorrow of those of us still alive.

Finally, I slept. Passed out on the rocks. And I wound up tangled with Alpha. Even as hot as it was, as painful as the heat pricked my skin, I painted myself against her. My arms wrapped around her. My hands on her sweat. But when I felt the bark on her belly, it woke me up with a blast.

I recoiled from her, afraid and throbbing. I rolled onto my back and stared up at nothing, waiting for sleep to reclaim me, my head resting on the padded pack of trees and my heart ashamed of this secret I knew, afraid that the secret might wake me over and over, again and again.

And as I lay there, part of me longed to slip off down the tunnels by myself and never look back. I could be alone without pretending to be something different. Alone like I'd been after Pop left. Those days spent on my own, days of dust and steel.

It had been harder that way, but hadn't it also been easier? To just drift on and keep lonesome and let no one near?

But even as I dreamt of these false freedoms, I was putting my arms around Alpha again, breaking down walls faster than my mind could build them, sinking down once more inside a bitter sleep.

Until Crow woke me with his hand across my mouth.

He squeezed my nose shut, clamped my jaws tight, and I couldn't make a sound as I struggled against him.

Then he released his grip, glaring at me to make sure I stayed quiet. And what? He wanted me to know he could still kill me? Needed me to see just what our friendship meant now?

But Crow was pointing up the tunnel, back the way we'd come from. I followed his finger, peering into the shadows. And then I heard it. A soft slap. A pitter-patter. Almost like the sound of dripping water. But not quite. More like the faint sound of footsteps.

I shouldered the plastic pack of trees, staggered up.

Kade was coiled around the sub gun, and when I tugged it away from him, his green eyes blazed open like he was about to yell out. But then, I reckon he saw the look on my face, because the punk stayed quiet. He glanced at Crow behind me. And then we heard the tapping sound again. This time a little louder. Closer.

I hoisted the gun to my shoulder, getting it ready. And then, stepping over Alpha and squeezing past Namo, I began sneaking back up the tunnel to see what I could find.

CHAPTER THIRTY-ONE

I rounded the bend with the sub gun clamped tight in my fingers. My hands sweaty on the grips. And I couldn't see much. Just black stone and the faint green glow oozing off the walls. But there was that noise again—the tip-tap patter. Then a shuffle.

The ground got loose beneath me. Gravel and rocks. I skidded and crunched and made too much noise. Grabbed the wall to steady myself. And then, as I peered up the tunnel, I thought I saw a murky shape flicker and bounce through the shadows, getting smaller. Fading away.

Or was it just my mind playing games?

I held still. Listened.

No sound now. No scrabble of footsteps.

I loosened my grip on the gun. And then I turned and ran back to the others.

"What is it?" Alpha whispered, eyes open wide.

"I don't know," I told them. "Maybe nothing."

"Could be Harvest," Kade said. "They could have followed us down here."

"All I saw was shadows." I shrugged. "That sound could have just been the ceiling dripping."

"Better keep our eyes open and keep moving," Alpha said, staggering up and catching herself at the wall. She called to Namo, waking him.

"I hope it is Harvest." Kade was eyeing the sub gun. "I hope some of those troops made it down here, so we can take them out. All of them. I couldn't ever kill enough."

"We're in no shape for fighting. We can barely walk." Alpha was pulling at Namo to get him to stand. And I reckoned that beast had been built for the cold and the high mountain passes, not for squeezing along these sweltering tubes.

"Let's help Crow back on top," Alpha said.

"You help him," I muttered, pushing off. "I'm gonna scout ahead."

I staggered on, the sub gun hung from my shoulder and jabbing my side, the pack of trees on my back, and the sweat dripping off me. I stumbled around one sharp twist in the tunnel after the next. But then a blast of red light was scorching my eyeballs, and a wave of heat was blasting my skin.

I shielded my face and pushed closer. Blinking my eyes open, trying to get used to the sting. It was like getting too close to the flame on a blowtorch. Reminded me of building with my old man, welding branches together in the tops of our trees.

And then I could see it, all up close and in person—the flame of legend, the molten rivers of myth. A moving wasteland of lava. Hell, it was like this was where all the lava got born.

"We've reached it," I hollered back at the others, but the heat burned my words right out of the air. So I just waited for them to catch up to me, as I stared out across the tumble and roar of the Rift.

The tunnel had ended on the high edge of a cliff. And below, everything was orange and gold and tar black and smoking. All of it bursting in bubble and flames. It was like being trapped inside an engine as its circuits got blown. Crackling sparks gushed upwards, then fell like a burning rain.

I could barely see the black cliffs that marked the far side. Must have been a mile across at least. And the slabs of lava rumbled and surged before me like a mighty river. Like blood boiling too thick for its veins.

I pressed back into the tunnel, waiting till I could see Namo's shiny eyes, his shaggy shape, and the silhouettes of bodies bundled upon him. I swear, you couldn't even tell which one of them bodies was dead.

"We're here," I called. "We made it."

Alpha slid down Namo's crusted fur, then staggered towards me through the heat, her skin coated in soot.

"We'll have to follow this ledge," she said, pointing along the top of the cliff. "See if it crosses somewhere. But I reckon there's something we gotta do first."

She stared down at the lava. Sweat and tears ran down her face. Then she went and untied Zee's body from the top of the mammoth and gently pulled it down.

The fiery light burned in Kade's eyes when he joined us at the cliff's edge. And Crow came crawling over, too, pulling himself along with his hands.

"Help me up," he whispered.

"You sure?" Alpha asked him.

"Course I'm sure. A Soljah stands for a funeral."

She got beneath him and hauled him upright, and then Crow was leaning on me, stinking of mud and sweat, his splinted legs quivering.

I had to hold him steady. I mean, he'd have pitched over the edge if I hadn't given him a hand. And as I steadied him against me, I checked out Alpha's handiwork—the purple thread woven around the busted brown bark of his legs. Looked like it was holding things together, all right. Almost looked like the fur had begun to fuse to the wood.

"Who's gonna say something?" Alpha had Zee bundled in her arms now, my sister's once-beautiful face covered in dried blood and cracked full of dirt. Her eyelids were drooped shut, as if she might only be sleeping. But, no. You'd have never thought that.

I kept waiting for Kade to speak up. It seemed to me like he would. But then I realized Kade was going to be too busy crying. He had his one hand hiding his eyeballs and his stump jammed in his mouth.

Waves of heat ruptured the air around us. Black rocks crumbled from the cliff, crusty and smoking, and they splashed in the lava and got swallowed in flames.

But beneath all the noise was a silence. And it was Crow that broke that silence in the end, his voice bright and clear. He weren't speaking, he was singing.

It was an old song my father had taught me, and I weren't much of a singer, but I joined in on the chorus. Alpha did, too.

"Now let me fly."

I remembered what I'd told Zee on Promise Island— that I was going to fix her. That I'd get trees growing around her and never leave her behind.

"Now let me fly."

I was going to grow her trees from these saplings stuffed in a pack on my back.

"Now let me fly to Zion."

But it hadn't been me breaking up the team, ruining everything.

I felt Crow slump against me, suffocating me, wrapping me in a sweaty cloak made of sorrow. And I began to sense this sorrow would destroy us. If we didn't stop the blame and the guilt.

"Now let me fly."

I put my arm around Crow's waist to help him stand taller. Started to think we were all trying to do our best with this task we'd been given. We were all bent beneath the same curse.

"Now let me fly to Zion."

Alpha let go of Zee's body, and my sister's hair fanned out and her limbs spun as she fell. And I had wanted to touch her one last time, even though she'd been made ugly, and as foreign as the first day I saw her.

But now she was twirling and tumbling. And I was holding my breath as she got further and further, and further away.

We worked our way out along the ledge, following the top of the cliffs the only way we could go. The burial had left us numb amid the buzz and sizzle. Cold amid the heat.

I glanced back along the cliffs, making sure we weren't being followed, remembering that noise that had sounded like footsteps, behind us in the tunnel. But all I'd seen in the tunnel was shadows, and all I saw now was the air shimmering like a fever, as if the heat was devouring everything in sight.

Kade stumbled into me, his eyes pointing straight down at the blaze, and I grabbed him, pulling him upright.

"You need to ride up top?" I called, yelling above the lava's crackle and roar. Crow was the only one still huddled on the mammoth, gripping its fur as it shuffled and swayed, keeping as far from the cliff's edge as it could.

"It's more likely to fall than we are," Kade shouted back at me. "I'm not getting up there. This is suicide."

"We have to follow the heat."

He cussed at me.

"Take my hand," I said.

"For what?"

"You're getting too sloppy."

"And what do you care?"

"Maybe I don't." I gazed into the inferno. "But Zee did."

His head slumped against his chest like his neck just got broke. And when he started scratching real bad at his arm, I remembered old Frost doing the same thing—reckoned it was a crystal-junky move and maybe Kade was craving a fix.

"It's bad, man," he said. "All of this. It hurts so raw, and feels so heavy."

"I know. Might get worse, too."

"There's worse?" He quit scratching himself, tried to smile. I could see his face fighting to do it.

"Take my hand," I told him, and when he did, our fingers made a fist.

We fought on. Above us, just smoke and jagged black rocks. And below us, the river of fire getting wider, and the far cliffs receding further each time I looked.

The lava was so bright it was blinding, and it singed your nostrils and droned in your eardrums, so you got full of it, became a part of it, moving inside the flame. And I started to reckon somewhere that lava would cool and turn into rock, and someday, perhaps, that rock might be mountains. For every end, there's a beginning, I guess. And maybe all that burns comes back.

And as if to mark this chaos and creation, people had once built walls here. Long ago, before their sky was encased in this hot, rocky tomb. Before the lava had burst forth and ruptured. Before the Darkness, I suppose. Before the stars fell from the sky.

Somewhere in those distant days, in the glory of the old world, people had built walls, homes and roads here at the dormant gates of hell. Because up ahead, below the ridge we were on, stood the singed carcass of a dead settlement. And while the buildings back in the lake had been sunk and frozen, these buildings looked like they'd been cooked alive.

They were just shells, really. Blackened ruins, surrounded by lava and stripped naked by fire. But it weren't the buildings that interested me, it was the slab of roads that was tethered to the city. A gnarled old network of highways that seemed to bounce and float upon the lava. A mess of old asphalt strips, clogged full of cars.

"There's our way across," I said, grabbing Alpha and Kade beside me. I pointed at the floating chunk of ancient roads that led out from the remains of the city to the other side of the lava. I felt Alpha lean against me like she was about to fall, and I shook her. "Come on," I shouted. "We're almost there."

The ledge we'd been working along led all the way down to the city, though it meant we had to drop closer to the terrible heat. We edged lower, turning rigid when the Rift roared with some new fury and lava shot up in towering spurts. Ash falling. Smoke everywhere. I could feel my bones baking and my brains getting fried.

I used the sub gun like a crutch, leaning on it as I staggered forward. And now and then, I still checked the path behind us. But if anyone had followed us down here, they'd have to be as near dead as us.

We hit the crumbling streets of concrete and embers, then struggled on through the city, making our way to the car-clogged highways that floated beyond the jumbled old walls. The buildings offered some protection, shielding us from the heat, and we stopped and rested amid them. Everything caked with rubble and painted with soot.

I was sore and suckered, the pack heavy against my sweaty spine. I went to spit but had no spit in me, so I just slumped there and listened to the Rift bubble and blow in the distance, like it was waiting on us, knowing we had to face it in the end.

Everything had looked black and empty inside the buildings, but I pushed myself to my feet and staggered closer to a broken window. The others called to me, but I waved them off. Just kept wondering if there was anything left inside this burned out shell. An old world can of food, maybe. An ancient glass bottle with some water inside.

I kicked out the last bits of broken glass from the window, prodding it clear with the sub gun, then shoved my way in.

The ash was so thick, I had to wade through it, and I knew right away the place had been picked over plenty. Probably got scavenged as soon as the Darkness began.

I worked my way deeper, though. Just in case something had survived. I climbed past counters and boxes, shelves that had long ago turned frail in the heat. Had been some sort of market once. In the days when there'd been more to eat than GenTech's Superfood. But everything fell apart when I touched it, and I realized just being in there was stupid. We needed to get out of the city, get across the lava, and get away from all this.

I heard scraping noises above me, somewhere inside the building. A shuffling sound. And I picked up my pace, finding the broken window and climbing back out. Figured that building was getting ready to tumble.

As we stepped onto the twist of highways leading out of the city, the ground shifted and swayed beneath us. Hell, this rocky chunk of tarmac bobbed in the lava the same way our old boat had once bobbed on that lake. Until the boat sank, that is. But I couldn't think about sinking as we began squeezing between the old cars and climbing across their remains, making our way through the scrap that choked the old road.

We crawled and jumped from the roof of one car to another. Namo and Crow lagging behind us, the mammoth shoving the charred metal out of his way. And we were a good ways from the city now. I mean, we were committed to following this slab of highway, no matter how much it spindled and swam. I could see where it reached to the cliffs in the distance, and we were getting there. Choked and staggered, but getting there. Long as this burned memory of the old world could keep us afloat.

I lost my footing and slipped through a car windshield. Alpha grabbed me, dragging me out through a coal-dust cloud. I felt the car shift, then slide a little. The rocks beneath us stretching. Buckling. The lava churning underneath.

I cinched the pack of trees even tighter to my back.

"He's too heavy," Alpha shouted, pointing up at the mammoth as he rumbled past us. That big ball of fur had his small eyes stretched wide, and they darted this way and that way, and he was moving all jittery, like the ground was scorching him. He was shoving the cars out of his way quicker now, and when they slowed him down, he'd damn near start hopping on the spot.

"Crow," I called. "Calm him down."

But Crow was already trying to hold the beast steady, and it weren't doing no good. And then Kade was hollering. He was up ahead of us, and I could hardly hear him above the roar of the lava, but he was screaming, pointing behind me.

I stared back, gazing across the tombstone traffic, studying the black cliffs and the black buildings. And then I saw it. In the city. All over the city.

It looked as if the walls were alive.

CHAPTER THIRTY-TWO

I thought my eyes were messed up. Either that or my brain. Looked like the buildings were melting. Crumbling. But the buildings were still standing there in the same damn place. Then I realized something was creeping down the side of them. And whatever it was, it was coming our way.

I could see the shapes crawling out of the city. Rushing across the broken old roads towards us.

"Go." I pushed Alpha before me. "Run."

"Crow," she screamed. "Move."

We raced across the cars. Fear mining some last strength from our bones. Namo storming ahead, stomping through the gridlock.

I reached Kade. Tried to help him move faster.

"No." He shook his head, staring behind me. "Start shooting."

I spun around. And there they were. Coming out of the shadows. Scuttling over the cars and trucks. And you wouldn't call them human. You'd never recognize them as that.

But that's what they'd been, I reckon. Once.

Now they were warped bones and scraps of skin, buried in ash and bulging blue veins. Eyes like something out of your worst nightmare. Hands and feet crawling over the machines their forebears had ground to a halt. Mouths like open wounds.

And what filth had they fed upon? For how many years?

I remembered the Kalliq forcing that injured mammoth down into the mud pit. Realized the sacrifice those people had made. Sending mammoths down here to keep these monsters at bay, I reckon. Because these devils sure looked hungry.

I fired a shot. Two shots. Conserving the few bullets I had left. Counting each one of them, and making each one count.

That pack of freaks howled as the sub gun unloaded. They quit coming so fast but were still pressing in. Baying and whining, like they were daring me to shoot.

I stole a look over my shoulder. Crow had Namo heading toward the cliffs in the distance. But I couldn't see Alpha, or Kade.

And when I turned back, the creatures had closed the gap between us. Just six cars back now. I fired another shot into the middle of them. But how many shots did I have left?

"Come on," screamed Alpha. She was somewhere ahead of me. They were all ahead of me. I was the only one left.

I tried backing up, but kept my eye on those spindled varmints. They were hissing and howling. Mangled teeth and swollen black gums.

And I couldn't move quick enough. They were scampering alongside the cars and weaving between them. They moved like the locusts in GenTech's fields, swarming towards me.

I fired two more shots into that pack of gristle.

Then I turned around and ran.

The slab was creaking and crunching. Cars were pitching and sliding across the road. I heard the creatures wailing. Felt their snatching fingers and teeth. I spun to face them. Fired a bullet. But they were pouring all around me now. There weren't enough bullets, and there weren't enough time.

"Namo," someone was screaming, "get on Namo."

I glimpsed Crow up ahead, holding the mammoth steady. Kade hauling himself up its side.

And there was Alpha. Kicking her way through the pile of ravenous freaks that surrounded her. Then she was reaching the mammoth, climbing up on it, and Namo took off moving again.

I felt hands at my thigh. My back. Pulling me under. They were on the pack. At my neck. Screeching in my ears.

I raised up the sub gun and let that thing loose. Plugging rotten flesh with lead and steel and no longer counting my bullets. And when I got clear for a second, I bolted as fast as I could.

I leapt from car roof to car roof, trying to catch up to Namo and the others. But the mammoth was full on charging ahead, clearing cars out of his way with his tusks. He was too fast. I couldn't reach him. And as he shoved the wreckage into piles behind him, it only slowed me down.

Then the road was shaking. Tearing and splitting. I could feel it wrenching apart beneath me. Separating.

And I was on the wrong side.

The slab shattered into a hundred pieces. The lava spinning us like a river, turning everything around. I watched Namo race across a piece of road turned to rubble. And then he leapt in the air with the others holding on tight.

He landed just high enough on the black cliffs at the far side of the lava. And he'd done it. They were safe.

But I was stranded.

And I had the trees.

Best thing going for me was I'd ended up on one of the bigger chunks of tarmac. Worst thing was the amount of company I had.

The creatures began to circle me. Snarling. Creeping closer. A pack of more than two dozen, hungry for one last meal. I aimed the barrel of the sub gun at them. But they kept tightening around me. Cinching in like a goddamn noose. They were fifteen feet away. Twelve feet. Ten.

I fired a shot at one that looked extra nasty. I fired another shot. And then that was it. I clicked the trigger, but the gun made a hollow sound. Empty.

Just act like you still got bullets, I told myself. Just act like you got plenty left.

But even if I could get through these creatures, how was I supposed to make it to the cliffs?

I glanced across the lava, spotted my girl and that beautiful beast. The mammoth that could leap fifteen feet through the air. The mammoth that had charged on to safety. Because there they all were. Safe. And there was no way they could help me now.

Think. Come on, Banyan. Think.

There had to be a way off this rock. Had to be a way to get free.

Me and you, Pop, I thought, feeling the pack on my shoulders. This is what it comes down to—the two of us together. Just like the years we'd spent drifting in our rusty wagon.

Wait. I stared at the steel remains of old cars around me.

That was it. That had to be it.

As I took off running, the creatures quit their formation, and they howled and shrieked as they closed in. But I hoisted the sub gun by the barrel and swung it around, waving it in circles like a club. I nailed the first creature in the jaws and sent it flying. I scattered two more as I sprinted to the center of this asphalt island I was stranded on.

Didn't have much time to make my selection. Just had to count on dumb luck. So I hit the side of a sedan and pried the door open. I kicked at the freaks behind me. Lashed out with the butt of the gun. And then, when I got clear for a second, I pulled the door wide and piled into the car.

I landed in seats made of leather, snapped the door shut behind me. But those things were all pressed at the windows. They were smeared at the windshield and gripped on the roof.

I slid into the driver's seat, squashing the saplings against my back. I was fumbling around on the floor. The dash. But the keys were right there in the ignition.

So now I'd see how good this salvage could do.

I cranked the key. But nothing. Just the screaming and scratches at the windows. And I couldn't look at those wretched faces. The gaping mouths and bloated eyeballs.

I cranked the engine, again and again. Hell, my old wagon sometimes needed plenty of times to get going. This weren't no different, I told myself. The damn thing at least had to be well rested.

Felt like the hundredth time I turned the key, the car buzzed and sputtered. And the next time, I eased the engine into a growl.

Then I pumped the accelerator. Floored it. And damned if a song didn't crackle out of the dashboard. Some jazzy number. And the howling creatures clashed with the happy tones of the music. And all of it clashed with the fear that was beating my heart.

I swung the car left. Then right. Smashing the other vehicles out of my way. And then I sped forward. The freaks on the windshield could barely hold on. I flipped on the wipers. Still swerving. Trying to loosen their grip. Doing anything I could to get a view and aim for the edge. Faster. Forward.

And then we took off.

That sedan never made it to the cliffs. Got close, though. Got more than halfway.

And then it nosedived into the molten roar.

I was already scrambling backward. I crawled across the seats and busted a hole through the rear windshield. Then I inched out and staggered on the tail end of that old sedan as its front end sank into the Rift.

The music gurgled and was gone beneath me. And I had seconds left before I went down the same way.

On the cliffs, a dozen feet too far, Alpha and Crow were screaming and pointing. And Kade was scrambling around, like he was searching for something to throw out to me.

I unhooked the bag then. Got it loose from my shoulders. I was ready to throw those saplings to as safe a spot as I could. And I would have gone down without them, though I'd have gone down screaming.

Only I didn't toss that bag to the cliffs that were too high, and too far. Because as my legs trembled and the lava swamped up red and closer, just inches from my boots, I held the pack over my head, and damned if something didn't reach out to retrieve me.

Namo.

The mammoth we'd traded for. The beast we'd dragged into hell. He perched his front legs on the cliff edge and reached down with his long, shaggy trunk, scraping the top of the pack and making the thing come unraveled so the saplings poked out in the fumes. Then Namo curled his trunk till he'd wound it tight to those saplings, and I held onto the pack and the clump of trees inside as the mammoth hoisted us into the air.

Not a moment too soon. And no moment lasted longer. As I floated up, the car disappeared beneath me with a juicy shower of sparks.

But then Namo was in trouble. The cliff edge was giving out beneath him, and he stumbled. Hunching backwards. And as he reared up on his hind legs, he lost his grip on me and the trees.

I ended up with one hand on the rocks and one holding the pack of saplings. My feet slip-slapping beneath me. Heat blowing up off the lava, making my grip on the cliff sweaty and loose.

I stared at the others, up on the remaining safe ledge above. Not too far, I reckoned. I could probably claw up there—if it weren't for this fistful of trees.

But it wasn't just Namo that could reach down to me now. I saw Alpha, climbing down and leaning towards me. Stretching and straining.

"The trees," she hollered. "Throw me the trees."

I swung up the pack. High enough she could reach it. And as she pulled it to safety, I held on, letting her pull me up, too—until the pack started ripping. If it tore too wide, the saplings would come loose, fall out.

I had to let go.

"Give me your hand, bro." Kade reached down. And just when I had nothing else to hold onto, I gripped hold of that bony stump at the end of his arm.

And then Kade was hauling me up the last part of the cliff, and I was scrabbling with my feet at the rocks till we were all the way clear.

I rolled away from the edge and onto my back, and I stared up at the faces squeezed together above me, Namo nudging at my chest with his trunk.

"For Zee," Kade whispered, and I tried to say something to thank him. I reached my hand up and gripped his arm again. I nodded and swallowed. And in the end, the only words I could muster were the same two he'd used.

"For Zee."

CHAPTER THIRTY-THREE

I felt like a lump of coal, but they dragged me up, and we huddled there for a moment, peering back into the painful glow, watching the remnants of the old world city and old world machinery. And soon it would fall, I thought, as I watched some of the wretched creatures crawl back inside their concrete shells. Soon it'd burn and be fuel to start over.

"This way," Alpha called, strapping the pack of trees to her back.

She'd found a tunnel. And as soon as we'd hustled after her and gotten Namo squeezed into the narrow passage, the air got cooler, softer. Easier to breathe.

We rushed on, fast as we could stagger, Namo bumping through the passage and bouncing Crow at the ceiling. And we were all sucking down air as the air grew sweeter. No more smoke. No more steam.

As the tunnel coiled through the rock, it kept getting cooler. And like the Speaker had told me—we'd followed the heat, and now we followed the howl.

It started as just a hum in the distance. But as we traveled further, the passage grew broader and the air began to rush towards us. Calling to us. Spinning at the craggy ceiling.

The passage opened up wider and higher until it became an endless cavern. Thing seemed to stretch on forever. And light spilled in up ahead. Rays of white and beams of blue, making it easier to see now.

Once we had plenty of room to maneuver, Namo started to saunter around at a pretty good trot. So we loaded him up, all of us climbing aboard and bundled together, holding on as the mammoth hurried through the open cavern, traveling beneath the roaring winds.

Was a lonesome place. The walls high and distant. The wind rushing above us, swirling and wailing and pounding like waves. The ceiling pushed further from the floor of the cavern—a half-mile high, then even higher. And as it reached upward, the rock gave way in places to patches of ice, making the ceiling twinkling and bright, as the sun found its way from the heavens all the way down here through some frozen part of the world above.

So we were past the Rift but still far enough north for things to be iced up for the winter.

Just gazing up at the frosty colors made me feel cleaner and mended. Though it made me feel even more thirsty, too. But that was all right, because as we drifted deeper into that bellowing cavern, leaning back on Namo's fur and bouncing along, his feet began to make a splashing sound. And before the sound even fully registered, Namo was guzzling at the pools, then spraying us with water straight out of his trunk.

We clambered down into the knee-deep water. Cool but not too cold. And it could have been frozen, for all I cared. I flopped on my belly and gulped down water till my belly was full. Then I rolled onto my back, looking at the high ceiling of rock and ice, listening to the music of those faraway winds.

"It keeps going," Alpha said, kneeling beside me. I gazed with her into the distance ahead, the pools all joining into one big stretch of water.

Hell, no, I thought. Don't let it be another damn lake.

But it didn't get any deeper. Even as the water stretched all the way to the walls around us, it stayed about knee high, and we could wade right on through, dunking our heads to drink whenever we felt inclined. It was good water. Clear and soft and sweet. I felt it charge through me, like it could flush out my brain.

And when evening came and light no longer seeped down through the ceiling, we had the strength to keep on walking. Taking hold of Namo's shaggy fur as we trekked alongside him, taking turns riding with Crow on the mammoth's broad back and sticking together, until we could stagger on blind no longer.

Finally, we rested. Namo stretching out on his side and us all stretched out on the side of his belly, rising and falling with each breath he took. Warm in his fur and from the heat of his body. Felt like being on a little island, surrounded by water and darkness.

Alpha reached out, finding my hand with hers, and I lay there a moment, feeling the great pulse of Namo's heart through my spine. Then I felt Alpha shuffle the plastic pack so the trees were between us. She'd been carrying them since the edge of those black cliffs I'd almost never reached.

"You warm enough?" I asked her, remembering the bits of Kalliq clothing we'd stashed in the pack.

We tugged out some of the mud-covered duds, bundled up a bit. Kade and Crow were already sleeping, so we draped a coat over them. And then we started checking the trees.

The saplings were still coiled tight together, but some of their thin stems had got split and some of the buds were mashed up, broken at the tips of their twiggy beginnings.

"You think they're all right?" Alpha asked, fingering the damage on a soft green stem.

"I think they ain't supposed to be stashed inside plastic. And look—the mud's drying out. That's what the Healer used to mend them."

Alpha scooted down off the side of the mammoth and scooped up some water, crawling back up on her knees as she cradled the water in her palms.

"Trees need water, right?" she said, slowly dripping some inside the pack. The drops glistened and beaded on the stems, got soaked up by the gray patches of mud.

At the bottom of the pack was the small last bits of my old man's remains, green and black and stubbled. And the fistfuls of algae I'd stored in there were still glowing faintly in the gloom.

"You want to eat some?" I asked Alpha, pointing at the moss.

"I say we save it. Who knows when we might find food down here?"

We laid down together again as Namo's belly grumbled and he let out a sigh beneath us, while at the same time, Crow and Kade began some kind of battle with their snoring, like they were seeing how loud the loudest could get.

"Thanks for carrying that pack," I said to Alpha.

"Of course. Can't do this all on your own, bud. We gotta share the weight."

"Reckon so," I said.

Because it sure does lighten the load.

Light dripped again through the icy patches above, waking me up. And when I opened my eyes, the first thing I saw was mountains.

I felt upside down. Confused. I shook my head and scrambled to my feet.

The mountains were pointing down at me, hanging from the high ceiling and making everything feel flipped the wrong way. Made me dizzy, looking up at them—jutting out of the stone, between the patches of ice, then jabbing downward, reaching towards the floor of the cavern. It looked like the rocky roots of the earth itself. And the upside-down peaks stretched as far as I could see. Spiraled and jagged, like endless rows of stone teeth dangling from the roof of a colossal mouth.

The Speak It Mountains is what the Speaker had called them. And it did seem like they were speaking, the wind making strange shapes and sounds as it danced through the peaks overhead.

These mountains were smaller than the ones we'd climbed in the snow, thinner and more twisted, though still a good quarter-mile from the top to their tips, and packed real close. So I was glad we didn't have to cross that maze of gullies and spires.

All we had to do was walk underneath.

I stood on Namo's shaggy stomach, peering out across the water, where the peaks were reflected. And the reflection made them look even more like mountains, seeing as it turned them the right way up.

I looked up to the peaks, then gazed down at their gleaming reflection, and it looked like two different worlds, instead of just two different views. I stood there thinking that was how we built the world around us. All from our own perspective. Even GenTech, even Harvest. They all had their reasons. It was a hard thing to grapple with and know what it meant. And I wished Zee had been there to help me think it through.

CHAPTER THIRTY-FOUR

As we traveled beneath the mountains, their peaks reached even lower, sometimes reaching all the way to the ground, so we had to steer around them, twist inside them. Getting caught in the wind now. And the further we wound our way through those dangling cliffs, the more fierce the wind seemed to howl.

We kept to the widest gaps, following the broadest routes between the hanging spires, so we could steer Namo alongside us, his long fur flying in the gathering wind.

And when it got too dark to navigate the rocky claws of the mountains, we set Namo down to rest again in the water, threading ourselves in the fur of his belly. Once more feeling his warmth and the rhythm of his breathing, pulling matted old coats over us to keep us from the wind, and not even speaking as we hunkered down for the night.

I opened the pack and felt the trees, making sure the stems hadn't gotten any more broken and that the healing mud was still slippery from the water Alpha had tended them with. Then I dug out the moss I'd gathered from the tunnels. It weren't glowing so much now, it was crumbled and flaky. And I passed some to Alpha, then split some between Crow and Kade.

We all chewed it down, though it left a rotten taste, powdery on the tongue. Then the fatigue pressed me flat, and I put my hands on my ears, trying to block the sound of the punishing winds.

A splashing sound woke me. And when I scrabbled around for the pack, I found it was missing—figured it must have fallen off the side of the mammoth, and the sound of the pack hitting the pool had been what had woken me up.

I reached down and groped through the darkness, trying to find the pack with my fingers, and when I realized the wind had stopped, I felt my body begin to unwind with relief.

But then the wind started up again, and it was even worse than before.

Almost sounded like it was made up of voices. People whispering. Thousands of them, all speaking over each other and confusing the words. The sound crept inside me like tiny fingers, wriggling in through my ears and spinning my brain.

But it weren't really voices. Just the sound of the wind. Told myself I was imagining things. Or maybe I was still sleeping. Dreaming.

I hurried down into the pool to search for the saplings, the cool water coming up to my thighs, and I felt it seeping through the remains of my clothes, caressing my bones and my skin, and it all felt much too real for a dream, I tell you that much.

But then why could I still hear those damn voices?

I put both hands over my ears, blocking out the terrible chorus of whispers, and I waded through the dark, splashing about. Couldn't find the pack anywhere, though, and just where the hell was it? Had the wind blown it clear across the damn pool?

Soon I was crashing around and getting desperate. I called out to the others, but they'd never hear me with the wind raging so loud. And that wind was playing tricks on me, turning me in circles. Got so I couldn't even find my way back.

I started running fast as I could through the water, my hands still clamped over my ears. And by the time I stopped, I was lost in the darkness, and completely alone.

I began to scream for the others.

"Wake up," I kept shouting, almost like I was shouting it to myself. Almost like I was still back there, sleeping on the side of the mammoth's belly, and this me that was out here wasn't out here at all.

Something half-solid hit the side of my leg.

I had to take my hands off my ears to reach down into the water. And then I found what I'd stumbled upon—the pack. But as I pulled it out of the pool, I realized the pack had come open and the saplings were floating free of the plastic, their limbs soggy and all matted together.

The wind sounded more like voices than ever now. Tumbling and urgent, and really freaking me out.

And I tried to shove the saplings back in the pack, pushing the good Kalliq mud back in place at the bottom, but as I groped in the dark, my hands got too slick. And every time I got the pack tied back together, it all just kept coming undone, and the saplings would start falling back out.

I held the shrunken last bits of Pop's face with my fingers as the saplings rattled and shook in the wind. It was as if the wind meant to snatch the trees from me, tug them away. But then, out of all the wind's whispering voices, one voice whispered louder than the rest.

"Banyan?" The wind curled the word around me. "That you?"

"Pop?"

"It is you."

"Don't." The word was sharp on my tongue. I thrashed around in the water, staring all around me but swallowed by shadows, blind in the dark.

"You're gone," I called. "You gotta leave me alone now."

"No." The voice trembled against me. "Not gone. Not yet."

I screamed into the wind, but it blew the words back at me, and they hit me and shattered everything I wanted to say.

So I tried again, even louder.

"What do I do?" I cried, as if the question had been chiseled inside me and to speak it now meant prying open my heart.

"You know." The wind wailed back. "You already know."

"No." I held the stump of trees before me, Pop's remains at their base like a broken skull. "How can I know without you here beside me?"

"I am beside you." The wind rushed through the thin, coiled saplings, shaking them so hard, I thought it might tear them apart. "I'm right here, son. I'm here."

"No, you ain't, damn you. You left me alone in that wagon. And look at what you left me to do."

The wind shredded the stone and clawed at the water, like a storm had broken out inside this black hole.

But now the wind was just noise. No more voices. No words.

"Wait," I shouted into the empty bluster and fury. "Come back."

I held the crumpled trees against me, clasping them to my chest as I knelt.

"Come back here," I whispered. "Pop. I miss you. I miss you so much."

The winds quit and the world turned silent, leaving just the sound of my sobbing and a wheeze in my chest. And I had to be careful not to break those saplings, I was hugging them so awful damn tight.

I tried to untwist my muscles. My breathing ragged as I tried to keep steady. And when I stared down into the pool, it was like there were lights on beneath it.

No.

Not lights. A sun in a sky.

I peered down as if from out of the heavens, gazing at a world that lay gleaming below. And I could see Waterfall City—the great falls, the thundering roar. And there were Pop's trees, along the banks of the Niagara. A forest. Leaves heavy in the mist and apples ripe for the picking.

But then my view got blocked. Covered by clouds. And when the skies cleared again, I saw the forest inside the Steel Cities. The trees creeping their way south, blunting the edges of buildings. I saw shantytowns sheltered from the wind, colored with green and patches of shade.

Next was the rusted forest in Old Orleans, the cypress and fern and Hina's statue. I saw it entwined with shrubby green foliage, as Pop's trees worked their way through the understory and whirled their way up. Every bit of brass and steel became covered and mended. The metal trees no longer shiny but muted and juicy as they soaked up the sun.

I saw the trees planted in the cornfields, immune to the locusts. I saw them on the streets of Vega, growing amid the buildings of the Electric City as the neon billboards flashed.

But in all of those places, there were folks on the outside. Hungry hands and mouths full of dust. I saw them on the outskirts of every last vision. They crept like shadows as they sank in the mud. And they were starving, though apples bounced on the branches and shone in their eyes. The new fruit was always too far out of reach.

The people growing the apples had plenty. They had full bellies and more food on the way. But the strugglers left out stayed starving. Trapped and broken. Just as wretched and wronged as before.

Didn't matter where the trees grew—with the Rastas or pirates, in the cities or on the plains. The story always spun out the same. There was always folk left hungry. Because there's always another GenTech, ain't there? There's always another man who'd be king.

I staggered through the water. Not even trying to see where I was going. The pictures in the pool faded. The words had all quit.

It was just me and the void now, like a couple old friends back together. And finally, I ran into Namo's shaggy trunk. It was whipping around in the water as the old beast rumbled and slept, and I traced my way around him, holding onto his fur so I'd not lose him. Then I pushed myself up and onto his belly. Still hugging the saplings against me as I crawled into a ball.

I did not weep as I lay there.

But at some point, I must have slept. Or fallen back outside the dream.

Sunlight crept down through the patches of ice above us, illuminating the peaks and the water. I blinked at the brightness, trying to ignore the ache behind my eyeballs and the rancid knot in my guts.

"Wake up, bud," Alpha said, grabbing my shoulders. "Quick."

"I'm awake," I told her, still slumped on my side.

"Then get up. Now."

I rolled over to face her.

"You look like I feel," I said. Her eyes were bloodshot, and her skin was clammy and gray.

"I can't find Crow," she said, and I realized now how frantic she sounded.

But there weren't no need to worry, I reckoned. The legless Soljah couldn't be too far away.

I was too quick sitting up and it made my guts spin. Something rotten came bubbling up. I leaned over and choked out a ball of slime, barely missing Namo's belly as I spat into the pool.

"What the hell?" My eyeballs seemed to throb in their sockets. But my guts felt better right away.

"Happened to me, too," Alpha said. "Puked as soon as I opened my eyes."

I stood up real slow, my legs tired and scratchy.

"I think that wind drove me mad," I said, looking about for Crow. Couldn't see him, though. And where the hell had he got to?

Kade came splashing towards us from behind the tip of an upside-down peak.

"I can't find him anywhere," he hollered.

"He's got the trees, bud." Alpha stood beside me, so pale, like all the blood had seeped out of her skin.

I stared down at the water. "You sure? I think the pack might have fallen off. I remember it happening in the night."

We splashed around in the pool, but that pack full of saplings was nowhere to be found.

"It's not here," Kade said, slapping his fist on the water. "Crow's got them. And we're wasting time."

"Well, shit. He can't get far," I said. "Not on those broken old stumps."

"Unless he's been faking it." Kade was trying to keep calm. Trying to breathe steady. But it wasn't working out too well for him. "Maybe he's just been biding his time."

"Faking it?" I said. "You've seen those things GenTech gave him."

"Come on. We'll ride Namo." Alpha was getting the mammoth to stand up. "We'll be quicker."

"Did you dream?" I asked her, as Kade climbed up onto Namo's back.

Alpha paused for a moment, like she was gathering all the strength inside her, and her face was like a ghost as she studied mine, measuring me in some new way with her eyes.

"I don't know," she said, in a way that weren't nothing like the girl I was used to. She stared at the hanging peaks, now silent above us.

"The Speaker told me we'd come here," I said. "Said this place can show you things you need to see."

Alpha just kept staring at the dangling mountains.

"You think it's true?" I asked her. She had goosebumps up her arms and her shoulders. "You cold?"

"I'm just scared, Banyan."

"I know." I put my hand on the back of her neck. Felt the scruff that had grown back on her head since GenTech had shaved it.

"I'm scared of what's gonna happen."

"What did you see?" I asked.

"Something all wrong." She turned to grab fistfuls of the mammoth's long fur so she could pull herself up top. And all I could think of was that bark on Alpha's belly. I imagined it growing and spreading in the spring, sealing her inside it like a wooden tomb. A disease, the Speaker had called it, when they'd shown me that woman in the corrugated coffin.

"It was me and you," Alpha said, not looking at me as she swung herself up.

"What was?"

But Alpha wouldn't say.

"Just a dream," I called after her. "Only a dream."

CHAPTER THIRTY-FIVE

I'd told them there weren't no reason to worry, but once we were rolling forward, I realized catching up to Crow would only be easy if we knew which direction he'd gone.

"He could be anywhere," said Alpha. "Those are some long legs if he's figured out how to use 'em."

My head quit aching, leaving me more room to worry. Crow had tried to leave me once already, after all, back when I'd wanted to stay with the Kalliq. Hell, maybe he figured there weren't room in my plans for him and his Soljahs, so he'd smuggled off with the trees, hoping to reach Niagara without us.

And what if he made it? Would the Rastas get fat on apples in the shade of their forests, while the rest of the world stayed sunburned and starved?

The winds kept silent as the peaks began to fade, receding into the high, stony ceiling and patches of ice. And as we traveled on, splashing through the water, we hollered Crow's name and peered into every nook and shadow. But we couldn't see him any damn place at all.

"What if he fell?" asked Alpha. "He could've drowned."

"Crow," I yelled, kicking at Namo to make him gallop faster, though I reckoned we were riding him right into the ground.

Kade leaned off the side of the mammoth and puked up a glob just like the one I'd spat out earlier.

"Better?" Alpha said, clapping him on the back.

"Feels like I'm coming off a bad batch of crystal."

"Reckon it was something in the water," she said. "Got us seeing crazy and feeling like crap."

But I remembered that dried-out moss I'd pulled out of the pack the night before, and wondered if it hadn't been something we ate.

"Look." I pointed across the water. There in the distance was the last peak. It sat out alone from the rest. No mountains beyond it or near it, just a big, jagged finger of rock jabbing down.

"The Speaker said the last peak points us home," I said.

"Then let's check it out." Alpha tugged at Namo's fur to steer him. "Maybe it'll point us to Crow."

The stone ceiling was becoming less and less patched with ice, so we were losing light as Namo crashed through the pool. Got closer, though, and we could see a figure beneath that last peak, dark and damp, bobbing on the water.

"It's him," I hollered, sliding off Namo and splashing forward.

The purple thread splinting Crow's broken legs shone through the gloom. I grabbed him. Pulled him towards me. He was floating face up, eyes closed, and his right hand was clasped tight around the pack full of trees.

"I told you," Kade said, coming up behind me. "The big freak is a thief."

Alpha shoved at Crow as he bobbed on the water. She slapped his face, then she glanced at me. "He's breathing."

She went to slap him again, but Crow's hand reached up and grabbed her, his fingers locking onto her wrist.

And when Crow's eyes came open, they were full of madness.

"The lion's mane," he roared, his voice brimmed full of tears and echoes. "I and I."

"Let go," Alpha said, trying to pull her hand free.

"I and I. In the blaze of God's dreadlocks."

"Stop," I yelled. "Let her go."

But Crow wouldn't let go. And his voice bellowed and sang.

"In the lion's mane. Through the dust and corn, leaving rivers behind us."

"He's breaking my arm," Alpha screamed.

I grabbed Crow's fingers, twisting them. Trying to bend back his knuckles. Kade was thumping him in the belly, but it didn't do a thing.

"An army," Crow moaned. "In the golden sunrise. And the Tree King buried beneath the shade of the South Wall."

"Banyan," Alpha wailed. Her eyes so wide and frightened. And I sank my fists in Crow's face and forced him below the water. Holding him under as he gurgled and twitched. He kept thrashing about, and I kept holding him down. He was dragging Alpha towards him.

But then he just quit.

He let go of her wrist, and she staggered clear. And as Crow's body went limp, I staggered back, too. I leaned down and pulled the pack of trees from his other hand, checking the saplings, then swinging them onto my back.

Crow floated up out of the water. Eyes shut now. And when his eyes bulged back and spun open, it was because he was coughing, and when he puked, the slime sprayed upward, then landed all over his face.

It was disgusting. And I went to turn my back on him. But he was sick, I reckoned. Just like we'd all been. Driven to madness by the water or the moss or this place.

I splashed water on him, trying to get him cleaned up.

He was crying. Sobbing and shuddering. "What happened?" he croaked. "What have I done?"

"Take it easy," I said. "You been walking a long way."

"No. I can't. Remember? I'm a cripple. You said so yourself."

"But you walked here. On your own."

"Don't leave me, Banyan," he cried. "Please. I know that you want to."

"Quit crying," I told him. "This all just some act?"

"He's faking it," said Kade. "I told you."

"Come on." I stared down at Crow as he floated in the shallow water. "Stand up."

"Where's Namo?" he asked, sounding real feeble.

"He's just over yonder. Let's see you walk over to him now."

"Why you doing this? You seen what GenTech done to me."

"But I seen where you're at, big guy. You walked all the way here."

"Don't know how it happened."

"Either you know you're faking or you've fooled yourself, too." I leaned down to him. "But you can walk. There ain't no doubt about it no more."

He found the bottom of the pool and tried to sit up. Tried to stand. Then he managed to haul himself against the jagged rocks of the last hanging peak and leaned against them, barely standing.

"Come on, damn it," I shouted. "Walk."

Crow took a step forward. Then another. He let go of the peak, and then he buckled and pitched.

And none of us helped Crow get back up. We just watched as he half swam and half crawled towards Namo, then pulled himself up the side of the mammoth, legs dangling beneath him.

"You go walkabout again," I called to Crow, "crazy or not, you better not touch these trees."

He stayed silent as my voice echoed around the cavern.

"Understood, Soljah?" I shouted.

"Yes, man," he called back, hardly loud enough to hear. "Understood."

"And this is meant to point somewhere?" Kade muttered, peering up at the peak.

"Supposed to." I felt its rough edges, fumbling around for some clue.

Alpha shook her head, still rubbing her wrist where Crow had grabbed her. "All it does is point down."

I ignored them. Just worked my way around the peak. And I made it all the way to the other side before

I got smacked in the shins so hard, I landed face down in the water.

I knelt and splashed around, my fingers groping for whatever it was I'd tripped on, and I found me a rusty piece of metal down there. Some kind of iron pipe. Rotten and flaking, but sturdy enough. Big, too. I could barely get my hands around it.

"Thing's sucking up water," I said, finding the pipe's opening, right beneath the rocks of the last hanging mountain. "Check it out. A pipe. Must be pumping the water someplace. I can feel it getting sucked up inside."

I tried tugging at the pipe, but the thing was bolted in place. And I'd no doubt the other end was also bound tight to something.

We'd just have to follow it to find out where.

CHAPTER THIRTY-SIX

Alpha splashed out in front, and me and Kade kept on behind her, Namo following our ruckus as we followed the pipe through the pool. Crow was slumped on the mammoth's back, and he seemed to have given up speaking as well as walking. He just belched and moaned, holding his stomach. Clutching at the beast as if Namo's legs had replaced his own.

The water began to get warmer. Thicker, too. Tasted dirty now. Full of silt. And it weren't much longer before I quit drinking it, no matter how empty my guts.

Then the water started drying up. We started stomping through puddles. And then, when the puddles were gone, we were slopping through mud.

By then, no more light seeped in anywhere, and we could hardly even see each other through the darkness. There was nothing to do but shuffle forward, gripping the iron pipe so you didn't lose direction and end up lost.

"You want me to take the lead?" I asked Alpha when I bumped into her back one too many times.

"Just move up beside me."

I quit grabbing at the pipe, started holding her hand instead.

"Hey, Kade," I called. "Get up here."

I reached behind me. "It's easier like this," I said. "We'll form a chain. You hold onto me."

"You're not gonna ask me for a poem, are you?" he said, taking my hand. His voice was bitter and coarse, but I thought I could hear a smile in there somewhere.

"Would if I thought you actually knew one."

"Hey," called Alpha. "You seeing this?"

I peered into the depths. Straight ahead and nowhere at all. But then I did glimpse it. A white light flashing. And right away, we were all slipping through the mud towards it.

We peered up at a small plastic lantern that had been stuck in the dirt. The light was faint and flickering, but it marked an entrance to a tunnel that led out of the cavern. The iron pipe we'd been following ran all the way inside.

The tunnel was wide. High, too. Enough space we could cram Namo through it. And as we traveled deeper into the tunnel, the walls became almost sandy in places, the mud of the cavern giving way to something closer to the dust I'd spent a lifetime breathing in.

But the tunnel weren't just dirt walls and a high ceiling. This tunnel was something folk used.

There were footprints running down it. And it was lit up. Every ten yards or so was the same sort of plastic lantern that had called to us through the dark. Each one of the old lanterns was dim and fluttery. And each one was connected to the next with thin red wire.

So there was power running down there. And you could hear water rushing in the iron pipe that ran along the wall next to us, whooshing and sloshing as it got pumped up from the pool beneath those upside-down peaks.

Juice. And water, and footprints. So, somewhere, there'd be people. It was just a question of when we might find them.

And who they might be.

We rounded a couple more bends, then slid down against the walls, exhausted. Our skin full of mud, but our bellies so empty, our muscles so weak.

Namo knelt down, and Crow crawled off the beast, carefully lowering himself to the dirt. Then he clawed his way over so he was next to me, his head in his hands once he leaned back on the wall. Alpha and Kade were slumped opposite, against the water pipe, the pale, plastic light chattery above their heads.

"Don't worry about it," Alpha said to Crow. She kicked gently at one of his splinted wooden legs, and the limb looked pretty solid now, purple thread all bound up with the bark, but that leg just wobbled when Alpha kicked it, and I don't think Crow even felt it at all.

"Hey," she said to him. "It's all right. We all saw crazy beneath those peaks." Alpha rubbed her wrist where the skin was bruised from him gripping it.

I glanced at Kade and wondered what he might have seen beneath the Speak It Mountains. And had it really been madness? Is that what it had felt like?

No. Not for me, anyway. Those mountains had shown me something I needed to see.

"Looks like we made it." Kade gazed at the dirt above us. "I've heard of tunnels like these under the Steel Cities. People hid down inside them in the Darkness, mining for a place to stay warm."

"I thought them was sewers," I said. "Concrete."

"Well, we're not near Niagara." Crow ran his hand along the wall behind him. He flitted his gaze quick between us, as if seeing if we'd still listen to him at all. "This dirt be too dry."

"Someone's got these lights running for something." Alpha had never looked so pale, her skin painted white by the flickering glow. "Should keep our voices down."

I scrambled forward so I was between the three of them. Then I began to sketch out a big square in the dirt.

Namo was rolled up on his side, flicking his trunk at my drawing and making these little sighing sounds. And the mammoth's breathing was the only noise in that tunnel, apart from the soft pulse of the water as it gushed through the pipe on the wall.

"What's this?" said Alpha, looking at the lines I had drawn.

"I been thinking things through."

I pointed at the top edge of the square. "Above this line is the Rift," I told them, then I scratched all the way across the bottom edge. "And here's the South Wall. East and west, we got the coasts, the Surge," I pointed, "here and here. So if we're under the northern Steel Cities," I marked a spot inside the northeast corner of the square, "then we're somewhere around here. And if we get out of this tunnel, I say we head straight for the Salvage Guild's headquarters."

"You want to go to the Guild?" Crow said. Maybe it came out louder than he'd wanted.

"Yeah. All those old world machines. Gadgets and tools. Weapons. I figure they'd be good in a fight."

"What fight you talking about, little man?"

I pulled the pack of trees off my shoulder. Laid it next to the map I had made. "For the first time in a hundred years, we got something to grow that ain't owned by GenTech. Right?"

With my finger, I drew a thick line right down the center of the map, showing GenTech's cornfields, running all the way from top to bottom. And to the west of the fields, I marked the only thing out there—Vega. The Electric City. The place GenTech called home.

"This is what they did with their power," I said, pointing to Vega. "They put it all in one place. Built themselves up by keeping other folk down. And now GenTech's gonna take these trees from us. They'll find us, no matter where we try to hide, and they'll take control of the apples like they control the corn. Then they'll keep control over everything. Keep us squashed and squabbling in the dirt. Keep us trading with them no matter how high their demands. It'll be business as usual. Unless we show them we're willing to stand up and fight."

"Us against the Purple Hand," Alpha said, nodding.

"Yeah," I said. "Us. All of us."

"Then we head to Waterfall City." Crow pushed himself from the wall and jabbed a finger in the dirt map, marking another spot in the northeast corner, further inland than the Steel Cities. "I know what it comes down to, man. Known it all along. But if we gonna start a war against GenTech, we gonna need warriors. Not old world machines."

"We'll head there," I said. "Right after we head to the Guild's headquarters and get them on our side."

"We should head to whichever one's closer," said Kade.

"No." Alpha folded her arms across her chest. "We should head to Old Orleans, bud. Like you said that we would."

"It's too far," I said, my eyes pleading with hers. "We'll get there, though. Later. I promise."

"You already promised. You and me, that's what you said."

"But it's like Kade's saying, we should go wherever's closer."

"So you lied to me."

"I didn't lie." I struggled to keep my voice down. "I just know now what we gotta do."

"And what do you know about starting a war?" she said. "We need to gather the armies from across the plains. Anyone got a score to settle with the Purple Hand, it's the pirates."

"We all got a score to settle," said Crow. "Not just your people GenTech beat down to nothing."

"That's it," I said. "That's what I'm saying—we don't need an army, we need every army. All of them. We have to share the weight." I pointed at the bag full of trees. "And then we all share the wealth."

Alpha shook her head. "There's only six of those saplings, bud."

"But they'll grow tall and they'll spread, and they'll keep on going. A forest for everyone. A forest growing apples for people to eat. It's like Zee said, we work together. Give people roots and branches, and it'll bind us as one." Wasn't that why Pop had taught me to build trees in the first place? To show people the world could still be something special?

And now I knew what sort of builder I had to be.

"I saw it," I told them. "Beneath the mountains. I saw what would happen if one tribe's more powerful than the others. Hell, we've all seen it happen, for the last hundred years. And I saw it happening all over again."

"Because of some vision?" This was Alpha. "That's what you're telling us? That's all you got?"

"What did you dream?" I stared right into those brown eyes of hers.

"It's not important," she said, looking away.

"Then why can't you say it?"

"Because it's crazy."

"And you're afraid it's the truth."

I needed her to believe me. To trust me. And I stared at the pack with a hole in my chest, knowing what it would come down to now. Knowing what I would have to do. Because they'd all need a sapling. Every last tribe. So I'd have to rip each tree from the others, breaking up the last of my father's remains.

It was Crow who finally said something. He stared at the pack, and he glared at me. And then he rocked himself closer to the map.

"We'll need the bootleggers," he said, drawing a squiggle to show the southern stretch of the Steel Cities. "If we all be going up against GenTech together."

"Bootleggers?" Kade frowned. "They've no weapons. No troops."

"True that," said Crow. "But they could feed our armies."

"The poachers could do that."

"Poachers?" Crow made a snort, and Namo got spooked behind me. "They can barely feed themselves."

"One for the Salvage Guild. One for the pirate armies. One for the Soljahs, and one for the bootleggers." Alpha still wouldn't look at me as she spoke. "That's two left. Two saplings."

"One left," I said. "I ain't letting the last one out of my sight."

"But what makes you so special?" Kade's green eyes flickered in the white light. "I thought it can't be anyone more than the next."

"I keep the last tree. The sixth tree. And if I die, you can pry it loose from my fingers." I didn't dare look at Alpha as I said it. I just thought of that patch of bark on her belly. Because I'd pinned my last hope of a remedy to that sapling. It was the last trick I had up my sleeve.

"So what about the fifth tree?" Crow stared at Alpha and Kade as he spoke, but he was talking to me. "You got that figured out, too, man?"

"Yeah," I said. Because I did have it figured. Crow was right—we'd need corn for our armies, at least until our apples could grow. But of course, GenTech had plenty of corn of their own. Plenty of food for their troops.

"GenTech needs crystal," I said. "The field hands and agents are all hooked on the stuff. So I say we take their supplier. The fifth tree we give to the Samurai Five."

CHAPTER THIRTY-SEVEN

Alpha shot me a stare, confusion on her face. But Crow had anger in his eyes.

"The Five?" he said. "The Samurai Five?"

"Tell them." I nodded at Kade. "Tell them what you told me."

Kade had hunched inward, as if bracing himself against a cold wind that no one else could feel.

"They make the crystal," he said, and he started scratching the back of his arm. Guess he weren't keen to talk about the poison he'd been hooked on. "Samurai Five make all of it."

"I know what they do," yelled Crow. "I want to know why the scum deserve one of our trees."

"Keep your voice down," I said. "Just listen."

"I was a field hand," Kade whispered, rubbing his fingers over his stump. "GenTech used the crystal to make slaves of us. All of us. They use it to make slaves of the agents, too."

"You think I don't know this, little man?" Crow turned to me, his eyeballs bulging out of his head. "I worked for GenTech, remember? I know more about them than any of you."

"Corn and crystal," I said. "That's how they keep their armies in line. And we can't control the cornfields, but we could cut off their drugs."

"Weaken 'em," said Alpha, nodding. "It's the first smart thing you've said."

"No." Crow sat back against the wall. Leaned his head on the dirt. "The Five are crooks."

"I heard they got honor." Alpha looked at Kade. "That they live by a code."

"They don't touch the crystal," Kade said. "I know that much."

"And that's it?" Crow ignored the others. Just kept staring at me. "Soljahs and salvage and the Samurai Five?"

"And bootleggers," I said. "And pirates."

"Not pirates." Alpha scratched a big X on the map, marking the plains, west of the Steel Cities but east of GenTech's fields. "The Army of the Fallen Sun, they called it. And we'll ride as that again."

"The Soljahs fought, too." Crow pointed at where he'd marked Waterfall City. "We made our stand against GenTech."

"Drop it," I told them. "The past don't matter. All that matters is what we do next."

I reached down and scratched out the map we'd drawn in the dirt.

"A blank slate," I said, glancing at Kade. "Remember?"

"All right, bud," said Alpha. "We'll do it your way. For now."

Crow might have gotten fired up about my plan for the fifth sapling, but he didn't look too tough when I was helping him climb back up onto Namo.

"Better hope these walls don't get any tighter," I said to him as he gripped the mammoth's fur.

"Keep hoping, Banyan. Seems like that's what you're best at."

Couldn't blame him for doubting me. Crow probably reckoned the trees would be safe in the hands of the Soljahs, and maybe he thought all the power would be safe with them, too.

Heading up those tunnels, Namo had to squeeze himself along where the walls got narrow, and Crow kept a tight grip as the mammoth wriggled and pushed, pressing down tight in its fur. Got so that big, shaggy beast was plugging up the passage behind us. But I strode out in front, the pack full of trees strapped to my back.

"Zee'd have been proud," Kade said, coming to walk beside me.

I pictured her bony shoulders, her long hair and pretty face. But then I remembered her being riddled with bullets. I remembered her shriveled and lifeless in my arms.

"I don't know," I said. "She wanted all the fighting to stop."

"Only one way to stop it. We rise up together against GenTech." Kade lifted his stump between us. "All hands on deck, right? I told her you could be a leader. I told Alpha, too. In the mountains, after you'd fallen off that ridge. I said people would follow you to the ends of the earth."

"Ah, you're feeding me a line."

"It's true."

"And what did Zee say?"

"This is the nicest thing I'll ever do for you, bro. She said you were the only one of us who was more important than the trees. You know, your sister was even more beautiful than she looked." Kade's voice had started falling apart a little. "She was strong inside, even if her lungs were broken. She was strong where it counted."

"I didn't know her, though. Not enough. Not like I should."

I turned to Kade, and the plastic lanterns strobed up and down the tunnel, painting him white and then black. And I wanted him to give me something more about my sister. Another missing piece.

"But why would she say that?" I asked. "About me being important?"

"Because she thought you could bring people together, if you ever got your shit together first."

I wasn't sure if I believed him. After all, Kade was the one who was so good at talking to folk. Not me.

But then Crow started hollering, and we peered back at him. Not much room to move in there, but he had his hands up, brushing the ceiling, showing us he could steer Namo just by moving his legs.

He veered left a little. Swung to the right.

"Look at you," Alpha said, and she gave him a whoop.

Crow tapped his chest, then he scratched Namo behind his big ears. "You know, this mammoth reminds me of I and I. Two big freaks, no?" He kicked his legs, and Namo sped up to a trot.

But then Crow slowed the beast all the way down, and he was twisting up at something. Fidgeting at the ceiling.

"Come on," I said. "Quit fooling around. And quit making so much noise."

"Still think we're under the Steel Cities?" Crow threw down a small clump of something he'd yanked out of the ceiling.

I bent down, scrabbling in the dirt till I had my hands on it.

"Roots," Crow said. "Reaching down from above us. We ain't under no Steel Cities. We be under the corn."

I peered at the dirt walls. The crumbly ceiling. Everything seemed to shake in the throbbing white lights. Then I stared at the mess of roots in my fists. Felt like tangled strips of plastic.

I remembered Pop showing me the corn's roots, when we'd been together in the cornfields, his hands digging into frozen dirt to reveal the wrinkled fingers of GenTech's crop. And it struck me that Pop had always been careful to show me the ends of all things—the Surge that rips at the coasts and keeps us landlocked, the twisted tips of GenTech's twisted plants, groping at the earth. Pop had wanted me to know I had nowhere else to go, so I'd better try to make this world better. Ain't no grass greener, he'd once told me. Since there ain't no grass left at all.

And now here we were, under the ground, and under the cornfields that kept the GenTech Empire fueled and well fed. The fields that run down the middle of everything, from up near the Rift all the way to the

South Wall. The towering rows of thirty-foot plants and the huge purple dusters—steel machines blading down one crop and reseeding for the next. Up above us would be agents and field hands and the place Kade had told me about, the Stacks, a cornhusk kingdom full of junky slaves.

"If we're under the cornfields," said Alpha, "then this is a GenTech tunnel."

"Irrigation." Kade tapped at the iron pipe. "The corn hardly needs much water, but it still uses some."

"You think it's some kind of maintenance passage?" I turned to him. "I mean, you was a field hand. Where do you think it comes out?"

Kade shrugged. "It probably runs up somewhere."

"It'll put us right in the thick of things," said Alpha. "Surrounded by GenTech."

"Surrounded by plants, maybe." Kade frowned. "The crops could give us cover."

"It's winter," I said. "Too cold for the locusts."

Crow stared down at us. "There be no point heading backwards."

"We move then." Alpha fixed me with a look. Fear in her eyes. "Quiet and quick. Ain't got one weapon between us."

"We have him, though." I pointed at the mammoth, and Namo curled his shaggy trunk towards my hand. "His hide's damn near bulletproof. And those tusks can do some damage."

"But then what happens? If we do find a way out?" Alpha reached up to Namo's belly, stroked his fur. "We take him out in the corn?"

She was right to sound worried. What would we do with the mammoth? Could hardly sneak him out through the fields. And even if we did, there weren't no way to ride him across the plains. Might as well drag a big old flag over our heads and wait for GenTech agents to hunt our ass down.

Cross that bridge when we come to it, though. That's what I told myself. Because before we could worry about Namo, we had to find an end to this tunnel. I glanced at the water pipe, wondering where it led to. I shielded my eyes from the flash of the lantern.

But then I quit moving at all.

I held up my hand to the others, held myself still.

Up ahead, I'd heard voices. And now there were footsteps. Creeping towards us through the dirt.

All I could think was how we should have Namo in front of us. We had to get behind him and use him like a shield.

I grabbed Alpha. Trying so hard to be quiet as I shoved her behind me. Then I turned to Kade. Reached for him, too.

But Kade wouldn't move.

He just stood there, his green eyes glittery, his whole body seeming to pulse in the busted white lights. I reached for his arm. Not sure what was happening. But he pulled it away from me.

And then he swung his stumped arm at me like a club.

He used it as a weapon. Clobbering me with it, like he was hammering me into the ground. And when I hit the dirt, Kade started grabbing at me with his hand. No, not at me—at the pack on my back. He was hoisting it off me. Yanking the straps from my shoulders. And as the footsteps pounded closer, the whole tunnel seemed to shake and spin.

I was face down in the dirt with blood in my eyes, and behind me, I could hear Namo wailing and Crow cursing. I rolled up and saw Alpha standing above me, her legs wide and fists clenched.

Kade was bounding down the tunnel away from us, his head straight and high. He had the pack held above him. And he was shaking it, spilling the saplings out of the plastic and into the light.

There was confusion for a moment. Hesitation on the faces of the approaching crowd.

"Kade?" one of them said, coming forward to grasp his hand. And then they all gathered around him, talking. Giving him a little space as he stood there, cradling the saplings to his chest.

And then there was cheering. Voices raised, loud and righteous. Shocked. But happy as a damn jubilee. And these weren't field hands.

They weren't GenTech agents, neither.

I knew what they were from their cornhusk clothes and their underground faces.

The crowd moved closer, and I heard them gasp at Namo, and still freaking out at the trees. And then they were descending on us. Jabbing at Alpha with hacksaws and knives and forcing her backwards. And Kade was above me, sticking his foot on my chest, a machete gripped in his fist.

"I trusted you," I whispered, peering up at him.

"Did you, though?" Kade's mouth hung open, his teeth all sharp and spitty. And then that poacher kicked my head so hard, my brain snapped loose as my eyes snapped shut.

CHAPTER THIRTY-EIGHT

The ropes were made of woven cornhusks. I could feel them, crunchy and rough, biting into my skin as they strapped my ankles together and bound my wrists behind my head.

I blinked my eyes wide in the half-light. Rolled off my back and onto my side, wobbled there for a second. Then I hit the dirt face first.

I spat the grime from my teeth. Tried to arc up and stare around the dusty cell. Every part of me was aching and cracked, all dried blood and bruises. It hurt just to move my eyeballs around.

The cell was brown and black shadows, but there was a brightness spilling in from the far end, and I rolled myself towards it. Slowly. Painfully. Finally squirming up against the iron bars of a door sealed shut with chains and padlocks.

I pressed my head against the bars and peered out at a long, empty passageway, where flickering white lights twitched on the walls. I spied other doorways. More sets of bars.

"Alpha," I called out, my voice all raspy, my throat swollen.

"That you, little man?" Crow's voice seemed to come from a cell halfway down the passage.

"Where's Alpha?" I moaned.

"In here someplace. Maybe. 'Less that bastard has her for questioning."

"Questioning?" I whispered. I banged my head on the bars. What questions could Kade have for us? We'd been straight with him, hadn't we? He'd been the one covering his tracks with lies.

"I'm so hungry," I called out. My guts were so empty, it made me dizzy, and that made everything feel even worse.

"They brought me water," Crow said. "Fed me corn with a spoon. They'll be back, you hang in there."

"No." My arms were tingling. Bloodless. Bound too tight. "I don't want their food."

"Ain't theirs, man. It's GenTech's."

"I don't want GenTech's food, neither."

"You gonna be hungry a long time, you wait for them apples to grow."

"Been hungry my whole life," I muttered. "Should be used to it."

I struggled up next to the bars so my back was against them. I strained at the cornhusk ropes. No use. GenTech grown and poacher woven. I slammed myself at the dirt, then rattled the bars with my knees.

"Save your strength," called Crow.

"For what?"

We were trapped down here beneath the cornfields. Locked inside this poacher den. And I cursed the filthy scum and their rotten colony. They were like the creatures at the Rift, I reckoned. Hardly human. And they had their dirty hands on the trees now. Every single one of those saplings. A hundred years of stealing from GenTech, and now they were stealing from me.

"They question you?" I asked, my head throbbing, my arms numb.

"Aye," Crow said. "They poked at me. Picked at me all over."

He meant his legs, of course. They'd made a freak out of him. I remembered how Kade had ogled the bark when we'd been freezing on the side of that lake. And I remembered how a poacher had once prodded Hina in the cornfields, his eyes full of disbelief at the beauty he'd found.

They just steal, I thought. They just scavenge. They're worse even than GenTech. All they do is take, and they don't give back a damn thing.

I sank back against the dirt.

"What they ask you?" I called out.

"About Promise Island, and how we ended up there. About your mother. And about your old man."

"What you tell 'em?"

"Everything. You will, too. You'll see. I'm telling you, don't fight them. Not now. Gotta bide our time."

"Yeah? That what you been doing?" I shouted. I mean, what a sick freaking joke. "Biding your time while you dragged your ass behind us?"

"Take it easy, Banyan."

"We could have used some help, you know."

"I couldn't walk."

"Walked good when you had the trees, though," I yelled. "And you could have done something in the tunnel. You had Namo. What happened to you being a warrior?"

"They were gonna kill you, man. 'Less I gave up."

There he went again, acting like he was my friend.

"So where is Namo, anyway?" I said, picturing the mammoth's big, shaggy face and small, blinking eyes. Was he one more miracle the poachers would let rot in a cage?

"Wait," Crow said. "I hear something."

There was a dragging sound and the clink of metal. Sounded like padlocks crunching.

"Alpha?" I screamed, struggling back to the bars so I could see down the passageway. "You there?"

Two poachers hobbled towards my cell. They carried long cornstalks carved like spears, and they wore the gnawed scars of locusts, the mark of the swarms. Hell, one of them had a hole in his cheek.

They jangled at the chains and locks, then yanked the door to my cell open with a rusty screech. One of the men jabbed his spear at my throat while the other leaned down with a plastic canteen.

"Better drink, boy," said the man with the spear.

I took a gulp of the water. Pumped up fresh from beneath that last damn peak, I guess. I sucked another gulp down. Then I sipped awhile longer. And when I'd gotten enough water in me, I leaned back from the canteen and spat in that poacher's face.

The man screwed the cap back on his canteen, and then he slapped me, hard. Bony fingers. Long, dirty nails. I didn't cry out or nothing, though. I'd made up my mind.

I wasn't giving these people a thing.

Crow's eyes shone through the bars of his cage as I got carried down the passageway by those two poacher guards. The other cells were too dark for me to see inside, though. And when I called out again for Alpha, no answer came.

As we turned into a new tunnel, the guards dropped me on the ground and began dragging me behind them, gripping the ropes that tied my feet together and bouncing my aching head through the dirt.

I could see the crooked roots of corn plants in patches above us, sticking out through the ceiling like flaky brown plastic, peeling and thready.

And these poachers were as busy and unruly as that tumbled mess of roots. I watched them all as I got dragged through the tunnels. They were everywhere, scrabbling around in their shabby rags. Barefoot, most of them. Their skin stained with dirt.

Clumps of folk worked their fingers inside oily salvage. Hordes of little kids ran around, crap in their eyes and snot in their noses. It was chaos and noise, and the whole place stank of old piss and sweat, and I hated each one of them. These bastards had stolen any chance that we'd had.

The two guards pulled me though the tunnels, prodding folk aside with their cornstalk spears. And none of those ragged freaks seemed to even notice, just kept their heads down and their eyes turned as I was dragged through the dirt. They were too busy working by the light of their crappy lanterns. Too busy digging and hiding and hoarding their corn.

Folks were sweating as they chipped away at the walls. Making more room to scuttle around with their mine carts and shovels and pickaxes, hidden from the agents and safe from the swarms.

And the folks that weren't digging were taking care of the poaching business. Stripping the husks off stolen cobs, boiling the GenTech-branded kernels in big vats of water.

There were women drying out the corn after they'd cooked it, sorting it in piles and boxes. There were others weaving tools and fabrics from the leftover stalks and husks.

And it almost reminded me of the Kalliq, the way these people used every bit, every precious last resource. But there'd been music and hope in the lives of that ice tribe. And there weren't none of those things down here.

We entered a chamber that was more sprawling than the rest. Even busier, too. Crammed full of people and busting at the seams. I mean, you never seen so many folk jammed together. Was like the worst shantytown, but bundled up and shoved under the ground.

High ceilings in this chamber, and nothing but shadow up there, beyond the white lights. The lanterns were connected by red wires that wrapped around the walls in a thin strip, and below those wires curled that water pipe we'd followed straight into this trap.

Middle of the chamber, there were rusty ladders and a mess of scaffold, and that jumbled tower led all the way up into the dark. Alongside the scaffold ran a pulley system. Nearly a hundred feet to the top, I reckoned. And I figured they'd have hatches up there. Ways out. But I couldn't see the folk working at the top of the scaffold. All I could see was the buckets coming down, filled to the brim with corn.

The guards hauled me through a crowd of scrawny poachers, and when I smashed into the side of an iron vat, boiling water splashed out, steaming on the dirt and scalding my skin.

But still, no one paid me no mind.

Then suddenly, the footsteps around me froze and all the work stopped. Even my guards quit moving.

For a second, the whole place was still.

Because a wailing sound was coming down from one of the side tunnels and echoing all around the chamber. And that sound weren't human. Not even close.

It was the sound of our mammoth. My old pal, Namo.

And I swore to myself, if they were hurting him, if they were causing him pain, then god help who was doing it. Because I didn't need another reason to hate these people. And I only needed one way to get free.

I got yanked to my feet by the guards. And up ahead, set in the dirt on a pair of hinges, was a door made of metal salvaged from the side of a crop duster, the faded GenTech logo in one corner of the once-purple steel. The guard with the hole in his cheek slammed a fist at the metal, pounding at the heavy door and shoving it until it creaked inward.

Then the poacher at my back shoved me forward. My legs were bound together so tight, I had to hop into the room.

And I mean, I call it a room, but all it was really was just a hole in the ground. There was a fire blazing in the center, flames crackling inside a ring of stone, and black smoke leaching up. And I counted nine poachers sat cross-legged in a circle around it.

Some of them had to turn around so they could face me, their eyes boring into mine as the old steel door got sealed behind me with a scrape.

I stared back into those wretched faces. Their features all creased and bitter. Chunks of skin missing. The women no fairer than the men. All of them were short-haired or greasy-haired or had no hair at all. Sunken eyes and scummy teeth.

They were like ugly brothers and sisters. Grown old before their time.

Except for one of them.

CHAPTER THIRTY-NINE

Kade made his most handsome smile as he looked at me. The red flames in the pit burned in his green eyes. He had on long robes made of cornhusks, the color of clay, but he hadn't gotten himself a wash or nothing. He was still painted with grime and grit.

Still, he looked a couple decades younger than the other poachers in that circle, and his teeth shone as he took a fistful of popcorn and shoved it in his mouth. I held his gaze as he licked his fingers and chomped his jaws. His eyes swaggering in their sockets.

"Said you were a field hand," I said. "In some cornhusk city."

"I was." Kade shook back the stiff sleeves of his robe and grasped his stump with his hand. "Until the blades took my fingers."

"So, no poems. No bootlegging. You just squirmed your way down here with the thieves."

"I told you, I traveled all over." He grinned, his mouth swollen full of corn. "A man has to do something with his life."

"This ain't living." I stared at the poachers who hunched around the fire pit. I watched them feeding the flames with cornhusks. The whole room smoky as it was foul.

"But it is you who is the thief," said a woman with metal bracelets on her wrists and slits for eyes. "If everything that's been said is true."

"I ain't a thief."

"Yet you stole," said another of the poachers. "On the island."

"What I took weren't GenTech's to begin with."

"Your father," said the woman with the bracelets. "He was a scientist. He worked for the Executive Chief."

"He was a tree builder. Worked for no one but himself."

"But he worked with your mother once," the woman said. "The Soljah told us. They both worked for GenTech."

"What difference does it make?"

"You said these trees belong to you."

"I said they don't belong to GenTech. And what? You want to give them to the people you been stealing corn from for the last hundred years?"

The woman gazed at me for a moment. Then she gazed into the fire. "We are establishing where these things came from, and who will come looking for them."

"Lord Kade told us these things will grow too strong for the locusts." This freak looked even worse than the others, ribs sticking out like a bony fist, a crown of cornhusks on his head. "He said they'll bear fruit."

Fruit. Just the sound of the word made me spin with hunger. I watched Kade, still throwing back his popcorn. Lord Kade, I guess I should say. The punk that was a poacher lord.

"Hungry?" he asked when he saw me eyeing his corn.

"What about Namo?" I glared at him. "What have you done with him?"

"But what of this fruit?" said the guy with the crown. "Have you seen it, boy? Did you taste it?"

"Hell, yeah, I tasted it. Tastes like cheese and maple syrup and every other flavor GenTech figured out how to brew. And it sits like a rock in your belly. Fills you up inside for a week."

"He's lying," Kade said. "The trees will grow apples. But he's never seen one."

"You sure about that, compadre?"

He started to say something about Zee, the things she had told him. But I cut him off sharp.

"Don't even say her name, you son of a bitch. You betrayed everything Zee stood for."

"You never even knew her." Kade's voice quivered with anger.

"Least I didn't pretend to. Least I didn't use her, like you."

He shot to his feet.

"Sit down, Lord Kade," said the woman with the world's thinnest eyes. She turned to the rest of her cronies. "They belonged to GenTech. They must have been made to grow fruit."

"But where do we plant them?" This from a man with a peeling red scalp. He dug his nails into the dirt beside him.

"A good question, Lord Baxter." The man who wore the cornhusk crown let out a sigh. Like he was all worn out, sitting there on his skinny ass by the fire. "A great gift Lord Kade has brought us. But a great burden also."

"Tell you what," I said. "I'll take them trees off your hands. GenTech won't even know they were here."

"Silence." Bracelets held up her hands, showing us her creased palms, her fingers like claws. "For too long have we feared the might of Vega. For too long have we dreamt of overthrowing the masters of the fields."

"Then this is our chance," rumbled Baxter, rubbing dirt on his scalp. "If these are the only ones. The last trees."

"He burned them," said Kade, pointing his stump at me. "He burned all the rest."

"And there were no others?" said someone who till then had stayed silent. "On the boat?"

"What of the Soljah?" piped up another. "Are there others like him?"

I thought of Alpha. The bit of bark stitched on her belly.

"We need the boy to tell us what he knows about growing them," said Baxter. "The Soljah said he's the only one that can."

And what was this? What lies had Crow told them? Selling me out and screwing me over? Or was he trying to buy me some time?

"It's not just growing them." Bracelets glanced around the circle. "We need help protecting them."

The man with the crown nodded as he watched the fire. "That's why I've summoned our allies," he said quietly.

The woman opened her eyes as wide as she could. "My lord," she whispered, fluttering her bracelets. "I should have been consulted."

Dude just shrugged.

"They will be here," said Baxter, his eyes fixed on the flames. Fingers still rubbing his scalp. "Before evening shadows."

"I can't agree with this course of action." Kade had sat his ass back down, and now he stared across the flames at Baxter and the guy with the crown.

The old prune lifted up the cornhusks on his head and scratched his thin white hair. Then he put the crown back on and closed his eyes. "I, too, wish this could be a prize for us alone. But we must share the spoils, if we are to survive."

"There are other ways, Lord Orlic," said Kade.

"None that offer safety. We need their help."

"Who?" I said, unable to keep quiet any longer. "Who you counting on?"

"An old friend." Orlic opened his eyes, fixed them upon me. "Or friends, I suppose, is more accurate. Pray you're still alive to meet them when they arrive."

"I don't pray for nobody."

"Very well." Orlic let out a big sigh, then straightened his crown. "Guards, bring the boy closer. It's time we found out what he knows."

CHAPTER FORTY

The guards dragged me inside the circle. Right up close to the fire.

"But I can help you," I told them, starting to get panicked. "We should all work together. Share the prize, like you said. Share the burden."

"Yes. Lord Kade told us how you intended to divide the trees." Bracelets wagged her finger at me, rattling her jewelry. "Pirates and Rastas. Bootleggers. The Samurai Five and the Salvage Guild. No mention of the poachers, who refuse to trade for GenTech's corn, and who battle agents every day of their lives."

"Battle? I've run into you people topside," I said, remembering what had happened in the cornfields, when poachers had got their hands on me and Hina, and a poacher had shot Alpha in the gut. "All you do is take. And then you scurry back in your holes."

"Enough," said Orlic from beneath his crown. "We'll not argue with you. You will tell us what you learned from your parents. You will tell us how to keep the young trees alive."

"I'd tell you to go to hell." I stared at all those rag-and-bone lords. "But it looks like you're stuck there already."

The boss man lowered his head, so all I could see was the cornhusks on top of it. And the others followed suit, bending their chins to their chests, like they were afraid of seeing something. Hell, I got plenty afraid, too.

Then the guards grabbed my fists and twisted me up off the ground a few inches, ripping the scraps of clothing that hung on my ribs.

And then, inch by inch, they pressed me forward. Edging my guts to the flames.

I wouldn't scream, I told myself. Not for them. Not for nobody. But the fire bit into me. It gnawed and sizzled, more sharp than hot. And I thought of Zee. Pictured her body spinning towards the lava, her hair blown out in strands around her like spokes on a wheel. And I'd told her I'd take care of the trees for her. I had promised I would. So now I was letting her down in death, as I'd failed her in life. And she'd wanted me to trust people, but I'd trusted Kade, and this is where it had got me.

The pain howled brighter. Fiercer and louder. But I grit my jaw and clamped every part of me shut.

"That's enough," said Orlic. The guards pulled me backwards, and I let myself breathe. "You must tell us, boy. Tell us these secrets you know."

I glanced down at my belly—bright red and scorched white and blistered. I choked back tears. Then I turned to Kade.

"Damn you," I croaked. "We could have made things different."

"He won't tell you," Kade muttered, refusing to look at me. "Unless it's to spare someone close to him."

"Which one?" asked Baxter.

"The only one we've not questioned." Kade stood, straightening his crispy robes around him. "I'll bring her."

"The girl?" someone asked him.

"Yes." Kade stared at me as he said it. "His girl."

I had secrets, but none the poachers wanted. I didn't know a thing about how to get them trees to grow. But Crow had given these freaks something to sink their teeth into. Maybe he was trying to get rid of me. Or maybe he'd thought it might keep me alive.

And it might, I reckoned. If I could think of something, I could trade these bastards for knowledge, and maybe they'd let us go.

But could I leave here without the trees?

I didn't know what should matter most. I didn't have time to plan or no one to talk to. I was stuck, held tight in cornhusk ropes. Facing cornstalk spears and that fire, sweat pouring off me and dripping into the flames.

And when Kade got back, he had Alpha gripped before him. She was tied up like I was, and I could see she'd fared no better than me.

I called to her. But she was blurred and busted, her eyes hardly open. She had a gash on her head and blood on her arms.

Kade wrangled her up beside me, right next to the fire. She had rags wound around her breasts and her belly, and Kade had one of the guards hold her up so he could start to unwrap her. Unpeeling the scraps from her beautiful skin.

I knew they'd see it. Once her rags were unraveled and her belly was revealed. The poachers would see the bark GenTech had spliced to her stomach, where she'd been shot by a poacher—hell, it was their bullet meant she'd needed patching up at all. And now these scum would poke at that bark with their filthy fingers. Study it with their underground eyes.

And then they would most likely burn her for her secrets, I reckoned. Just like they'd burned at me.

"It's all in the timing. In the spring," I lied, picturing the body in the caves of the Kalliq. The dead woman encased in a wooden shell. "You got to know when to plant them."

Kade quit what he was doing. A single scrap of clothing clung to Alpha's body. Like a bandage hanging on a wound.

"When?" said Baxter.

"The first full moon after the snow melts." I just kept making stuff up. "Certain time of night."

Orlic nodded, like what I was saying made perfect sense to him. "Tell us more."

"Not till you let her go. You can keep me here," I said. "You let her go, and I'll help you."

"And give up the one way we can get you to speak?" This was Bracelets. I could feel her thin slice of eyeballs upon me. "You are in no place to negotiate. But we know now how to make you see reason. Guards, help Lord Kade take them back to their cells."

They threw Alpha in a cell, and then hurled me back inside the one I'd woke up in. I landed on my back, staring up at the dirt like I was stuck in a grave.

Kade strode into the cell and slammed the door shut.

"Leave us," he told the guards. "I have a debt to settle with this one."

He wound the chains back in place, fumbling around one-handed until he got the locks sealed. Then he stood over me, blocking the light from the doorway. My eyes got used to the dark quick, though, like I was subterranean already, as used to life underground as these filthy poachers.

I watched as Kade reached inside his cornhusk robes and pulled out a small nylon pouch and dropped it beside me. Then he reached into his robes again and plucked out a knife.

"What you gonna do?" I whispered. "Kill me?"

"And let you off easy?"

"Can't believe you waited this long. That's what you been itching for, ain't it? Except you needed me. Needed all of us. Acting all high and mighty all the damn time, when you're the lowest sort of scum after all."

"So this is it?" he said. "That's all the fight you have in you?"

"Untie me, you cheating bastard. I'll show you a fight."

He knelt beside me. Took the knife to the back of my head and started slicing apart the rope that bound up my hands. My wrists popped free, and I waited as Kade set to cutting the ropes from my ankles. But soon as my legs could move, I swiveled up and bore down on him, pummeling my fists in the knots of his spine.

He spun and wriggled, and I had him pinned down, but Kade was stronger than me. He got the knife between us, grasped in his one bony hand.

"You messed with my sister. And you was gonna burn my girl," I said. "So go ahead and stab me. I'll kill you with my bare hands and that knife in my gut."

"No," Kade whispered. His face all wrong.

I punched him in the mouth. "That's for lying to me."

Then I punched him again. Harder. "That's for Alpha."

Again. "For Crow."

I pulled my fist back. "And this one's for Zee."

But I remembered my sister pulling at me when I'd been beating Kade on that cold beach full of skulls, at the side of the lake. And it distracted me, remembering Zee. Feeling the look that had shone in her eyes.

And then I heard Kade. Hissing and cussing.

"Keep quiet," he kept saying. "Get off me. They'll hear."

I wrapped my hands around his neck. "Drop the knife."

He took the blade and stabbed it in the dirt.

"Let me speak." It was like I'd squeezed the words out of him. His face was all twisted and red. "I had to make certain. Put on a good show. We can't have them doubt me."

I took my hands off his throat. How do you trust someone who's been so full of lies?

"I was gone so long." His voice was all shredded, and he sucked at each breath. "And I'm young. Just a nobody. It's only the trees that got me onto the Council."

I watched as he pulled himself back to the wall, wheezing and choking. He'd started sweating, and he smeared a dirty hand across his brow.

"Come on," he said, trying to breathe normal. "Save your anger. You have to see what I'm doing."

"But these are your people."

"The trees." He shook his head. "They're not safe."

I crept to the cell door and peered out through the bars. I called for Crow. Alpha.

No answer at all.

I rubbed my ankles, worked at my wrists. Then I glanced back at Kade.

"So spit it out, Cornhusk."

"We have to save them," he said. "The saplings."

"You're gonna give them up?"

"I want one of them. You aren't leaving me with nothing. But the rest can't stay here. Not now."

"Why? These old friends of Orlic's that are coming?"

Kade covered his face with his hand.

"Who is it?" I asked him, and he made a moaning sound. "Tell me, damn it."

"He made it," Kade said.

"Who?"

"He got out of that crater."

"Harvest?"

Kade winced when I said the man's name.

CHAPTER FORTY-ONE

Kade wiggled a tooth free from his gum, then flicked it across the cell floor as he slumped against the wall beside me.

"Harvest's a hard man to kill," I said. "Hell of an ally you poachers rustled up."

"He's not my ally."

"So, what? You a poacher or ain't you? Shit, how am I supposed to believe a word that you say?"

"Orlic used to pick corn with him."

"They were field hands?"

"Used to be," Kade said. "Harvest clawed his way up through the ranks. Started to work as an agent."

"Then what? Decided he could do more damage on his own?"

"They say he knew GenTech needed bodies, so he started to snatch people off the plains, trading them for machinery and the army they made him."

"Right," I muttered. "The replicants."

Kade scratched his left arm, rubbed its stump. "I want to see every one of them dead. You know I do. All of them. All of him."

"So how come your people trust him?"

"Because he never touched the poachers. In all the years he spent taking people, he never bothered the people down here. He knew our location—could have sold us out to the agents. Traded us all." Kade shook his head. "But half the people here were field hands once. Just like him."

"Well, you sure made it nice and easy for him, didn't you? All the trees in one place."

"No. I'm going to kill him. I'll make him pay for what he did to Zee—for everything." Kade sucked at his torn lips. "I don't know. Maybe Orlic's done us a favor."

"A favor? We'll be surrounded."

"There's still a chance."

"Ever feel like you're all out of chances?"

"We can't give up," he said. "Not yet. I told you Zee said you're important. That you could bring people together. She said they'd believe in you because you'd never give up, no matter what."

"Right. A real glutton for punishment."

"They made contact with Harvest the day before yesterday. We still have some time."

"I was out for two days?" I felt the cuts on my face. My head bruised and swollen. "You poachers kick a guy good when he's down."

"It's no worse than you've dished out to me."

"So we're even now?"

"Come on. We need each other." Kade reached out his hand. "I cared about her, you know. Your sister. I still do, man. I can still feel what she was like." He breathed slow and deep, like he was giving all he could to keep steady. "She was like one of the saplings. Fragile and special, but strong when it mattered the most."

"You were leading us into a trap."

"I didn't know we were going to end up in these tunnels."

"But we did," I said. "And you'd have stuck Zee in the flames of that pit, if that Council told you to do it."

"You can't say that."

"You did it to me." I pointed at the burns on my stomach. "You'd have done it to Alpha."

"I called your bluff, that's all."

"That ain't all, and you know it," I said. "And I ain't shaking your one lousy hand."

"You still need me, bro."

"Stop calling me that."

I looked at him. Dressed up in his cornhusk robes. A poacher and a thief.

But hadn't he also been a friend to me? Hadn't he pulled me out of harm's way when I'd needed it, yanking me clear of the lava when I'd been slipping off the side of that cliff?

"We have to get the trees out," he said.

"For Zee?" I scowled at him.

"For everyone. It's like you said before. Everyone rising up together to take on GenTech. With me on the Council, I could get the poachers on board. These tunnels could come in handy, going into battle against the forces of Vega. And the poachers have food for the troops—more than the bootleggers could ever provide."

"I don't want to hear no more of your talking, unless it's you telling me a plan to get out of this place."

"Our scouts contacted Harvest's people out on the plains. They said he'd be here by nightfall on the third day, so that means tonight."

"Well, shit."

"He'll have a small group with him, but not too many. He'll want to keep a low profile in the fields, stay out of sight so he can sneak through the corn. He's on good terms with GenTech, but he won't want to draw their attention—he wants those trees for himself."

"But even if he don't bring an army, how do we get the trees past your people?" I said. "There's thousands of them."

"That's why we have to be stealthy."

I thought about it. Stealthy weren't something we'd been real good at. But I reckoned it had to be worth a shot.

"And you'll come with us?" I asked him. "If we get out?"

"No." Kade shook his head. "It can't look like I helped you escape. But I keep one of the trees here, and I'll rally the poachers to our cause. I belong here. They took me in when no one else would have me."

I wondered then if Kade and I were so different. We'd both been born to struggle, and both wound up on our own.

"They broke me," he whispered. "The crystal. These people got me clean."

"All right," I said. "Stay in this hole if you want to. But how do I get the hell out?"

"I'm working on it."

"Work on it faster. And you gotta tell Alpha and Crow. Whatever you come up with."

"I'll tell them. Just be ready when the time comes."

He staggered to his feet, robes rustling. He retrieved his knife and that small pouch he'd thrown on the floor. Then he handed them to me and started working at the locks on the door.

"What's this?" I asked him, squeezing the little nylon bag.

"It's for your belly," he said, not turning around. He clinked and rattled the locks until he got the door open. "If someone peers in here, try to make it look like those ropes are still on you. And keep the knife stashed down in your boot." Then he stepped into freedom and sealed me inside.

After he'd gone, I concealed the blade like he'd said to and backed into the shadows, winding the ropes around my legs in a way so that I could kick them loose quick. Then I tore open the pouch Kade had given me, and damned if it weren't full of that good Kalliq mud the Healer had packed around the saplings and roots. Kade must have scooped up some of it, though there hadn't been a whole lot left. Must have figured I needed it bad, I reckon. And I did need it. I grabbed that fistful of gray slime and smeared it on my belly, rubbing it into the patches of red, the blisters and black.

The mud felt soothing, like a cool hand in a fever, and I let its goodness seep into me, cutting the sting. And I almost busted out crying as I sat there in the cell, remembering the Healer telling me her name, her beautiful smile falling away as her body turned stiff in my arms.

I wondered how deep Kade's feelings for my sister had run. Had he cared for her like I cared for Alpha? Yeah, I thought. Maybe he had. And maybe I was going to lose my girl, like Kade had lost his. Now or come springtime, no matter how hard I fought against it.

I felt shut down as I slumped there in the darkness. It was like I'd never been more trapped. GenTech above, poachers crawling all around me, and King Harvest creeping through the corn with his copies, heading straight for the trees.

CHAPTER FORTY-TWO

I came awake in a panic as the metal hinges screeched, the door to my cell flying open. I hoped it was Kade. It had to be Kade.

But it was Baxter.

He stood there for a moment, illuminated by the lights behind him, scratching his bald red scalp, then chewing on his fingernails. Looked like he was making his mind up about something. But then he gestured in the guards.

They found my ropes untied and began binding the cornhusks back in place until Baxter stopped them. "There's no time," he said. "Just bring him. Now."

The passageway was loaded with poachers, some with cornstalk spears, others carrying machetes. They had other cell doors yanked open, and I watched as they dragged Crow out through one of them. His arms were bound up tight, but his legs were free. And as the guards shoved him around, I saw Crow could stand again. He was even able to walk.

Up ahead of us, they hauled out Alpha. She was conscious now and thrashing around. And Kade had said he'd tell the others the plan, but what was it? Just sit tight and wait, he'd said. And where the hell was he now?

"Come on," Baxter called to the guards. "Let's get moving. Quick as we can."

A spear jabbed my back, pushing me along, and then they bundled us out of the passage and down through the tunnels. Hell, they practically ran us around the place. Half pulling us, half pushing. We were all shoved up together, about a dozen guards surrounding us, with Baxter out in front, his flaking red scalp leading the way.

"What're you grinning at?" I said, glancing up at Crow.

"I be walking, man," he said. And sure enough, he was moving them legs pretty smooth.

"Yeah, well, you're walking into a whole mess of danger."

"Least I ain't being carried. And look at these things now."

The purple thread Alpha had cut off the side of our mammoth had done more than bind Crow's legs back together—it had started to grow shaggy all over the bark.

"So, what? Now you're a furry sort of freak?"

"Almost like Namo be here with me," he said. "Giving me strength. I feel all right about, too. Like a lion, no?"

"Look at you, being all positive."

"And I can feel my legs getting stronger. I can feel it more each minute that goes by."

"Better enjoy this walk then. Seeing as it might be our last."

"Banyan," Alpha called, trying to push through the throng to reach me, but the poachers kept holding her back.

I craned my neck, trying to catch another glimpse of her. And I remembered again how it had been a damn poacher who'd shot her in the cornfields. And now she had that GenTech bark on her belly. The start of a disease.

And what about Crow? His legs seemed to have been somehow altered, changed by the fur they'd been splinted up with, but would he still suffer the same fate as the woman who'd been all wrapped in bark, sealed up and suffocated in the spring?

I had one hope of finding a way to stop that from happening to Crow, to Alpha. I had one desperate idea, that final trick up my sleeve, my plan for the last tree. But to fix anything, to put my plan into action, to find a cure, I had to get out of here, and I needed those saplings.

So where the hell was Kade when we needed him?

"I have to tell you something," Alpha called. "Banyan. It's about what I saw."

"Silence," said Baxter.

I saw Alpha try to wriggle free of the guards that were holding her.

"Beneath the peaks," she cried. "Beneath those mountains."

"Guards," Baxter yelled. "Keep them quiet."

One of those filthy grubbers smothered Alpha's mouth with his hand. There were too many of them surrounding us, rattling their weapons. Not a thing we could do.

I glanced up at Crow, and he was gazing straight ahead, and he'd quit smiling. Maybe he'd remembered what we were up against. Or perhaps he was remembering the things he'd seen himself below the Speak It Mountains. The vision he'd been screaming about when we found him in the water. Something about a lion's mane and an army, and something buried beneath the South Wall.

We entered the sprawling chamber with the high ceilings and the scaffold. Poachers everywhere, milling around and keeping busy. But there were too many of us to be ignored now. The workers quit shucking their corn and digging their ditches, their rusty mine carts rolled to a stop. Folk watched us awhile, then wiped the sweat from their faces, and then they turned back to their backbreaking work.

The heavy steel door to the Council's chamber was already cracked open, and the guards shoved us towards it, then squeezed us inside. The room was just as smoky and foul as before—the fire still roaring in the center, flames and shadows dancing across the Council's faces. I looked around for Kade. But then my eyes found the trees. They were right there near the fire. The last six saplings.

And they were dried up and shriveled in the dirt.

Looked like if you grabbed that bundle of sticks, they'd turn to ash in your fingers. The last bit of Pop was like a punctured sack, as if he were now no more than a wilted womb, or the remnant shell of a swollen seed, the bark brittle and ruptured.

"What the hell?" I yelled, shoving guards out of my way, wrestling their spears from my path.

"Let him closer," said one of the lords.

They'd set the trees in the middle of the circle. Laid them on top of the plastic pack, right beside the flames.

I collapsed on my knees before them.

"We think it's cold," said Baxter, when he saw me tug the clump of saplings away from the smoky pit.

And he was right. The saplings felt cool to the touch. Like they were sucking the life out of my fingers.

"What happened to them?" asked Kade, kneeling beside me, all crunchy in his cornhusk robes. And it seemed to me like the trees were as dead as the husks Kade wore wrapped around him. Just as dead but twice as fragile.

And I had no idea what to do.

The tank had protected the trees. The liquid and the lights and GenTech's science. And when the tank was shattered and the liquid was gone, the Healer's wisdom had nursed Pop's saplings back to health.

"The Kalliq mud?" I said.

"That's all of it." Kade pointed at the patches of gray powder that clung to the parched stems. Looked like everything had been squeezed dry and used up.

I reached to my belly, and the dried mud flaked off the burns where I'd smeared it. Nothing left we could give to those saplings. Nothing around us but crappy corn roots in the ceiling and mile after mile of dust.

"Did your mother warn you, boy?" Orlic asked, gazing at the trees from across the fire. "Did she say this might happen?"

I glanced back through the guards, searching for Alpha.

"Something to do with GenTech's science?" said Kade.

"It ain't science," I told him. "It's nature. It's life and death."

"So they are dying," Orlic muttered.

"Of course they're dying," I said. "Any fool can see that."

We needed Zee. She'd spent more time with my mother than I had. She'd hung around on Promise Island, watched the Creator at work. And she'd read books about the old world. She knew about the way things had been.

I thought of all the things my father had told me. About the way life was before the Darkness and the locusts, before trees were only welded from steel and woven with plastic and wired with lights.

"All I know is they need water," I said. "Like the corn. Water and the sun."

I stared at the saplings. Here lay my hope of saving Alpha, and Crow. And these were the trees we were going to surround the whole world with? The trees I was going to break up so we could bring folk together? One world. One forest. It was like Zee had told me, we had to all work to make that happen. We had to trust each other. All of us. And it had to start now.

"Bring water," Baxter called out. "Quickly."

I curled my fingers under Pop's remains, lifting him real gentle, holding the wilted bits to my chest. "We gotta get up top. He needs sunlight."

"But the moon is rising." Harvest's voice crept in through the doorway. "And all is now dark."

CHAPTER FORTY-THREE

The room was silent for a moment, but for the crackle of the fire.

"I should thank you, tree builder," Harvest said.

Everyone had swiveled to face him. He stood in the doorway, his skin as pale as his drab plastic clothes, and he seemed to blend with the dirt down here. Just a streak of gray staining the brown.

"Yes." He nodded and rubbed his hands together. "I'm grateful. They're still waiting for you in the north, you know. GenTech. Looking rather desperate about things, plugging the passage through the Rift, and not wishing to lose hope that they'll find you. And how would I have gotten these trees past all of those troops? GenTech has begun not to trust me, it seems." Harvest tried to smile, but his scarred face couldn't do it. "Of course, I don't trust them, either. But now you've saved me the trouble of smuggling the trees home."

"They're sick," I said, holding up the bundle of saplings. "They need help."

"So do you, tree builder." Harvest stepped into the room, and six of his replicants filed in behind him. "So do you."

I glanced at Kade, hoping he had a plan and he just hadn't told me. I peered through the poacher guards for Alpha. Crow.

"Harvest," Orlic said, standing. "We're much obliged for your haste." He actually said that. He thanked him.

"But of course." Harvest had begun striding towards me. "The very least I could do. Though your hospitality is not what it was, I must say. I would have preferred my men to remain armed upon entry."

I remembered what Kade had said about the king having once been just a field hand. So I guess he'd learned to speak fancy as he worked his way up the line. Because that's what he talked like—real fancy, like a rich freak from Vega. Instead of like a thief who'd been born to work in the fields.

Man was a fake. A slave who had made slaves of others. A king that built himself an empire by snatching folk from their families and homes.

And he was more than all those things. Because he'd stolen any chance I had of knowing my sister. And now here he was, coming to steal any hope we'd had the nerve to hold onto.

I watched the replicants behind him, the carbon copies with their lifeless eyes. And what was it Hina had once told me? GenTech could copy the body but not the mind. So what about the black pit of the king's soul? Did that get copied, too?

Two poachers staggered into the room behind the Harvesters, carrying an iron vat, water splashing on their filthy clothes. The men froze for a moment, but Kade beckoned to them, and slowly they shuffled towards me, half dragging their vat through the dirt, their arms looking like they might snap from the strain.

As Harvest stepped closer, I took the frail saplings and coiled them inside the pack, being as careful with them as I could.

He stopped when he was just two feet from me. Then Harvest searched me over with his beady eyes, the crusty scars hanging off his face, the skin like melted plastic.

"You've fought bravely," he said. "But the trees belong to me now."

"Hang on, old friend." This was Orlic. "There's enough to be shared between us."

"Be quiet, you fool." Harvest's eyes stayed glued on me as he snapped at the poacher lord. Then he held his hand out towards me.

I extended the pack towards him, my fists shaking. And Harvest reached out with his wretched fingers. The saplings almost in his grasp.

And that's when I dropped the pack and grabbed him by the arm.

"They need sunlight," I said, pulling him towards me. "Not shadows."

I yanked Harvest forward. Hard. Then whipped him past me with every bit of strength that I had.

And I hurled that murdering bastard right into the fire.

I scooped up the pack and shouldered it as I pulled the knife from my boot. It was like one movement how I did it. And then I was darting forward. Slicing my way through the poacher guards and heading for the Harvesters at the door.

There were screams behind me, and I turned my head for an instant, saw Kade grappling with Harvest in the fire, his cornhusk robes going up in flames. Other poacher lords were trying to break them up, but I couldn't think about the fact that Harvest was still alive and kicking and Kade needed my help. Because up ahead of me, the replicants were closing in and closing their empty hands into fists.

No weapons. Not this time. So I'd see what these boys could do in a bare-knuckle fight.

I charged past the two poachers with the vat full of water, and I swung my knife at the Harvesters, trying to get some space so I could make for the door.

I called for Crow. Hollered for Alpha. But I couldn't see nothing except those dull copies around me. I couldn't move the knife fast enough. They were getting closer, ready to rush me all at once.

I slammed into the one between me and the doorway, stabbing at him as the others pressed tight, their hands at my neck, fingers grabbing at the pack.

I spotted Alpha. Her arms still bound in the cornhusk ropes, two poacher guards holding her back. And she was straining and screaming, but I couldn't hear her above all the damn noise. And I couldn't do nothing for her. The Harvesters were crawling all over me. Tightening their grip, like they were all fingers of the same giant fist.

I slammed and bucked, and we smashed into the dudes with the vat of water, spilling it clear across the dirt with a crash.

But then I heard a new sound. Above all the turmoil. I heard a bellow and a boom. And then the Harvesters were being peeled off me, one after another. They were being ripped apart and thrown through the air.

I broke free. Spun around, so I could see what was happening.

And it was Crow that was happening. Holy shit, it was Crow.

Bide our time, he'd said. Save our strength. And you best believe he had meant it. Because he weren't just standing, or walking, and he weren't just towering ten feet tall. He was spinning and kicking. Mowing down Harvesters and poacher guards with those big purple tree-legs. His wrists were still bound together, but it was like he didn't even need them—dude moved like a blur, mammoth and tree and man all mixed up together.

And nothing could stand in his way.

I yanked at the straps of the pack, cinching it against me as I raced over to Alpha. Sliding into the dirt and slashing her ropes apart with my knife. She grabbed two machetes off the ground and leapt up beside me.

But there was Kade and Harvest, dragging themselves out of the fire and rolling in the dirt to extinguish the flames. Kade's robes had gone up in smoke, leaving him all red and singed at the edges. But Harvest's clothes had just seemed to melt against him, leaving him more smoke-like than ever as he scrambled to his feet and stared into my eyes.

It was Kade I wanted to get a good look at, though. How could we get out of here without him?

"They'll head for the scaffold," he yelled, though the poacher lords were too frail to run after us, and all the guards had been beat down by Crow.

Kade stared at me, trying to make sure I was getting the message. "They'll head for the scaffold," he screamed. "They'll head for the fields."

Didn't need to tell me a third time.

We bolted through the door as Harvest rallied and the poacher guards and the replicants began squirming upright. I hacked my blade at the ropes on Crow's wrists, setting his arms free, and he jammed the steel door shut behind us.

"What about them?" cried Alpha, pointing into the sprawling chamber.

The workers had turned still at the sight of us, but slowly they began hoisting up their shovels, flicking open switchblades, brandishing hacksaws and pickaxes. And there were so many of them crowding towards us. A whole mob between us and that tower of ladders we needed to reach.

"Hope you saved some of that strength," I said to Crow.

"Just stay behind me. Both of you. And give me one of them swords."

Alpha threw a machete up to the Soljah, and damned if he weren't something, stepping in front of us, like he was putting us all on his back.

I tugged the pack even tighter to my shoulders, felt the remains of Pop hang against me.

I'll get you out of here, I wanted to tell him. I'll get you some water. Show you some sun.

"What about Kade?" asked Alpha.

"He ain't coming with us," I said. "But he wants a tree. He told me."

"No," Crow said as we inched forward. "I'm not leaving a tree with these scum."

I had my knife in a white-knuckle grip as the crowd shook their weapons and tools and marched closer. And it weren't just those poachers ahead of us, neither. The steel door was rattling and clanking. And once it flew open, we'd be surrounded. Too many poachers on too many sides.

And Harvest, of course.

Unless Kade could figure out some way to kill him.

"Give me your knife, bud," said Alpha, taking one hand off her machete.

"I'm gonna need it."

"No time to argue. You trust me or not?"

She reached her hand out, and I gave up my blade, just as this battle was about to go down. But if there was one person I trusted, it would always be Alpha.

She pitched the knife at the closest dirt wall. The blade spun through the air, and when it hit the wall, it sparked up and smoked as it sank. She'd cut those red wires. Busted the circuit. And one by one, the white lights that lit up the chamber blinked out like broken stars.

Until every star had turned black.

We plunged forward through the darkness just as the door peeled open behind us. I could smell the smoke from the fire pit. Hear the yells of the poachers. And then I heard Harvest's voice, too.

I could sense the mess of bodies before us. Blades and shovels, ready to strike. But we kept charging, blind and desperate. Alpha letting out a battle cry that seemed to turn things bright for a moment. Her voice setting the darkness ablaze.

Then we hit the first wave of poachers. I could see their shapes in the gloom. Metal scraped upon metal. Sharp steel clanged and clashed. Crow and Alpha slashed their machetes, fending off the poachers' tools, hacking a pathway through the mob, until we were swallowed and wriggling inside it.

The three of us kept spinning, punching and thrusting, and we never quit moving. But once we got through the crowd, we weren't at the scaffold—just a dirt wall, and we were cornered against it.

Crow spun around with one leg out, knocking folk back like they were nothing. Giving us a little time to escape.

"Wait," I yelled, still at the wall. "Crow, wait."

I'd hit something. Stubbed my foot on the old iron pipe that ran all the way up here, pumping the water from beneath those upside-down peaks.

"Bust it open," I screamed, and I kicked at the pipe so it rang out in the darkness.

Crow took two giant strides and was right there beside me, swiping behind him with his machete as he took aim, and then boom, the pipe crunched and crumpled. He kicked it again. Two more times. It punctured, and he smashed it wide open. There was water everywhere, gushing out of that pipe so fast, it damn near smacked me onto my ass.

But I stayed on my feet as the dirt turned to mud. Slippery and thick. I started to try to push through the crowd. Head down. Flailing around with no way to see. I just followed Crow, battling onward. I could hear Alpha behind me. But I lost my footing.

And then I went down.

CHAPTER FORTY-FOUR

I hugged the bag of trees against me as the water pooled all around. Feet trampling and stomping me. I was trapped beneath the mob and the mud. I called out. Screamed. And then Crow was above me. Stooping down and grabbing me up with one hand.

I landed in a pile on his shoulders as he busted through the dark. It was chaos. Carnage. Crow had the machete in one hand and his other hand clenched in a fist. But it was those legs of his that made him unstoppable, whirling and kicking, crunching every bone and skull in our path. Freak of science or force of nature, either way, all I could do was hold on.

I peered back through the darkness. Watching behind me. Searching for Alpha.

"Crow," I called, but he knew what I was thinking.

"No, man. We gotta go," he yelled. "We gotta take care of business."

And that's what Alpha would do. She'd push on for those saplings, even if it meant leaving one of us behind. That's what she'd been trying to tell me—that this thing was bigger than me and her being together. It was bigger than all of us in the end.

We hit the scaffold, and Crow was swinging up the side of it. I crawled off his shoulders and made my way onto that column of plastic and steel. And then there I was, climbing upward, my old man on my back, just as I had once been on his back, bundled in a blanket, bouncing around as he worked.

I peered up at the blackness that hid the way out. And below us was the gnashing of weapons and the flashing of steel. A mob raging and the water rising. A hurricane trapped in a hole. I hung there for a second, staring down at the frenzy, like I was caught between two versions of me.

"Crow," I shouted. And this time there was no question. No hesitation.

There was only something that I had to do.

I unhitched the straps from my shoulders, hoisted the pack from my back. And I didn't look up as I held up that bundle. I just waited till Crow had it and the weight disappeared.

"Take care of him," I said, staring down at the war we had started. An army of poachers against an army of one.

"All right, man," Crow said. "You take care of you."

And then he was gone, racing up the ladders.

But I wasn't leaving no one behind.

I slid down a few sections of scaffold, grabbed onto a rope from the pulley, and leapt off the side. Swinging out through darkness. Sailing back into the fight.

I landed in the thick of things and ended up on a poacher's back, and he snarled beneath me. I wrestled him for the shovel he was holding.

I wrestled him, and I won.

"Alpha," I screamed. But too much was happening. I thrashed around, trying to keep the scaffold close enough so I'd know where it was.

The water was coming thick and fast, up to my knees now. Folks were yelling and running. Trying to grab up buckets of corn.

Then gunshots cracked in the air above us.

"Bring him to me," Harvest called, firing another shot high over the storm of bodies. "Find the boy and bring him. Now."

I crouched down in the water, scooped up a fist of mud, and smeared it on my face. In the dark and the dirt, I could be just another poacher, I reckoned. So I stood back up, tightened my grip on the shovel. Things were getting quiet now. Folks were still scrambling about, but they were too frightened to make much noise.

Son of a bitch had a gun. Total game-changer. And I reckoned the poachers might rustle up more firearms—they'd sure had guns when I'd run into them topside.

I glanced up, hoping Crow had almost made it to freedom. Hoping he'd made it out into the corn.

"Tree builder," Harvest called. "Did you think I wouldn't recognize your friend?"

I stopped breathing.

"Took me a moment." Harvest's voice was clear as it was cruel. "But I remember the face of anyone who tries to kill me. And how could I forget this would-be sniper from the crater? Dirty red hair and angry green eyes."

So Harvest had recognized Kade. And now he was going to try to bait me with the life of some poacher who'd betrayed us. Some punk who'd lied to us.

But Kade was also the struggler who'd hauled me up the side of the rocks and saved my life at the Rift.

"Let him go," I hollered, shouting real loud so that Harvest could find me. I was the one he wanted. And I couldn't hide in the dark while he put a gun to Kade's head.

But all of a sudden, the darkness was ending. The lights flashed back on the walls and burned bright all around us. A blast of electrics, like the last gasp of a world coming back to life.

And that weren't the only thing that happened.

There was a trumpeting sound. One more miracle. Because it weren't just the trees that we'd found, after all.

Namo came crashing out of a side tunnel like a rumble of thunder. He had his tusks pointed straight ahead and his head bowed low. And riding on his back, her machete held high and her face splattered with blood, was Alpha.

I spotted Harvest through the crowd, maybe twenty yards from me. His deformed face unable to contain its confusion as it wrinkled and clenched. He had Kade pinned next to him with one hand, and his other hand gripped a revolver—a crummy old world weapon, not

Harvest's usual style, though this gun could kill Kade all the same.

The lights pulsed on the walls, illuminating the poachers' faces, full of shock and wonder, their eyes stretched wide with fear, as Namo galloped onward, surging through the mob and the muck, splashing through the water, Alpha waving her machete, her battle cry melding with the wail of the beast.

Harvest trained the gun on the mammoth, and Alpha pinned herself down in the thick fur, holding on tight. He let off a shot, then another. Emptying his gun of its bullets. Each bullet cracking and booming and bouncing right off.

"Kade," I screamed, my voice lost in the sound of the stampede. He was grappling with Harvest as the mammoth bore down on them.

"Move," Alpha shouted, but I knew Kade weren't moving. There was no way he could let that bastard run.

Kade punched Harvest in the gut and sent him spinning. Then he clutched Harvest with his one hand, holding him steady, as Namo skewered a tusk straight through the king's chest.

The mammoth roared as he lifted his head, and when he ground to a halt, he reared up and threw Harvest's body high in the air.

Harvest landed in a heap, and the crowd cleared away, fleeing from the dead man and the unchained beast.

But I'd seen Harvest killed before. I'd seen him shot dead by Jawbone. At least, that's what I'd thought I had seen. I ran through the mud and the water, shoving my way through the bodies. I reached Namo and stroked his side, letting him know it was me that was there.

Then I crept up to the mangled heap, turned Harvest over. His chest had been gouged open. His lungs were pierced and crushed. And his jagged face rippled with agony. Every part of him shaking as he choked on one last breath.

Kade knelt beside me with his hand clenched in a fist, as if he were still holding Harvest. As if he were throttling him and meant to never quit watching him die.

"You fools." Harvest coughed and shuddered. His scarred features all ruptured with pain. "Now nothing can stand in GenTech's way. They will take the trees. And they will crush you. All of you."

The light drained from his eyes, and then he was still. But it had been there—the spark, like the scars, that let me know it had really been him.

I spun up to face Alpha. The shovel still clamped in my hand.

"He's gone," I said.

"Told you we'd kill him."

"No." I pointed the shovel up at the scaffold. "I mean Crow."

CHAPTER FORTY-FIVE

Kade called an end to the fighting. He rounded up what was left of the Harvesters, and he put the poachers to work, patching the water lines and digging ditches to drain the flood. He had Namo led away, then took me and Alpha before the Council, and there we huddled around the fire pit, facing the anguished looks on their sunken faces.

"Crow's gone," Kade said. "Killed six entrance guards and took one of Harvest's speeders. Disappeared through the fields."

"He'll go east," said Baxter. "Head for Niagara."

"Moves fast when he gets his hands on those trees." Kade stared at me. "Doesn't he?"

"It's all right," I told them. "He'll keep them safe."

"Yes." Orlic's face was a thorny scowl below his cornhusk crown. "I'm sure he'll deliver them safely to the Soljahs."

He was pissed, of course. We'd killed his old friend from the cornfields, and Crow had made off with the saplings. But these poachers couldn't punish me and Alpha. They knew it. And I knew it.

We were the only hope they had left.

"I'll bring you one," I said. "I'll bring one back here. I promise."

"And what makes you think the Rastas will give one up?" Orlic took a handful of cornhusks and threw them in the fire.

"Because we're gonna band together," I said. "Rise up against GenTech. You, too, if you'll join us. Imagine it—getting out of the dirt. Enough food for everyone to share, and no one tribe to control it. Imagine forests growing free. Clean air, clean water. Plenty to eat."

There was doubt on their faces. There was doubt in their eyes. And I started to ask myself the same damn questions. Would the Soljahs be willing to work with the rest of us? What sort of welcome would we receive if we made it across the river and reached Waterfall City?

But Crow would be there, I thought. And I'd trusted him before, so now I had to trust him again.

"Kade will go with you," said Bracelets. "He'll go with you and make sure one of the trees comes back here."

"Kade helped them kill Harvest," said another. "How can we trust him?"

"You saw him put that gun on me." Kade stared at Orlic. "And he'd have taken what he wanted and left us with nothing, if it had been up to you."

"Return with a tree, lad," Orlic said to him, his eyes softening as they studied the fire. "And you will be pardoned. But you'll never sit on this Council again."

"We'll take the rest of the speeders they came in on." Kade touched the burns on his arms, from where he'd wrestled Harvest in the fire, and I couldn't see his eyes, but I reckon they simmered full of rage. I heard him try to breathe through it. A poacher lord for three days, and now his robes had been turned to ashes, and he was in rags again. Just like us.

"What about Namo?" I said.

"The mammoth?" Orlic frowned.

"He could prove useful," said Baxter.

"He already has," I told them. "And you should let him go."

I couldn't argue them down about it. They wanted to keep the beast chained up and put him to work. And in the end, there weren't no way he could come with us, anyway, I reckoned. Nor was there a way he could get home. Hell, for all we knew, every mammoth had perished in that battle between the Kalliq and the Harvesters, and Namo had no home to get back to at all.

I had Orlic swear they'd keep the chains off him. That lord needed me too much not to give me his word. And I didn't know how much faith I should put in that poacher's word, but what other choice did I have?

He let the three of us take Namo back down the tunnels, leading the mammoth to a spot where he could stay out of the way. Alpha leaned her head against him as she staggered along, worn out and busted as I'd ever seen her. Covered in dirt and blood, and her grip still on her machete, as if at any moment, the poachers might turn on us again.

We got to a crappy dugout, and Kade set down a bucket of corn, the tiny GenTech logos on the kernels the same purple as the mammoth's fur. It was tight in there. Namo had to keep his head stooped, and it weren't no place fit for him.

"He's gonna get lonely," I muttered.

"But he's safe," Kade said. "And what else can we do?"

I stared up at Namo's big, shaggy face, and he just blinked down at me. Then I reached up a hand to his trunk, patting him as he brought his head close to mine.

"We'll come back," I told him. "Get you out of here."

"You think he's all that's left?" Alpha asked. "The last of the mammoths?"

"I sure hope not." I thought of the walls tumbling into the Kalliq's crater. The bullets and rocks raining down. Harvest had got out, though. So maybe some of the Kalliq did, too.

"Kids will come and see him," Kade said. "There are good people down here."

"Bet they put him to work." Alpha shook her head. "Soon as we're out of sight."

I leaned against Namo, and I'll be damned if that big ball of fur didn't wrap his great trunk around all three of us, curling us against him and holding us close.

"There'll be hell to pay," Alpha whispered, her voice muffled in Namo's fur. "If these bastards eat him."

"These bastards are my people," said Kade. "And they'll show him respect."

Namo pressed us even tighter together, then uncoiled his shaggy trunk and stamped his way into the corner of the dugout. There was hardly enough room for him to turn around.

And he was like the trees, I reckoned. Something beautiful left behind. So there'd have to come a time when he was no longer hidden. You don't do the world any favors if you hide things away.

"No one's gonna eat him," I said, though my voice trembled as we started back through the labyrinths, and I wondered if I'd ever have a chance to see that mammoth again. "Reckon you gotta have faith in folk."

"Yeah?" Alpha said. "How's that working out for you?"

"Reckon it's too soon to say."

"And what about Crow?" she said. "You think he's gonna give up those trees when we get there?"

"Guess you're gonna have to leave persuading him up to me," I said.

"What the hell does that mean?"

I felt Alpha staring at me, but I turned to Kade.

"We'll catch up with you," I told him.

"Don't get lost," he said, pushing past us, and I waited till he'd disappeared around the bend.

"You know I don't want to do this." I couldn't even look at Alpha as I said it.

"Do what?"

"Split." The word came out weak, when I'd meant to sound strong.

"Split?"

"You and me," I said. "We gotta say goodbye."

CHAPTER FORTY-SIX

I stood in that tunnel as the white lights throbbed on and off again, as if they were counting the seconds until one of us could speak.

"What're you talking about, bud?" Alpha said finally. She tried smiling, as if I'd been joking. But her mouth couldn't make the smile last.

"You have to gather your armies. Every pirate on the plains who can fight. Once GenTech finds out people are banding together, that we've got the trees, we're going to have to be ready for them. And I gotta get to Waterfall City. Make sure those saplings get split up, for everyone, like we planned."

"We'll do it together."

"There's no time."

"I'll make time."

I put my hand on her face. "All I want is to be with you. You know that."

"Don't—"

"I love you," I said. And I needed to keep steady. I took her in my arms, to feel her against me, and so she'd not see if my tears started to fall.

"Then why would you leave me?" Alpha trembled as I held her. She was sobbing so hard, and there weren't a thing I could do.

"I have to."

"Because of the trees."

"Because of the people who need them. Because everyone deserves them. It's bigger than us. And it ain't fair, none of it's fair. But it's the world we got given and the one chance we've got."

"But I need you, Banyan. And I love you, too, damn it." She said it softly, and the words I'd waited for cracked beneath the weight under which they were spoken. "I should have told you sooner. I should have told you all along."

"No. I should never have started this to begin with." It came out faster than I could think. "I fooled us both with this feeling. Wanting some life that we can't have. It's like you said, just something out of an old world song."

"But it don't belong to the old world." She pulled away from me. Put a finger on my lips. "I belong to you, Banyan. And you belong to me. And I'd do it all again, all of it. Just to know you. Just to spend this time by your side."

I was worn down and torn up, and I couldn't move a muscle for fear I might fall.

"We'll be together again," I whispered, her finger still pressed on my lips.

"The pirate clans are all over the plains. It'll take weeks to unite them. Months."

"We ain't got months."

"No." She turned her face to the dirt wall. "You're right. We got no time at all."

The poachers quit working when it came time for us to leave. They stood in the dirt with their tools and their corn, and even the Council pried themselves away from their fire. It was a silent affair. Solemn as a gray-rain dawn. Kade had me and Alpha climb with him into a big, empty bucket at the base of the scaffold, then he gave the signal, and poachers started working the ropes and pulleys, hoisting the three of us into the air.

The pulley system creaked and clanged, and I wondered if the whole thing might fall apart. But Kade said it'd be all right. Said it had held a lot more than our weight, was built to keep hauling poachers and corn for a whole lot more years to come.

So we got dragged up the side of the scaffold, staring down at the dirty faces. I spotted Orlic, Baxter and Bracelets and the rest of the Council, all huddled together in their cornhusk robes. And I wondered how Namo was doing. Did he miss us? Did he miss his old buddy Crow?

I pictured the Soljah heading east, purple wood legs wrapped around his stolen speeder. And would he remember me when the time came? Would he still believe in the things I had said? That we had to gather the tribes together. And to do that, we had to break up the trees.

Hurt to admit it, but I reckoned I'd no idea what Crow would do. Nor did I know how much sway he would hold with the Soljahs. And if the Soljahs wouldn't share the saplings, what would come next?

Alpha stood beside me with her arms crossed, and she seemed distant already. And I would lose her. For a while. Or forever. Because that's what falls upon everyone. Every step you take gets you closer to the end.

"Almost there," Kade said, and I glanced at the top of the scaffold, where ladders pointed straight up into a hole in the dirt.

Still the bucket hoisted us higher, till we were enveloped by the earth and bound by darkness, black as a grave, the smell of soil rich and damp. And the only sound was the squeak of the rusted bucket and the creak of the cornhusk ropes.

We pushed up through a thatched panel of husks and dirt. And when we broke out beneath the sky, the red sun filtered through the crops hardly at all, but it was enough to bloom through my insides and turn me blind for a moment.

I kept my eyes shut as I turned my face to the light, felt its fingers on my skin as if it were tugging me closer. As if it might hold me against it and never let go.

And when my eyes got used to being aboveground again, I could only blink at the huge corn plants that towered above us, thirty feet high, tightly packed stems and dark green leaves, dusted with the dirt from the plains. I peered up at the stalks—so damn straight, and planted so damn close together. Nothing like the ragged six saplings. Nothing like my thin, twisted trees.

I remembered how sickly those trees had looked when I had seen them last. How drained of color and life they'd appeared. But Crow would have gotten them water and given them sunlight. Plenty of water in

Niagara, after all, and plenty of sun in a world where shade's so hard to find.

A handful of poachers emerged from the corn, stepping out from the plants around us, their feet not making a sound.

"My lord," said one of the men. "I hear you're leaving us."

"I'm leaving," Kade said. "But I'm not a lord anymore."

He asked three of the men to hand over their shotguns. He gave one to Alpha, and he gave one to me.

Then they led us through the corn, pushing at the stiff leaves, working our way between the tight green stems, until we reached a narrow service road. Abandoned, by the looks of it, the surface rutted and broken. Little patches of snow in the ditches. Frost gleaming in the dust.

Too cold for locusts then. Good crossing season at last.

There were three ATVs on the side of the road, covered with old cornhusks and stems. We hauled the dried remains off the vehicles, dusted them down.

"Here you go," Kade said, handing us GenTech masks to protect our lungs from the landscape. Alpha pulled hers down, hiding too much of her beautiful face. But I just hung mine loose from my neck, as if the dust could do me no more damage.

"We follow this road through the corn," Kade said. "It winds east till it pushes us out to the plains."

"Then let's stop there." Alpha straddled her ATV and propped her shotgun under her leg. She glanced at me. "To say goodbye."

"Keep your eyes open," Kade said, and he threw us each a pair of goggles.

"Don't worry," I muttered, climbing onto my bike and pulling the goggles down over my head. "They're open every second of the day."

We never saw any agents as we rode down that road. We never saw any dusters in the distance or field hands in the corn. All I could see was Alpha ahead of me and the dust raging high all around us, and I plowed through the ditches and deep sand, my face once again all covered in grit. It felt good, to be honest. The dirt thick on my tongue, crunchy in my teeth. Hell, maybe the dirt was the closest thing to a home I ever had.

At the edge of the cornfields, the tall plants stretched west behind us, and they spread north and south far as the eye could see. But the landscape just gave up to the east, where everything was crumbled dirt. We stopped the ATVs, letting the dust settle as much as it could.

"We're pretty far north," Kade said. "Niagara's about due east of here."

"Well, compadre." Alpha pulled her mask and goggles up onto her head, approaching Kade then slapping him on the shoulder. "A general needs an army, so I'm dropping south to start building one. And I guess this is it."

"A general, huh?" He smiled, as if remembering he'd called her that, but you could see his heart weren't in it. "I suppose I'll be seeing you on the battlefield then."

"I hope so."

"You know, I've been trying to find the right way to thank you." Kade gazed back into the corn. "For killing that monster."

"You held Harvest still," Alpha said. "All I did was point Namo the right way."

"No." Kade climbed off his bike. "He had a gun at my head, and I'd be dead if it wasn't for you."

"He had a gun on me, too, once. Remember?"

"Yeah." He choked the word out. "I do."

"I miss her, too." Alpha took Kade's face in her hands, making him look into her eyes. "But we'll fight for what Zee wanted. And there'll be more sorrow, but the hurt's to be lived with, you hear me? Don't go getting yourself killed."

"You underestimate me."

"And you'll take care of my man for me?"

"Like he's my own brother," Kade said, glancing over at me.

I was still sat on my ATV, and I yanked my goggles down around my neck and stared east at a world that now seemed foreign. Everything altered since when I'd last seen it. As if the way things were stitched together had all been undone.

"Come on, bud," Alpha said, striding past me. "It's time."

I slid into the dust and followed her over to her bike, and then we stood there, a cold wind picking up the dirt around us as the sun beat down.

"I need to tell you something," she said, taking my hands but avoiding my eyes. "And you ain't gonna like it."

"You don't have to tell me."

"It's about what I saw. Beneath the peaks."

"No," I said. "I don't want to know."

"I was in a forest, bud. A real forest. It was all tangled and dusty, but there were leaves on the trees. Everything all green and thick."

"Don't sound so bad." I tried smiling.

"It was all wrong, though. I was trapped in there."

"You were just dreaming," I said, but I'd turned tight and cold inside.

"You couldn't see me. You were running through the forest and screaming my name. And I was trying to tell you I was there, right there, but no matter what, you still couldn't hear me. It was like the words wouldn't even come out of my mouth."

I couldn't look at her now. I glanced back at the wall of corn behind us. The dust. The sun. Anything else.

"It don't mean nothing," I said.

"Yes, it does. It was a warning. My own mind telling me that I'll lose you if we don't remember this." She put her hand on my chest. "You mustn't forget. Okay? And I won't forget, neither."

"I won't forget it," I said. Because how could I tell her the real meaning of her vision? The real future that the world had in store.

"I'll send word," she said, trying so hard to hold it together. "To Waterfall City. Let you know when the Army of the Fallen Sun is ready to rise once again."

"We'll go wherever you want." I tried to smile as I said it. "Just me and you. In the end."

"See those trees bloom. Leaves and apples and everything. In the spring, right?"

"Right," I said. "In the spring."

I stepped closer. Pushed her rags above her stomach and wiped off the dirt. I put my hand against the bit of bark GenTech had sewn into her, and I let my fingers rest there a moment, as if I might conjure some spell. Then I pulled her towards me, shielding her with my body.

"I'll be your pirate queen," she said, her voice shaking. Her breath so warm on my neck.

"Course."

"And you'll be my tree king."

I forced a smile, even though she couldn't see me. Even though her face was buried in my chest.

"Aren't you gonna kiss me?" she asked, and I held her face in my hands, wiped the dust off her skin. Then I kissed her lips and her neck and her shoulders. I held every part of her against everything I had.

"Hurry," I whispered. Swallowing back tears as I watched her mount her speeder. Feeling ripped out and empty as she tugged down her mask.

And then she was tearing off beneath the burning sky and the plumes of dust, and the sound of her engine was the only thing left behind. And perhaps I should have let my tears loose, when she'd still been there to see them. But I'd wanted to look strong so she'd remember me that way, as if I could stop time or make the world stop spinning long enough to jump off. But the world would keep turning and time would keep moving and with spring would come life, and with life would come death.

But if I could get back those trees, there might still be a way forward. Because if Alpha was sick, there had to be a remedy. And if the bark was a disease, then there was one tribe that might know the cure.

END OF BOOK TWO

ACKNOWLEDGMENTS

As the journey of this story gets bigger, so does my list of people to thank.

My agent, Laura Rennert, provides me with brilliant support, and she edited this book with me, back and forth and back again, making it infinitely better. Others helped make it better, too: Jenny "Sassafrass" Kapke, Eric Dinkel, and MG Buehrlen all pitched in with their thoughts at important stages in the process. My dad, my mum, Annemarie Carzoli, and Mike Stjernholm all gave very useful feedback. My copy-editor, Pamela Feinsilber, went above and beyond, as we got near the end. Lara Perkins was on top of logistics that would make my head spin. Taryn Fagerness, my foreign rights agent, connected the story with people in different countries around the world, and I'd like to acknowledge everyone involved at the publishing houses in those countries, too.

I'd also like to acknowledge the booksellers, school teachers, librarians and book bloggers who were so supportive when the first book in this trilogy hit the shelves.

A big thanks, also, goes to every reader that got in touch with me after reading Book One and wanted to know when they could read Book Two.

I'm grateful to my family and my family of friends, who are always so enthusiastic and supportive. And my incredible wife, Allison Benner, helped me hugely with this story, and even more importantly, she makes the story of my own life better in every single way.

ABOUT THE AUTHOR

 Before he wrote stories, Chris Howard wrote songs, studied natural resources management, and led wilderness adventure trips for teenagers. Born and raised in England, he currently lives in Colorado with his wife. Visit him online at www.chrishowardbooks.com.

OTHER TITLES BY CHRIS HOWARD

ROOTLESS

Made in the USA
Charleston, SC
04 November 2015